A Taste For Man

A Taste For Man

Ross J. Burns

Murphy & Lightner

Murphy & Lightner

Cover design by: Elizabeth Burns

atasteforman.com

ISBN 978-0-578-91913-3

para mi Anchoveta

Chapter One

Amara

It was somewhere in the gray maze of strangler figs and mangroves. Hiding was easy in the convoluted roots and limbs. Each tree made a forest within the forest. He couldn't see it. He couldn't hear it. He could, however, feel its enormous presence as clearly as he could feel his own breath. Julian Hamilton knew this particular male well. He had been observing him for months. He was the biggest male Bengal tiger Julian had seen in his more than 12 years in the jungles and forests of southern Asia. He was also, by far, the most aggressive and dangerous.

Julian was downwind, so not knowing precisely where he was didn't make him nervous. Cill, the fidgety man crouched next to him, made him more than a little uneasy.

1

"Were you listening when I said this one ate a full-grown man for dinner and dragged his four-year-old home for dessert?" Julian asked. His deep, throaty voice made the warning all the more potent. Cill responded with a dismissive wave of his hand. Julian shook his head in disbelief.

Cill, who claimed to be a writer for National Geographic, was clearly bored and uncomfortable after spending 16 hours cooped up in the hot, elevated wooden box. At times, it was unbearably uncomfortable, a steam room on stilts. He pushed his back against the wall and blew a bubble with his gum. He popped the bubble loudly and slurped it back into his mouth. After a welcome minute of quiet, Julian spotted the tiger. He stared at the regal creature appreciatively for a few moments before he elbowed Cill.

"There he is. Eighty meters to your right."

Cill quickly turned around, raised his binoculars and looked out the little window of the blind. He scanned the area. "I don't see him."

"He went behind a tree. Give him a second."

Cill nearly dropped his binoculars when he saw the huge head and dagger-like teeth in full frame.

"Oh my god. He's, he's, he's. . ."

"Magnificent," Julian said.

"Yeah, that."

The beast turned sideways, giving Cill a different view.

"And he's fucking huge," Cill said. Nerves had crept into his voice.

"He eats well."

Both men followed with their binoculars as the tiger walked directly toward the blind. When he had cut the distance between them in half, he disappeared. Cill nervously searched the forest.

"Where the hell did he go?" Cill asked, jittery nerves giving way to moderate panic.

"Just calm down and keep quiet," Julian whispered. "Let the tiger do his thing."

Cill shuffled around in the blind, creating a commotion that caught the animal's attention. The tiger peeked out from behind a mangrove tree and aimed his laser-like gaze through the window of the blind and straight into Cill's nervous green eyes.

"Oh, shit," Cill said as he quickly turned away from the window.

"Stay calm," Julian said, his voice measured and unruffled.

At that point, Cill was anything but calm. He reached for Julian's Savage Model 110 leaning against the wall. Julian was quicker and grabbed the rifle. He pulled it close to his chest. Julian was always the only one to have a gun. He never let any of his clients carry one.

"Don't even think about it," Julian said.

Cill pushed his back against the wall. He took several quick and nervous breaths.

"Shit, shit, shit. Where is he now?" Cill asked.

"I don't know," Julian said as he scanned the forest with his binoculars. "But if you would shut up he might do us a favor and leave us alone."

Julian's warnings had no effect on Cill, who whipped around and stuck his head out the window of the blind. He saw nothing. "Aidan, where the hell is he?" he yelled toward another blind 60 meters to his left. "Aidan, help!"

Aidan was Cill's photographer, or so the two men had claimed. With his two big bags of camera equipment, there was little room for him in the same blind with Julian and Cill.

"Shut up! You'll get us all killed." Julian demanded as he grabbed Cill by the shirttails and pulled him inside the blind.

Just as Julian released his grasp from Cill's sweat-soaked shirt, the blind shook on its posts. A second, more forceful jolt followed. Both men looked below. Three feet away were the enormous front paws of the Bengal tiger. Its legs were only halfway extended as it pushed against the spot where one of the support posts met the base of the blind eight feet off the forest floor. As the massive cat pushed, the blind swayed back and forth. The support post cracked. It held for a couple of seconds and collapsed. The rickety blind listed toward the unsupported corner and crashed to the ground. Its walls blew apart on impact. Julian and Cill landed hard on the forest floor and helplessly bounced like rag dolls to within a couple feet of the tiger. Julian froze completely, the rifle still clutched tightly in his hand. Cill, in full panic mode, quivered uncontrollably.

"Easy. Easy," Julian calmly whispered even as the tiger was baring his teeth and hissing.

"Oh, shit, oh shit, oh shit," was all Cill was able to spit out as he tried to scoot backwards slowly.

"Stop. He'll never let you get away like that. Stay still. Look him in the eyes," Julian said with quiet force.

Instead of following Julian's directions, Cill rolled to his left, turning his back to the tiger. The move was suicidal, an open invitation for the tiger to attack. The tiger lunged and hammered its front paws onto Cill's back. With its claws set deep, the tiger savagely tore at flesh and bone.

"Shoot it! Kill it!" Cill yelled frantically, his neck craned awkwardly so he could fix his desperate, pleading green eyes on Julian. The rifle stayed tight against Julian's chest. He didn't raise his weapon, not even an inch. Blood bubbled out of Cill's mouth as he tried to scream for help.

Filled with awe, not terror, Julian watched the tiger clamp its sharp teeth into Cill's shredded flesh. Cill lay limp in the mud, a gurgling, bloody mess. The green of Cill's eyes rolled back into his head, leaving only lifeless white.

The tiger abruptly swung his head toward Julian. Their faces were just inches apart and Julian could see his reflection in the tiger's big yellow eyes. The tiger released a threatening growl, low and loud. Hot tiger breath and spit hit Julian's face. Startled but unafraid, he held his ground. The tiger turned around, sank his teeth into Cill's back and continued feasting on bloody strands of muscle and ropy tendon.

Julian heard a gunshot. The tiger winced, lifted his head and growled. It couldn't have been Aidan who had fired. He didn't have a gun. Or did he? Julian looked toward the other blind and saw Aidan 50 meters away, pistol raised and closing in at a run. Julian stood up and calmly walked toward Aidan with his hands up.

"Don't shoot him! Please don't shoot the tiger. I beg you," Julian yelled. He was desperate.

Aidan didn't slow. He aimed his gun. He pulled the trigger—twice. The first bullet hit Julian two inches below his left clavicle. The second hit an inch below the first. Both bullets entered him, ripped open the flesh on his back and exited his body. The second just missed tearing apart his heart. He fell to the ground. His world went black.

***

When Julian first regained consciousness, it was fuzzy and lasted only a few seconds, but it was long enough to feel the tiger licking the gunshot wounds on his chest and back. He didn't see the single drop of blood that fell from the wound on the tiger's face and landed in the center of the spot where a bullet had torn him open. He could certainly feel it. That single drop of tiger blood hit him like a sledgehammer pounding a red-hot spike.

"This isn't happening," he thought. "I must be hallucinating."

He felt an intense nausea in his gut. It surged and swirled through his body until it reached the back of his eyeballs. Everything was black again.

***

Cill and Aidan had shown up unannounced a few days earlier in the tiny village of Nurnashmari, deep in the Bangladeshi Sundarbans. They said they had been down river and someone had recommended Julian as a guide. Julian, who took on clients semi-regularly, though none since he started working in Nurnashmari, initially turned them down. He was generally mistrustful of people and he didn't want to show anyone the tiger he had been observing. On the subject of tigers, Cill and Aidan appeared to know what they were talking about. Yet, something wasn't right. The ultra-thin watch on Aidan's wrist triggered Julian's usual suspicions. He knew the watch. It was a Vacheron Constantin. His grandfather had worn one. It was a pricey accessory to be wearing in one of the poorest places on earth where time meant essentially nothing.

Aside from the expensive timepiece and the ominous pronunciation of Cill's name—with a Celtic hard C— these two gave Julian no more reason than intuition to view them as anything but legit. They had a business card from National Geographic as proof they were on assignment and only wanted to photograph and study the tiger, not kill him. They were offering quite a bit of money for Julian's services and agreed to Julian's other, non-negotiable terms: a substantial donation to the people of Nurnashmari, and the continued secrecy of the tiger's location. Julian unenthusiastically accepted their offer. However, he felt obligated to warn them of the special dangers presented by this particular male. The tiger was born to kill and did so for sport. He also ate and dismembered his prey on the spot, often before the prey was even dead. It was a highly unusual habit for a tiger. It was as if killing wasn't punishment enough. This tiger insulted his prey by piling on his domination. And, of course, his preferred flesh was human.

After the first 20 minutes in the blind with Cill on the first day, Julian felt profound regret. The opinion of Cill he had reluctantly settled on had been way off the mark. Cill appeared to know a lot about tigers, but he was too fidgety. The chewing gum was what really gave him away. No wildlife journalist hoping to observe a man-eating Bengal tiger would chew gum with an open mouth. Even worse, he blew bubbles. When the bubbles popped they emitted a waft of artificial watermelon flavor. The Nat Geo business card was probably a fake. It was easy to make a fake business card. These days anyone could do it.

Aidan also demonstrated a fair amount of tiger knowledge and experience. The opposite of Cill, Aidan was calm and quiet to the point of being cold. The barrier of reticence he put up was unnerving. Julian felt like he was being surveilled. He was kicking himself for trusting someone who wore a $20,000 watch that did nothing more than tell the time of day. Still, the two men had accepted quite willingly that Julian would be the only one to carry a rifle. They said they didn't have any guns anyway. That was the most important qualification for Julian. He would use his own rifle in only the most desperate situation. For Julian, no situation could ever be so desperate, but it was bad for business to tell his clients he would rather let the tiger kill them.

***

The second time Julian came to he felt weak and struggled to sit up. As he looked around he realized he was in a new and unfamiliar place. There were no remnants of the destroyed blind. Cill's mauled corpse wasn't there, nor were there any blood or body parts on the ground that would suggest it had ever been. Julian was groggy and confused. How long had he been there? More importantly, how had he gotten there? Had Aidan dragged him? Was it someone else? Was it the tiger?

"Aidan?" Julian called out. "Is anyone there?"

There was no answer from Aidan or anyone else. Julian tried to stand. He was too weak. He lay back back down on the ground, closed his eyes and fell asleep. He was still asleep when he felt something hit his hip. Startled, he opened his eyes. The tiger was standing so close he could feel his hot breath. Julian wasn't afraid. He didn't understand why he wasn't, he just knew he didn't need to be. On the ground at his hip was a bloody human arm. The giant tiger gently nudged the arm toward Julian, inviting him to eat. Julian saw the Vacheron Constantin watch still strapped to the wrist.

Julian heard the muffled sounds of other tigers. A female and two cubs picked at the flesh of a one-armed body. The female looked up. Julian waved at her as if she were human. He realized the senselessness of his wave and put his hand down. The female went back to gnawing on one of Aidan's legs. The two cubs looked up. Both had a patch of black fur between their eyes. In the black were orange flames. They were twins.

This particular male *pantera tigris tigris*, commonly known as a Bengal tiger, had been terrorizing the village of Nurnashmari and its people for over a year and a half and had earned an almost mythical reputation. He never allowed himself to be trapped or snared, though many had tried. The people of the village, feeling they had exhausted every option, tried to kill the tiger several times. The tiger had been shot with a rifle on at least six occasions, yet it simply would not die. The villagers called him Amara, a Bengali name that means "immortal."

When Julian first showed up in the village, not far from the border with India and not close to anything, the villagers pleaded with him to help them trap or kill the tiger. He always declined, saying he would help them protect themselves. He was only there to observe. "Tigers are endangered. Humans are dangerous," was how Julian justified placing greater value on the life of a tiger than on a man's, even his own. He wrote an article about Amara for Frontiers in Zoology called "The Man-Eating Tiger That Refuses to Die and Deserves to Live." In the article, Julian was upfront with his views about there being no circumstance where killing a tiger, no matter how dangerous, was acceptable. The article caused a heated discussion in the animal biology community. He was ridiculed as often as he was applauded. While in Khulna to load up on supplies, Julian read online that the controversy he ignited over this notorious tiger in an intentionally undisclosed location in South Asia was picked up by the Associated Press. Julian instantly regretted writing the article. He never thought the article would blow up the way it did. One critic compared him to "whacko militant anti-abortion activists." He didn't care what others thought of him. His main concern was he had jeopardized what he wanted most for the tiger: his safety. He knew people like Cill and Aidan would show up looking to write stories about the tiger, but he was trying to prove a point. In the end Julian had accepted their offer out of fear that if he didn't the two men would strike out on their own and end up killing the tiger, getting killed by the tiger, or both.

Julian was liked by the people in the village. He was generous and helpful with everyone, but his refusal to help kill Amara was a contentious issue. No one in the village took Julian's side. All of its residents had a family member or close friend killed by the tiger. Amara had killed 17 villagers. Cill and Aidan raised the count of confirmed kills to 19. A fisherman hauling his skiff ashore, a woman nursing her child, an old man whittling a spear hit so hard by a vicious swipe from behind that his head dangled from one single strand of ligament. Fat, thin, tall, short, it didn't matter. Amara had a taste for man.

Chapter Two

Mercy

Julian was in remarkably little pain. He moved his shirt to get a better look at the holes ripped into his chest. The wounds were clean. He couldn't see them, but he could feel the exit wounds on his back. Aside from preventing possible infection, medical attention could wait. He wasn't particularly hungry, and he certainly wasn't going to eat human flesh. He had become unusually thin over the past months, but he wasn't so desperate as to gnaw on a human arm. He was a pescatarian anyway. He was a vegetarian when he arrived in the Sundarbans, a lifestyle easy to follow when he was in southern India, but if you weren't willing to eat fish in Nurnashmari, you went hungry. Water was at the top of his list of needs. As remarkable as his most recent experience with Amara had been, he didn't think the tiger would be able to fetch him drinking water. His body was telling him he needed hydration and his mouth felt like he had eaten sawdust.

Julian got to his feet and took a few wobbly steps. When he finally got his bearings, he was certain it had been Amara who had dragged him there. Who else could it have been?

His years in the forest had taught him many things about surviving in it and how to find his way out of it. Once he found the creek that led to a second creek that led to the village, he would be able to find the skiff he had beached and tied to a mangrove. From his skiff he knew the way to his blinds and the water bottles in his pack. What he didn't know was what else he would find there.

"Goodbye, friend. May you live forever," Julian said to Amara as he left. Amara growled softly, almost affectionately.

It took a half hour to find the creek and half that to get to his skiff. From there he went to the blinds. The first thing he saw was Cill's partially-eaten body. Based on the size of the maggots feeding on his putrid remains, Julian guessed that Cill had been killed by Amara two days earlier. It was only a guess. He never had to perform a forensic diagnosis on a human corpse before.

The pack that held his water bottles was just a few feet away. He opened one of his bottles and drank it in one long pull. His thirst slaked, he rifled through Cill's pack. There was a notebook with a few irrelevant, inane scribbles. For someone supposedly writing for National Geographic, Julian had expected to find notes more interesting than partial lyrics to Led Zeppelin's "Immigrant Song" and juvenile doodles of cars and handguns. In a small outside pocket was a big pack of watermelon flavor Hubba Bubba.

Closer to the blind that Aidan had been using, Julian found a Glock 19 on the ground. He found six spent shell casings within a 10-foot radius of where he had found the pistol. He could only remember hearing three shots, one that hit Amara and two that hit him. Julian took the Glock and left the shell casings where they lay. Inside the blind were Aidan's two bags of photography gear. In one of the bags was an Android satellite phone and charger. The lock screen said there were five missed calls. It didn't give any more information than that. He put the phone and charger in his pocket. Upside down on the floor was Aidan's camera with a 600 mm lens. Julian scrolled through some of the photos on the camera. Just a few minutes before Cill died, Aidan had captured three images of Amara from his spot in the blind: one of the mighty tiger's tail and two of his left ear. The photos were so poorly composed they looked accidental. After thoroughly searching the area for any clue he could find, Julian put all the gear in the blind that was still standing and tried to get comfortable inside. He was tired. He rested.

Julian had an odd thought when he woke. Even though Aidan had tried to kill him and Amara, Julian wished he were still alive. Julian had questions for the reticent bastard. He would have to go back to the village. Maybe there were answers in the hut where Aidan and Cill had left the rest of their gear.

He considered how he would explain Cill's and Aidan's deaths to the villagers. It would be easy to just tell them the tiger attacked the two men, killed them and ate them. That was Amara's modus operandi. It wouldn't come as a surprise to anyone. There was no need to mention he had watched idly as the ferocious man-eater clawed and devoured

Cill, or that he had enjoyed the spectacle. He knew that part of the tale wouldn't go over well with the villagers. Two details that would be hard to explain were the bullet holes in his chest and back. He resolved to keep them a secret for as long as he could.

He waited until late to return to the village. He needed to search the hut where Cill and Aidan had stored their stuff and spent the first night. Fahd, the villager who owned the hut, was Julian's harshest critic and the most fervent supporter of killing Amara. When Julian first arrived in the village, Fahd took an immediate dislike to him. Julian had done nothing to provoke such a sentiment. The only thing he could think of was jealousy. Many of the village women had stared at Julian shamelessly. Julian avoided Fahd whenever he could. He knew better than to ask him if he could go into the hut where Cill and Aidan had stayed. He had no choice but to sneak in.

On most nights Fahd could be found waiting for Amara in front of his hut with an old Smith and Wesson Model 19 revolver in his right hand and a bottle of contraband rum in his left. That night was no exception. Julian had been in the hut and he knew there was an open space between the thatched roof and the rear mud wall big enough for him to fit through. He waited for Fahd to be in his cups, which was usually a given by 11:00, and walked quietly behind his hut and over to the other. He climbed the wall and slithered through the gap without a sound. On the dirt floor were three duffel bags. Using a flashlight, he went through every seam and stitch of the two dead men's bags and the clothes he found in them. Most of the stuff in the bags was of little interest to him. There were, however, two somewhat revealing items in one of the bags: a well-worn Chicago Cubs hat and a T-shirt advertising Chubby Wieners, a hot dog place on Western Avenue, in Chicago. Julian thought it odd that the man who shot him in the Bangladeshi jungle might be from his hometown, especially when both Aidan and Cill had claimed to be native New Yorkers. Something else he found proved he had been lied to. Under the straw mattress was a soft case with a disassembled Savage Model 110, just like the one he owned.

Julian would never shoot a tiger, but by carrying his own Savage 110, he was able to keep others from bringing a firearm they might use to shoot a tiger in panic or for poaching. He never imagined any of his clients would bring a handgun as protection from a tiger. The only reason Julian could think of for Aidan to carry a handgun was to kill a human, someone like him. The Glock was a poor choice to kill a tiger. He supposed that if they killed him first, they could conceivably take his Savage 110 and use it to kill the tiger. There was a hole in the poaching theory. Poachers preferred to trap tigers and club them to death. A bullet hole lowered the value of the skin. Maybe killing him was just as important as killing the tiger. That didn't make sense either.

Nothing in the hut gave any indication of who the two men really were. It didn't seem possible they had no identification with them. He had checked everything in the hut and the blinds. He had even brushed aside the maggots so he could dig through Cill's pockets. Then it hit him. There was another set of pockets he hadn't checked.

***

Julian slipped himself and the case with the rifle through the gap above the rear wall of the hut. By then Fahd was asleep, chin on chest, Smith and Wesson in the dirt. Julian walked to the riverbank without worry of waking him. He paddled back up the creek. He went past the spot where he had tied up before and continued to the spot he knew to be just a thirty-minute walk to Aidan's body, or what was left of it. He lashed his skiff to a tree and slept with one eye open until dawn.

Walking out of the jungle the day before he never felt the need to worry about his safety. His experience with Amara was confusing. It was also reaffirming. Since he was a young boy he had known he had a special connection with tigers. His twin sister, Lara, had it, too. As children one of their favorite things to do was go to the Lincoln Park Zoo to see Molly, a Siberian tiger that was born at the zoo in 1997. They were only nine years old when Molly was born, so it was like they grew up with the tiger. They used to tell their mother that Molly recognized them when they went to visit her. Their mother thought they were joking. They weren't. There was always a glint of recognition in Molly's eyes when she saw the twins.

When he was young Julian was obsessed with tigers the way many young boys are obsessed with stegosauruses and triceratops. There were posters of tigers on his bedroom wall, stuffed tigers, plastic tigers and books about tigers, lots of books, everything from Jim Corbett's classic Man-eaters of Kumaon, to Kipling, to picture books. Lara's interest wasn't so conspicuous. Hers was more internal. When they were 11 and studying for a spelling bee with their father, he quizzed her on a word.

"Reincarnation. R-e-i-n-c-a-r-n-a-t-i-o-n," she said proudly.

"What does reincarnation mean?" Julian asked.

"It's when the soul of someone who dies comes back in another person's body," their father said.

"Or animal," Lara added. "When I die, I want to come back as a tiger."

She said that more than once.

When he started at the University of Chicago he chose animal biology as his major. He knew it would be a few years before he would branch out to specialize in tigers. A few semesters of general biology would always be useful. He was in no rush. He often wondered if he would have been better off staying in school, if he would have been better prepared for his time in the jungles and forests of Asia with more than just two years of undergraduate biology classes. He was sure now that wasn't the case. After months and months of observation, he knew Amara better than any tiger he had ever observed, and he had observed nearly a hundred. He was pretty sure Amara knew him, too. Julian was almost always hidden in a blind, but there were times when he felt Amara was watching him as much as he was watching Amara. Whatever it was that created that chemistry, he was sure it could never have been taught in a classroom or lecture hall. After more than 12 years of searching he finally found the tiger that confirmed his special gift. Or maybe it was the tiger that found him. So what if the tiger was a vicious man-eater? The circumstances were extraordinary. So was their encounter.

He was fairly sure Amara escorted him back to his skiff the day before, though Julian never saw or heard the tiger. That wasn't unusual. Walking back into the forest would be different. He didn't have Amara as an escort, nor did he expect Amara to be in the place he was going. Male tigers are solitary, territorial creatures. Amara had gone to the den to share his kill with one of his mates and her cubs. That's it. Males don't spend much time with other tigers. It was also unlikely there would be a second male in the area. Amara would never allow it. Julian wouldn't discount the possibility of a run-in with the female he saw eating Aidan. A female Bengal could kill him as easily as a male could, especially if there were cubs to protect.

Tigers are far from the only danger in the Sundarbans. Crocodiles lurk in the muddy waters. Burmese pythons, king cobras and red-tailed bamboo pit vipers stalk the forest. Crocodiles wouldn't cause problems for him in the forest once he found a safe place to land his skiff. Disturbing a resting cobra or pit viper was his main concern. He left the two Savage Model 110's in the skiff and took the Glock, which wouldn't be much good for hitting a striking cobra, not for a poor shot like him.

When Julian arrived at the den, there were no tigers to be found. Aidan's body and severed left arm were there, though little meat was left on his bones. At least the tigers hadn't eaten his clothes. Julian went through Aidan's pockets. There was nothing but a lens cap in Aidan's pants pockets. In a shirt pocket he found a packet with a glow-in-the-dark condom, which made him laugh audibly. He looked around the den. He saw nothing else that looked like it once belonged to or had been used by a human. He thought he might never find out who Aidan and Cill really were. In a fit of frustration, Julian kicked Aidan's shredded corpse. It moved an inch, just enough to reveal a small brass buckle attached to a thin strap. Julian flipped over the fetid corpse with his foot. On the ground was what looked like a money belt with a thick pouch. Inside the pouch was currency from Bangladesh and India, and $3,000 American. Also inside the pouch were two passports. Cill was

Cillian O'Brien. His place of birth was Oak Lawn, Illinois, a Chicago suburb. Aidan was also born in Oak Lawn, and his last name was also O'Brien. Aidan was 16 months older than Cill. Maybe people would believe the O'Brien brothers being killed and eaten by the same tiger in the Sundarbans was just the luck of the Irish.

He left the passports, two of the hundred dollar bills and 4,000 Bangladeshi Takas, about 50 bucks, in the pouch of the money belt. The $2,800 he took was more than what they owed him. He figured the bullet holes in his chest were worth at least that much.

The spot where Aidan's body laid was so deep in the forest it saw almost no human presence. Not even the honey hunters went there. Odds were if anyone did eventually stumble across Aidan, that person would find nothing but bones. Julian wanted the body to be found, or at least he wanted people to know Aidan had also been killed by the tiger. The less explaining he had to do, the better. Dragging Aidan's partially disassembled body back to the blinds was impractical. To provide proof of Aidan's death and an easy way to identify him, Julian picked up the arm with the ridiculously expensive Swiss watch and carried it slung over his shoulder as he headed back.

After 15 minutes of walking he got the same feeling he had when he thought Amara was following him the day before. Several times he looked around for Amara. He never saw the tiger. He leaned against a tangle of tree roots. He raised his water bottle to his lips and tilted his head back to drink. When he lowered the bottle, Amara was standing 10 feet from him. Both man and tiger stood silent and motionless. Amara stepped gingerly toward Julian. The tiger was clearly hurt. Julian hadn't noticed it the last time he saw Amara. He slowly dropped to his knees and let the tiger come to within a foot of his face.

"Hello, Amara," he whispered to the tiger. "I was hoping you would come see me."

Julian adjusted his route so he could walk side-by-side with Amara all the way to the collapsed blind. He would walk back upstream to get his skiff when it was time to say goodbye. Things at the blind looked pretty much as they had the day before. There was no further evidence of any human presence. The only change was the advancement of Cill's decomposition and the stench that accompanied it. Julian made one change to the scene. He dumped the arm into a muddy clump of exposed roots ten feet from Cill's corpse.

The pair continued on to the other blind. Julian climbed the ladder. Aidan's camera gear was as he had left it, which was the way he wanted it to stay. When he climbed down from the blind, he found Amara flat on the ground, struggling to breathe. Julian sat beside the tiger and examined Amara's body closely. He found a gunshot wound in Amara's leg and one in the chest. He couldn't believe those two shots and the flesh wound on the tiger's face could take out the great, the immortal Amara. There had to be another. There was. It was in the tiger's abdomen, right by the liver. Such a shot could cause Amara's liver to slowly fail and eventually kill him. It could take days, or even weeks. Knowing Amara, the latter seemed more likely. If it took too long, the tiger would eventually lose its ability to hunt and starve to death before the gunshot killed him. No matter how long it took, it would be unpleasant. The thought of Amara suffering for even one more minute was unacceptable. He knew he had to do something he had vowed never to do. In this circumstance, it was absolutely the right thing to do. He just didn't know if he could do it.

Julian pointed the Glock between Amara's eyes. He held it there for 30 seconds. When his hand began to shake uncontrollably, Julian lowered the gun. Amara lifted his front leg and put it back down. Stunned, Julian looked into the eyes of the tiger. They were saying, "End my suffering." He was sure of it. He raised the gun, looked away and pulled the trigger. The tiger's body went limp. Amara was dead. Julian's body seized. He couldn't move a single muscle, not even to blink. After just a couple of seconds, the paralyzing grip was released. He dipped his finger in Amara's blood and painted tiger stripes on his face. He looked to the sky and let loose his rage with a ferocious roar.

***

The tiger weighed over 800 pounds and Julian couldn't move him more than the few inches it would take to fall into a grave directly beside it. Using pieces of lumber from the collapsed blind, Julian dug an enormous hole. He had to make it deep enough to withstand the heavy monsoon rains that would start soon. He would have one and only one chance. It took hours before he was satisfied with the hole's depth. He dropped the Glock in the grave. He used one of the posts from the blind for leverage and pried at the tiger's body until it dropped. With every foot of dirt he filled back into the hole, he compacted it. When he was finished he scattered leaves and twigs around the area to camouflage the grave.

He looked down at the earth that concealed the body of the dead tiger. His seething anger was joined by a profound and painful sadness, a feeling he had felt before. When he killed Amara, it felt like part of him had died, both physically and emotionally. Before he turned to walk away, Julian, the mild-mannered animal lover, made a promise to Amara. "I will find whoever made me do this to you and I will make them pay."

Chapter Three

Butterflies And Dancing Elephants

There was still at least an hour of daylight left when Julian approached the village in his skiff. He didn't want anyone to see him, so he drifted into a bushy section of mangroves a hundred meters beyond the edge of the village. There he planned to wait until long after dark. From his vantage point he could easily spy on the village with his binoculars. Unfortunately, the conversations the returning fisherman were having on the muddy banks of the river were inaudible.

After he had been waiting in the mangroves for half an hour, he saw a bigger boat heading up the river and toward the village. It was the same boat that had brought Cill and Aidan when they had showed up a week earlier. Two white men got off the boat and stepped into the soft gray mud. Using his binoculars, Julian could see that one of the men was tall, at least 6'4", and had a deep scar running from his left temple to the corner of his mouth. He had a face that frightened small children. Ex-military Julian thought. The shorter one had a Caesar haircut and wore blue framed glasses that made him look like an aged-out hipster. Julian could see the one with the blue glasses was drenched with sweat, scratched himself frequently and generally looked uncomfortable. He walked in the mud gingerly, as if trying to keep his shoes clean. The tall one appeared to handle the challenges of the Sundarbans with relative ease. A dark-skinned man, most likely a Bangladeshi translator, jumped off the boat. They approached some of the fisherman and showed them photos on their phones that could only have been of Cill and Aidan.

All the fishermen nodded. One fisherman pointed towards Fahd's hut in the village. Another pointed into the never-ending forest. The man next to him pointed in the opposite direction. It would be suicide for the two men to venture into the forest in the dark. Fahd's hut was all they would get that night. Julian knew that nothing in their hut would raise any immediate suspicion that anything untoward had happened. Anyone would think they had been sleeping in the forest, as they had done with Julian several times. Nor would these two new men learn anything specific about where Julian had taken them. Julian had never shared the location of his tiger-watching spots with anyone in the village.

When it was late enough, Julian paddled his skiff to the riverbank in front of his hut and went inside. It was clear the two new men had searched his hut, but they hadn't tossed the place. He slunk across the village to check Cill and Aidan's hut. It was surrounded by foliage and trees that allowed Julian to get close without being seen. He could hear the two men inside well enough to know they were speaking English, but he couldn't follow the conversation. He could only pick out choice words like "shithole" and "motherfucker." A few minutes later the tall one with the scarred face stepped outside, took out a satellite phone and tapped in some numbers. Worried he was trying to call Aidan's phone, which was in his pocket, Julian quickly took the phone and smothered it in his armpit. The phone didn't ring.

"Hey, it's KP," scarface said into the phone. "Some villagers told us that they've been out in the forest for a few days. They're probably sleeping there, which isn't so unusual with this fucking Julian guy." He listened as the person on the other line spoke.

"Of course we checked his place. He's not there. Neither is his boat." KP was clearly agitated by what he was hearing on the other end of the call. "I've already called the motherfucker five times. I never should have let those two take the lead on this."

KP held the phone away from his ear, not because he was being yelled at, but because he just didn't want to listen anymore.

"You already know what I think. He's probably dead, but until I'm sure, I'm going to treat him as a threat, no matter how little he might know. We need to tie this off. I'll give it one more week." Again he held the phone away from his ear. "And you can forget about the tiger," KP said before abruptly hanging up the phone. He kicked dirt in anger.

Julian didn't know what to make of the new men. Two things were clear. They knew his name and they were taking orders from someone. But why were they in the Bangladeshi Sundarbans? Did they come to poach a tiger? These guys didn't fit the typical poacher profile. For one thing, they were white and American. All the poachers he had seen were Asian and worked for complex syndicates run by the Chinese. In his years of experience Julian had come across many poachers. He had worked tirelessly to stop poaching and he had created a few enemies along the way. Payback was a possible motive, particularly by the Kunming syndicate in Yunnan Province. He had helped the Indian authorities put a dozen members of the syndicate in jail. He received a few threats, but no one had ever tried to make good on them.

None of the poachers he had seen had been white Americans, nor had any of them tried to kill him. He'd heard stories of American poachers in Bangladesh and India. He couldn't confirm any of the stories, nor had he ever seen or met any personally. What he did know was the two dead guys were brothers born near Chicago. One brother liked watermelon flavored gum and Led Zeppelin. The other wore a ridiculously expensive watch and was a deadeye with a Glock. They didn't work for National Geographic. That was clear. It wasn't a lot to go on. He knew the duties assigned to these two new men included making sure he was dead and bagging a Bengal tiger. They weren't going to get the tiger, that much was certain, and he wasn't going to give them the chance to complete their other duty, not here at least. He had more respect for the villagers than that. He didn't know where he was going, but he couldn't stay in Nurnashmari.

Julian hurried to his hut. He stuffed his passport, a couple select research journals, the money he took off Aidan and some food into his backpack. On a small shelf next to the door was a cracked mirror and a single chess piece, a black queen. The piece looked unfinished and crudely carved, as if he had made it himself. He put the queen in his pocket. He caught his reflection in the mirror. He barely recognized himself. His face was gaunt, filthy and smeared with blood. His hair and beard long and unruly. When he first moved to Asia he was a handsome, fresh-faced 20-year-old. As recently as a few months ago the women of the village were eyeing him appreciatively. Now, anyone who didn't know better would never believe he was only 32 years old.

He went to the river, got in his skiff and started paddling quietly. The only plan he had was to head downstream.

***

On a map, the Sundarbans of India and Bangladesh look like a wall chart of the human lung. Enormous rivers split into primary, secondary and tertiary bronchi and minute bronchioles of fresh and brackish water. Getting to this tiny pocket of the world's largest river delta was more than difficult. It was as deep in the forest as you could get. Julian knew that unless they used a seaplane, Scarface, the one who called himself KP, and the one with the dumb blue glasses would have needed several days to get there from Dhaka or Kolkata, even with guides and good boats. The same would be true for Julian to get out of there. As the crow flies, Kolkata was closer than Dhaka, but harder to get to. It didn't really matter where he went. He would go anywhere someone was willing to take him, whether that was India or Bangladesh, upriver or down. He would motor as far as his gas supply —which was quite small—would allow and start paddling until he ran into someone with a bigger boat.

He was well clear of the village when the satellite phone rang in his pocket. Julian had no intention of answering it, still, he wanted to see if there was a caller ID. He pulled the phone out of his pocket. There was no name or number. All it said was "Chicago, Il." That was enough information. Finally, he was sure of where he was going. For the first time in more than 12 years, he was going home.

***

When he hit deeper water, Julian killed the motor. He threw the satellite phone in the river. He disassembled the two Savage 110's and scattered the pieces so there would be no chance some fisherman would find enough of them to put one of the rifles back together. He pulled on the motor several times to get it started. It wouldn't turn over. He checked his gas can. Empty.

For three exhausting days he paddled down river until he traded his skiff for a ride with some fisherman with a bigger boat. They took him to a village where he could get a ride with more fisherman with an even bigger boat. After two days of helping them fish, they dropped him off in India, where he boarded a large sight-seeing boat headed up the Bidyadhari River to Gadkhali, a town where the road to Kolkata starts, or ends, depending how you look at it.

In Gadkhali he bought a ticket to Kolkata on a bus that had no room for him inside. He climbed the ladder at the back of the bus and joined 20 other men seated on the roof. It wasn't his first roof-ride in India, and it was only 80 kilometers, but it was a three-hour, white-knuckle, hang-on-for-your-life ordeal. Any bus ride in India, cross-town or cross-country, could be exhausting and unnerving. In the middle of this one, however, Julian added the complication of feeling ill. There are dozens of reasons why one might feel ill on an Indian bus, many of them digestive. Julian had experienced all of them. One thing he was certain of was this time it wasn't motion sickness. He was running a fever and sweating profusely. His hands were so clammy and damp that he frequently lost his grip on the rusty cargo rail while going around a curve and thought he was going to be thrown from the bus. He managed to hold on every time, though a couple of times he needed the help of fellow roof-riders.

Near Sudder Street, an area of Kolkata frequented by budget-minded foreign tourists, Julian checked into a room at a hotel he stayed at when he was in the city for supplies or to connect with the rest of the world. He collapsed on the bed and was asleep before he could close his eyes. In the middle of the night he woke with the hottest fever he had ever experienced. Skin-scorching temperatures were accompanied by intense hallucinations. Every color in his room inverted to its opposite. His blue backpack was orange. His green pants were red. The yellow towel on the back of the chair was purple. The elephant in a photograph on the wall came to life and started dancing with the desk lamp. The elephant morphed into a crow and began circling the room. Faster and faster the crow flew, cawing every time it passed Julian's bed. A tiger crashed through the window and swallowed the crow. The tiger jumped on the bed, stuck his enormous face into Julian's and let out a terrific roar. A single monarch butterfly flitted out of the tiger's gaping maw. The butterfly was followed by a pulsating swarm of flies buzzing like a room full of bandsaws. Julian leapt out of bed and scraped frantically at the hallucinatory flies burrowing under his eyelids. He vomited on the floor and fell next to it, where he lay asleep, soaked with sweat for another 10 hours.

When he woke it was if he had never been sick. He felt completely normal. Better than normal. He remembered every last detail of the previous night's hallucinations. His recollections were so vivid and lucid that he questioned whether the carnival of elephants, crows, tigers and flies hadn't been real.

His stomach was bottomless. He spent much of the morning feasting on kosha mangsho, rosogolla, kati rolls and other meat dishes he had only sampled in his years of being a vegetarian, which appeared to be behind him. He went to an internet cafe to check his email. The four-month list of messages was long and intimidating. He didn't bother to read them. He logged into the website of his cell phone provider and bought more minutes. He left the cafe and stepped onto the noisy Kolkata sidewalk to call his brother, whom he had not talked to in almost a year.

"Holy shit," his brother Simon said.

"Just calling to let you know I'm coming home," Julian said.

Simon said nothing.

"Simon, are you there?" Julian asked.

"Yeah. Sorry. I was just waiting for the punchline."

"I'm serious."

"Why now? I mean, do you need a place to stay?"

"I don't know what I'm doing yet or how long I'll be there. It could be a while."

"You know you're always welcome."

Julian's hems and haws gave away his reluctance to stay with this brother.

"Or I could buy you a place this afternoon. Downtown? How about something in Winnetka or Evanston?"

"Of course I'll stay with you," Julian replied, reminding himself Simon was family.

***

Honey collecting is dangerous business in the Sundarbans. The bees are some of the most aggressive in the world, there are crocodiles and poisonous snakes to deal with, and, of course, there are tigers. From April to June, many of the Bangladeshi and Indian fisherman in the Sundarbans put fishing on hold to make money collecting wild honey in the forest. Every year it makes for a profitable side hustle, and every year dozens of honey gatherers are killed by tigers. If you're going to get killed by a tiger, odds are it'll happen during honey season.

KP and his blue-spectacled partner, Declan McCauliff, had been hanging out at Fahd's hut for five miserable, sweaty days when they heard the commotion at the river bank. There were 10 men from the village surrounding a man who had returned from a honey foraging trip. They were all shouting in Bengali, peppering the man at the middle of the circle with questions. KP and McCauliff couldn't understand a word. They looked to their translator for an explanation.

"He found a body," the translator said.

"Whose?" KP asked.

"He's not sure. The man looks white, definitely not local, but it's hard to tell because there isn't much left of him."

"Offer the guy 500 Takas to show us the body," KP told the translator.

The honey forager who discovered the bodies gladly took them up on their offer and led them into the forest and to the body of the dead man.

In the downpour of the first monsoon of the season, KP and McCauliff stood over the carcass. They held their shirts over their noses to block the stench. The body was in an advanced state of decay, but KP had no trouble recognizing it, or at least the one green eye that was still in its socket.

"Tough luck, Cill," KP said.

"Take a look at this," McCauliff said.

KP turned to McCauliff. He was holding up Aidan's arm by the band of his Vacheron Constatin. McCauliff took off the watch, wiped it down, and put it on his own wrist. KP shook his head in mock disapproval.

"A souvenir for his mother," McCauliff said.

"Yeah, so she'll never forget he was a thief."

***

Simon Hamilton was different from Julian and Lara. His siblings were twins, so naturally they would look alike, but they had similar personalities, too. Simon's personality was so different from theirs that when Julian was a kid he thought Simon must have been adopted. There was, however, a remarkable physical resemblance and the siblings were sometimes confused as triplets when they were teenagers. Julian loved his brother as much as he loved his sister, though Simon's personality sometimes caused sibling strife. Simon was wound tightly and from a young age had a lust for wealth. It seemed to dictate most of what he did with his life. There, however, one constant, unwavering similarity: Julian and Simon adored their sister. Lara was beautiful inside and out. She was the high school class salutatorian, finishing seven class ranks ahead of Julian. She was the sweetest girl Julian had ever known, which was a lot to say about your sister.

After Simon graduated from Vanderbilt, he immediately went to work at an investment bank. He spent his days on the 75th floor of the Willis Tower turning a big pile of money into a bigger pile of money. The three siblings had large trust funds they could access when they turned 20. Simon could have chosen any career he wanted. He could have been a painter, poet or park ranger and still lived like a king. He chose the job on the 75th floor with million-dollar bonuses for making rich people richer.

Simon spent his money on Italian automobiles and motorcycles, luxury Caribbean vacation homes and art from all over the world. As for Julian, he didn't care much about money or have much use for it. When he was 20 years old he withdrew $10,000 in cash from his trust account, bought a pair of boots, a decent camera, some outrageously expensive Zeiss binoculars and a one-way ticket to India. As a favor, and for some small commissions, Simon looked after Julian's accounts. Julian never asked about them and told his brother he didn't want to know. During the 12-plus years he had been gone, he dipped into his accounts a few times. He would go off the grid for months at a time. There was one stretch while he was in Burma that he didn't talk to Simon for over two years. Despite the infrequency he wasn't completely out of touch with his brother or the rest of civilization. He had a credit card, a cell phone, and at times, a satellite phone. He occasionally dealt with research associates and scientific journal editors. He knew he had enough money to stay afloat for a long time, but he didn't need to know exactly how deep the well was. Now that he was going home to the big city, maybe he'd need to know more.

Chapter Four

The Mag Mile

It's doubtful Fahd or anyone else from Nurnashmari would have recognized Julian walking through the terminal at O'Hare International. While in Kolkata, he had gone to a street barber for a shave and a haircut. In a public market he bought some black silk pants and a matching shirt. On his feet were simple imitation leather khussas. The toes didn't curl up and there were no embellishing shells, mirrors or beads, but the shoes were decidedly Indian. The overall look was subtle, almost elegant. He was dashing. A trio of Lufthansa flight attendants with wheelie bags stared as he passed. His brother had taken the morning off from work, something highly unusual for Simon, to collect him at the airport. Julian didn't want to look like a hippy returning from a 12-year acid binge on the sub-continent. His groomed appearance was one less thing for him and Simon to argue about.

Simon had no trouble recognizing his brother standing at the curb in front of terminal five. The two hugged firmly for what felt to Julian to be as long as a minute. He had missed his brother and his brother had missed him more than either of them realized. He hadn't seen his brother in more than 12 years and now, oddly, he felt closer to him than he ever had.

"No bags?" Simon asked after noticing Julian carrying nothing but his blue backpack.

"I left in a bit of a hurry."

Almost immediately after buckling his seatbelt, Simon peppered Julian with questions about what he'd done since the last time they had spoken for longer than a half minute. In Julian's answers there was no mention of being shot or being befriended by a tiger that had just killed and eaten his clients. When Simon asked him why he came back, Julian was deliberately vague, saying only that he had loose ends to tie up.

"I thought we were going to your place," Julian said when Simon didn't go north on the Edens.

"We are," Simon replied.

"You guys don't live in Lake Forest anymore?"

"I don't. Vanessa still does. I bought a little place on Pearson," Simon said.

"You got a divorce?"

"Separated."

"But you already bought a place?"

"We'd been separated for almost a year. It seemed silly to keep renting."

"I'm sorry. Of course, I've never met her so I really can't really comment."

"I invited her to dinner tonight so you can pass judgement over a glass of Malbec."

Simon admitted to his brother that he still loved Vanessa and they had been talking about a reconciliation. He didn't want to blow it.

What Simon meant by a little place on Pearson was a corner luxury apartment on the 63rd floor at Water Tower Place. The apartment had views of Michigan Avenue, the lake and the city's iconic gothic revival landmark Water Tower. It was impeccably furnished. The walls were a celebration of abstract expressionism, with works by de Kooning, Gorky, Kline and other lions of the movement. Julian's eyes feasted on the display. A Rothko in the living room grabbed Julian's attention.

"Mom's favorite," Julian said.

"And Lara's," Simon added.

"How the hell did you get this?"

"I didn't steal it, if that's what you mean."

"Of course that's not what I meant."

"I bought it."

"It belongs in a museum."

"It makes me feel good. It's comforting."

"You can't just buy it because it makes you feel good."

"I had just separated from Vanessa. I needed something. Some company. I admit it was a highly unusual and controversial situation.

Rest assured, they were well compensated for it. Besides, I said I would give it back in two years and they get to keep the money."

Julian's displeasure with his brother was obvious. Simon was quick to deflect.

"Despite your well-documented distaste for wealth, I've been taking good care of your assets. Whether you like it or not, you're a very rich man. Blow it all on saving tigers if it makes you feel better. It's not that different from buying a painting."

"I don't want to talk about money now. I just want to think good thoughts." Julian said. He stared at the Rothko and got lost in purple. Simon went to his side and stared into the painting. Despite their disagreement over the painting's acquisition, its allure was something they could both agree on. After a long moment Simon broke the silence. "You didn't come from the farthest corner on earth just to give me shit, did you?"

"Of course not. I'm sorry."

"Then why did you come back?"

"I made a promise to someone. I need to make good on it."

"That's all you're going to tell me?"

"For now."

***

Julian awoke from a long nap. He rolled over to face the table at the side of the bed. On the table was the black queen, angled in such a way that it looked like she was keeping watch over him. He got out of bed and put the chess piece in his pocket.

He wandered into the living room and was surprised to find a blond woman on the couch. His brother had gone to work to let him rest.

Julian thought he would be alone, yet there she was reading a book about birds.

The woman stood up when she saw Julian. She was as tall as he was.

"Sorry. I have a key and let myself in," the woman said.

"You must be Vanessa," said Julian as he rubbed the sleep out of his jet-lagged eyes.

She offered Julian her hand, which he took.

"Sleep well?"

"I've been sleeping on straw mats for years and that bed felt so good."

Vanessa was a six-foot-tall Southern California postcard. She played college volleyball at U.C.L.A and was on the U.S. national team. After retiring from the team at 30 she attacked her new career in finance with the same fervor she had for volleyball. A year later she met Simon at a conference in New York and it was love at first sight. Within a month of meeting, Vanessa had left her home and job in California and moved in with Simon. A year later they were married. Julian was invited to the wedding. He didn't go. He was in Burma and didn't even know about the wedding until the couple had celebrated their first anniversary. The closest he had come to meeting Vanessa was speaking to her on the phone once for less than a minute.

Simon came home and apologized for being late. "Where should we go for dinner?" he asked them.

"I'm good with whatever Julian wants," Vanessa said.

"I can't believe I'm saying this, but I'm really craving a fat, juicy steak," said Julian.

"Great. Gibson's is just a few blocks from here," Simon said. "We can walk."

Julian had just cut into the first bite of a bloody 24-ounce T-bone when Vanessa asked what his plans were and how long he was going to stay. He had already told himself that everyone he knew was going to ask him that question and still he hadn't prepared an acceptable answer, fictional or true. He didn't want to tell everyone that he came home to find the person who wanted him and Amara dead. There were too many details to that story that he didn't want people to know.

"I'm thinking about starting a foundation either to help tigers across Asia, or maybe the mentally ill and homeless in Chicago," Julian said.

"I knew it. You came for the money," Simon said only semi-sarcastically.

"With the kind of money you have you could do a great deal of good," Vanessa said.

It started as a ruse, but this little storyline of starting a foundation was beginning to sound like a pretty good idea to Julian. It wasn't exactly new to him, but it would have to wait.

"I've done a lot of work managing endowments and I know tons of people in the not-for-profit world. I could help if you want," Vanessa said.

Julian thanked Vanessa before he turned to his brother and said, "How much money are we talking about?"

"You really want to know?" Simon asked him.

"I really want to know."

"Well, the last time I checked, which was right after you called from Kolkata, it was $450 million, give or take a few million."

Julian was stunned and silent.

"You've been gone for a long time, brother."

"And Simon is very good at his job," Vanessa said.

Julian wasn't unfamiliar with wealth. For his first two decades he lived a comfortable and privileged life. He went to private schools in the North Shore suburbs. There were European ski vacations, spring breaks on St. Maarten and summers at the family's lake house in Northern Wisconsin. The wealth he experienced growing up was more about opportunity than liquidity. Until he was 20, he had little access to cash and his parents required he always have some sort of part time job.

After Julian left for Asia, he committed to a life of frugality. He always knew the money was there if he needed it. He did his best to forget about it while he was chasing tigers. It was one of the reasons he communicated so infrequently with his brother. He didn't want to be reminded of it, and if there was anything talking to his brother made him think about, it was money. Tucked away in the back of his brain was the thought that someday he would return home and need something to get started. Of course, he didn't need $450 million to live in Chicago. He had held onto the money because he didn't want to do anything rash. He wanted to donate and use the money responsibly. He never thought he would be away as long as he was. He hadn't considered how dedicated to studying and protecting tigers he would become. Finally, vengeance made for a good reason to come home.

Over the long, leisurely dinner Vanessa and Simon delved into their marital woes more than Julian expected. Their marriage counselor had encouraged them to talk openly. They lived in the city before they were married and the first couple of years after. They moved to Lake Forest, where they thought they would raise a family. After a year of trying to have a baby, Vanessa found out she was sterile. It turned out Simon was, too. Since they couldn't have children, they worked all the time. They both struggled to stay awake on the train home, then spent an hour or so knocking around their David Adler-designed mansion on Lake Road before it was time to go to bed so they could be rested to do it again the next day. An emotional gap formed between them. He moved to the city. She quit her job managing portfolios and started coaching college volleyball. They had spent the last year trying to figure out what went wrong. They still went out together occasionally, but it was hard work rebuilding their relationship.

"Sell the damn house," Julian said. Simon and Vanessa had the same funny expression of recognition, as if they were both saying to themselves, "Why didn't we think of that?"

"Speaking of houses, who's living in the Evanston house?" Julian asked.

"Some guy from Malaysia bought it a couple of years ago. I'm not sure if he ever moved in. Bill Westermeyer called me just last week to let me know it was going on the market soon and asked if I was interested."

"Maybe you could buy it," Vanessa said.

"I could never live in that house again. Too many good memories there," said Julian.

"I know what you mean," Simon said.

"Time to make some new ones," Vanessa said as she raised her wine glass.

"Clink and drink," Simon added. They all did.

To Julian, Simon and Vanessa seemed to get along terrifically for a separated couple. He was envious. He admitted to them that with the exception of six-week fling with an Italian animal biologist he worked with in Satpura National Park in India, he had been emotionally, romantically and sexually alone for the past decade.

"Got any friends who might be interested in a filthy rich tiger nerd?" Simon asked Vanessa.

"Isn't that what every girl's looking for?" Vanessa replied.

Julian saw Simon and Vanessa holding hands and making faces at each other on the walk home. When they were a block from Simon's building, Julian, like he would do if Simon were his college dorm roommate who needed the room for a few hours, told his brother he wanted to walk a little longer and that the two of them should go upstairs without him. He had a key. He could let himself in.

Julian walked south on North Michigan Avenue, the Magnificent Mile, or simply the Mag Mile, Chicago's version of The Champs Élysées. It was after 10:00 and the stores were closed. Still, there were people out walking and enjoying a warm early spring evening, just like he was. It's unlikely those other people were having the same experience Julian was having. Michigan Avenue didn't go completely dark when shops closed, far from it. But there was no denying his night vision was like nothing he had ever experienced before. His visual acuity was off the charts. He could read the small print on street signs half a block away. From across the wide street he could see clearly the small Fila logo on a man's hoody. A rusty rattletrap Datsun pickup drove past. The old man driving had a black patch over his left eye.

Julian could see a blue twinkle in the right. Every little architectural detail jumped out at him. The Grotesque sculpture of the monkey above the fourth floor of the Tribune Tower. The bright white terra-cotta of the Wrigley Building clock tower. The reflections off the giant glass walls of the Apple Store, which he had never seen before. Everything popped. He had always thought his hometown was beautiful, day and night. His amplified vision gave him a new and greater appreciation for it.

When he reached the river, he walked down to the Esplanade and over to Lower Water, where there was considerably less artificial light. His new enhanced night vision worked there, too. To get back to Simon's apartment he took the less trafficked, darker Fairbanks Court, only partially because it offered another test of his vision. The stronger pull was some previously undiscovered instinct telling him to seek stealth.

Johnny, a tall, skinny young black man with a luminous smile, no more than 22 years old and dressed in a gray uniform, was working the night doorman's shift when Julian returned. Johnny pulled open the front door to the lobby and greeted Julian.

"You're Mr. Hamilton's brother, right?"

"True. Though this is the first time I've ever admitted it. I'm Julian."

"And I'm Johnny. You two look a lot alike."

"We get that a lot."

"Your brother is one of my favorite tenants."

"Is that right?" Julian asked.

"Most generous tenant in the building, specially round the holidays. Nomsayin?"

"He'd be second most generous if I moved in."

"And when will that be?" Johnny asked with an endearing grin.

"Me in a posh place like this? I don't think so," Julian said.

"What's the point of having coin if you ain't gonna' spend it?"

"Good point."

"And, keep this on the down-low, but I've got a scratch arrangement with a real estate lady. Nomsayin?"

"Not really."

"I scratch her back. She scratches mine," he said while rubbing his fingers together.

"Got it."

Johnny slipped a business card out of his pocket. "Just tell her Johnny sent you."

Chapter Five

A Slap In The Face

"How are you feeling today?" Olivia Van de Weghe asked the old man as she put a small tray of vitamins and a shot glass of bright orange liquid on a round mahogany table.

The old man sitting in the blue wingback chair next to the small antique table lowered the tablet he was using to read the Chicago Tribune. "Fantastic. Do I ever answer differently?" he asked.

"You didn't always answer that way."

"No, but those days feel like a lifetime ago.

The old man raised the shot glass, took three deep breaths, acknowledged Olivia with a tilt of the glass and threw it back. His lips puckered when he swallowed and his body heaved when it hit his belly.

The 89-year-old man was often confused as Olivia's grandfather. It was an understandable mistake given the 54-year age gap between the two. The old man, Edward Van de Weghe, was Olivia's father and the founder of VanPharm, a pharmaceutical conglomerate that had made him exceptionally wealthy. The business had also nearly killed him. Two years earlier his arthritis had become so debilitating and he was so desperate for relief that he volunteered to take part in a trial of one of his company's new drugs, Tribathalmate, a biopharmaceutical that never made it to market. Nine people in the trial died. Dozens more became gravely ill, including Edward, who, had he not been founder of the company, would have been told he was ineligible for the trial because of his advanced age. Edward flirted with death in the ICU for two months. The fiasco almost killed the company, too. Edward retired as president and CEO, a position that for years was purely titular, but stayed on as Chairman of the Board.

Olivia's shirt was open down to the one button on her suit jacket. She was tall and striking, a "life is cruel and unfair" kind of beautiful. She buttoned the jacket and gave it a tug to straighten its line. Her look was provocative and professional at the same time.

Edward clicked twice out of the side of his mouth. His way of saying she looked good.

Olivia smiled. She bent over and gave her father a light kiss on his cheek. "I'll see you this evening."

Letty, a pretty young woman in a servant's uniform, met Olivia at the bottom of the grand staircase and handed her a travel cup of coffee and a sleek, black leather attache.

"Que tenga buen día, Miss Olivia," Letty said.

"Igualmente," Olivia replied with a smile.

She walked down the hall to the garage where she parked her carmine red Porsche Taycan Turbo S. She backed the car out of the garage, put it in drive and stomped on the accelerator. She raced down the long driveway that wended its way past a pool, a tennis court and stables, where a chestnut mare and her foal whinnied as she flew past. She barely slowed down as she approached the opening iron gate. The instant the gap was wide enough, she shot through two imposing stone columns and exited the estate.

Olivia always had a heavy foot and was one citation away from having her license suspended for the second time. She did like to drive fast. It's why she bought the Porsche. Her recent efforts to slow down were working, except when her father was fresh in her mind. That made slowing down impossible. The bright orange liquid she singlehandedly developed had saved his life, but most days she wished he would just die already.

***

Julian stood under the Loop tracks at Adams and Wabash and watched puffy clouds float across the blue sky. He had walked the 18 blocks from his brother's apartment and the "L" stop was his final destination. He didn't go any further than half-way up the stairs to the platform. He simply looked up at the heaping white billows. Occasionally he fixed his gaze on the trains as they passed above him, but it gave him an ill feeling in his gut. He had ridden the Green Line frequently when he was at the University of Chicago and knew all the stops. To the south of Adams and Wabash were Roosevelt, Cermak, 35th, Indiana, and on and on all the way to Ashland and 63rd. He had loved riding the trains.

As a kid they meant freedom and independence. Their significance now wasn't so optimistic. The "L" trains, particularly the Green Line, would forever remind him of his sister's death. He hadn't been on one since. Despite his aversion to trains, he was drawn to them like a bee to nectar.

He had been standing on the stairs for 10 minutes when he heard a woman's cry for help. Julian looked over the handrail. On the sidewalk below, a short, muscular man in a striped tank-top slammed a middle-aged woman to the ground. She hit her face on the concrete as she fell. He grabbed her purse and ran off, dragging her several feet until the woman let go. She lay there on the sidewalk motionless, her right cheek smushed against the concrete, a line of blood on the front of her cream colored dress. She looked lifeless.

Yet another undiscovered instinct took over and Julian jumped into action. There were several people on the stairs blocking his path back down, so Julian leapt over the rail. It was more than 10 feet down to the sidewalk, a jump he never would have made if he had taken even half a second to think about it. He landed close to the woman sprawled on sidewalk.

"Are you okay?" Julian asked the woman, who was slowly coming around.

"I think so. But he took my purse."

Without another thought, Julian took off. The short, muscular purse-snatcher was already halfway down the block and headed toward the Art Institute, no doubt hoping to disappear behind the museum and into the crowd in Grant Park. Julian sprinted after the man. He had never run so fast in his life. Speed came effortlessly. His strides were long and powerful. He caught up to the man, pounced on the his back and rode him to the sidewalk like a rodeo cowboy on a steer. Julian stood up keeping one foot firmly pressed on the man's back. The man tried desperately to get up. Julian wouldn't let him. He had him pinned. He took the purse out of the man's hand, grabbed his foot and dragged him back to the bottom of the stairs at the train platform. Police were arriving on the scene when he got there.

"We appreciate your help, but you know you could have broken your leg or worse jumping off the stairs like that," an officer later told Julian sternly.

"I'm sorry officer. I wasn't thinking. I just reacted," Julian said.

"Well, don't do it again. I don't want to fill out paperwork all day just because you weren't thinking."

Ordinarily, Julian would have been submissive and more apologetic with the officer. Today, he really didn't care. He almost resented the officer's disapproval. He told himself that he would do it again.

After the police dismissed him, he wandered over to Grant Park where he got the urge to run. The park and its walkways were crowded with people, but Julian needed to run. The speed at which he could run was invigorating. He jumped over railings, bushes and bike racks. He felt like a kid on a playground as he raced through the park. He drew stares from passersby. There were plenty of joggers in the park, all of them jogging in straight lines and staying on the path. They didn't vault over trashcans and park benches with giant grins on their faces. And none of them was wearing what looked like silk pajamas and slippers. He realized he needed to go out and buy some new clothes.

He sat on a bench at Cloud Gate, the city's famous bean-shaped sculpture in Millennium Park. He thought about his unusual, almost superhuman speed. He couldn't make sense of it. He hadn't done any proper exercise in years. Although he was technically outside when he worked, the work he had been doing with the tigers was sedentary. He spent most of his time sitting in a little wooden box eight feet off the forest floor. He had recently been shot in the chest twice. He was jet-lagged. He had always been a slow runner. His brother and his sister had always been able to run faster than him. For his entire childhood they teased him about it. He enjoyed his newfound speed, but he was baffled by how it had just shown up.

The area around the sculpture was packed with people of all colors, shapes and sizes. An older Asian woman in polkadot overalls was bent over trying to take an upside-down photo of her reflection in the Bean's polished surface. Julian could hear her make soft, struggling grunts, like a puppy.

A red-haired, freckle-faced boy was arguing with his little sister over who got to push the stroller.

"Jacob, let go. Mom said it was my turn," the young girl said.

"Go suck a walnut," the boy said to his sister.

"It's the only diet that's ever worked for me," a tall woman in tight jeans told her companion. "I lost 13 pounds in a month."

A tremendously overweight white man with a bushy beard wearing a mechanic's jumpsuit walked a tiny black dog smaller than his shoe. He called the little dog Hurricane. Julian could hear him as if the fat man were standing right next to him. He could hear everyone as if they were standing right next to him, but they were scattered all around the plaza.

First it was his vision. Now speed and hearing. They were all improvements, but they were also disconcerting. He needed to see the only person in the world he knew who might understand just a sliver of what was going on. Hopefully, she would be willing to see him and not throw him out on his ear.

***

Julian felt nostalgic as he walked across the University of Chicago campus. It was a warm spring day and the ivy that covered so many of the campus's gothic buildings was brilliant green. The blossoms on the redbud trees were bright pink. He saluted the gargoyles at Cobb Gate. He went out of his way to pass the Harper Library Tower, the Rockefeller Chapel, and the Smart Museum, where the Rothko painting that now hung in Simon's apartment had lived. His mother frequently took him, his sister and brother to the Smart, where she and Lara would stare deep into Rothko's purples and reds.

Julian found the building he was looking for, the home of the School of Biological Sciences. He had had many classes in the building during his two years at the University. As he climbed the stairs he was reminded of happier, less complicated times. He didn't regret what he had done with his life over the past 12 years, though he did wish he had been offered more options.

Julian rapped on the door of a second floor office. Black letters on the door's frosted glass window indicated the office belonged to Dr. Lourdes Villegas, Ph.D. A tall, thick young man in a black beanie and stinking of cannabis opened the door.

"May I help you?" the young man said.

"I'm looking for Lou," replied Julian.

"Who?"

"Sorry, I mean I'm looking for Dr. Villegas."

"Is she expecting you?"

"No. If she knew I was coming she would have told me not to."

The young man looked confused.

"Just tell her Julian Hamilton is here to see her. Please, it's important."

There was a glint of recognition when the young man in the beanie heard Julian's name. "I'm Dan, one of Dr. Villegas's research assistants. She's in the lab. I'll take you up."

Julian followed Dan up the stairs to the third floor and down the hallway to a heavy fire door. Like the door downstairs, the words "Dr. Lourdes Villegas, Ph.D." were printed on it. Dan opened the door and gestured for Julian to enter. One side of the long room housed a dozen or so work benches and stools with wheels. On most of the benches were compound light microscopes and assorted analysis and testing machines. The other side of the room was dominated by multi-level shelves filled with beakers, Erlenmeyer flasks and pipets. Lourdes was seated on a stool at the farthest work bench, her eyes pressed against the ocular lenses of a microscope.

"Someone here to see you, Dr. Villegas," Dan said.

Lourdes wheeled around on the stool and stood up. She looked across the room. She had been staring into a microscope for several minutes and her eyes weren't letting her see clearly. As Julian came into focus, she couldn't believe what she was seeing. She took several steps to get a closer look. Julian smiled. Her recognition triggered a wave of emotions in him, the first of which was guilt, which was followed by sadness, relief and a tinge of joy. The emotion that stuck with him most, the one that was most comforting, was desire. She was, after all, the only woman he had ever loved. He had burned for her. He felt the same nervous excitement he felt the first time he met her.

Back then she was simply Lourdes Villegas, a skinny freshman at the University of Chicago. They met in a cell biology class first semester. The class was in a large lecture hall and on the first day Julian was seated a few rows behind Lourdes. He learned little from that day's class, having spent the entire hour staring at her profile. He was smitten. After class he followed her out and caught up with her in the foyer outside the lecture hall.

Meeting girls was always easy for Julian. When he was 12 and just becoming curious about the opposite sex, Julian asked his father what he had said to Julian's mother the first time he met her.

"Hi, I'm Robert," was his father's answer.

"And that line worked?" the young Julian asked.

"Of course it did. It's the only line you'll ever need. Introduce yourself and be yourself. Keep it simple and everything else will fall into place."

It was good advice. As a 14-year-old high school freshman, Julian tried out the line on a half-Japanese girl in his algebra class. She was tall and had bleached blonde hair and a ring in the side of her nose. The first day he saw her she was wearing a Nirvana T-shirt and ripped jeans. Julian and his friends initially thought she was one of those untouchable I'm-cooler-than-you girls who over-populated the North Shore. She wasn't like that at all. She was just cool, and easy to talk to. The girl responded with a simple, "I'm Yasko," as if her father had given her the same advice. Julian was so excited about the ensuing conversation that he went home and bragged to his father about his accomplishment. Julian's father patted him on the back and told him he was proud of him. His father always knew how to make Julian feel good about himself. By the end of that first week of school, Julian's friends referred to Yasko as Julian's "hot Asian girlfriend." By the end of the semester Julian's father was dead from pancreatic cancer. Diagnosed in October and gone by December.

The line didn't work every time like his dad suggested it would. It worked with Lourdes, though. Within two minutes Julian knew her name, that she was first generation American-Peruvian from Stockton, California, and she loved running, The Big Lebowski and The Clash. Ten minutes later they were having lunch together in the cafeteria, where she blamed her penchant for foul language, which Julian found charming, on being the atheist child of hyper-Catholic parents. Profanity was forbidden fruit and Lourdes binged on it. Cursing became a habit she could never break.

By dinnertime they were having sex in her dorm room with no regrets. They dated for almost two years, every day as good as the one before it. Then Lara was killed. Lourdes had just gone back to Stockton for a few weeks during summer break. She did what she could from across the country to help Julian through the ordeal. He sank deeper and deeper into depression and eventually stopped answering Lourdes's calls and texts. He dropped out of school and within seven months he disappeared completely. He wasn't even on the same continent.

When she was 20, Lourdes looked much like she did now. Of course, she was older, but time had been good to her. Her body, sinewy and strong, had hardly changed at all, neither had her sense of style. She always looked like she was about to go for a run or had just finished one. In her college days, she had a closet full of tracksuits. Her collection had grown substantially since. However, when the occasion called for it, she could wear the hell out of a little black dress. She could make heads turn when she wanted to. Most of the time she really didn't care.

When Julian learned Lourdes had received her Ph.D. from the University of Chicago, he sent her a note of congratulations that included little personal content. As soon as he had pushed the letter through the slot in a Kathmandu post office, he regretted it. He even asked inside if he could get the letter back, but they wouldn't allow it. In turn, she sent him a note. Her note said even less than his. It was just an acknowledgement of his acknowledgement. At least she had written back. A year later she wrote him again and asked him for a strictly professional favor: collaborate with her on a paper. It was published under both their names, hers first, in the journal Animal Behaviour, titled "The Effects of Habitat Loss on Familial Behavior in Large Cats." Her input was biological, his was behavioral. All of their communication while working on the paper was done through email and they had rarely spoken to each other since shortly after his sister's death. Their written communications, however, had turned friendlier and more familiar. She hadn't forgiven him, though she was no longer furious.

"Well look what the cat dragged in, or should I say tiger?" Lourdes said.

"Hi, Lou. Sorry for just showing up like this."

"No, no, no, don't apologize. It's much more dramatic this way," Lourdes said as she circled him tauntingly with a smile that made it obvious she more interested in seeing him squirm than affronting him. He stood still and let her play her game.

"I see your acne's cleared up. Last time I saw you, you had a mess of pimples," she continued.

"I was stressed out and not taking care of myself."

"Kinda skinny, too."

"Okay, I know I deserve this." Julian said. She was quick to cut him off.

"Can I slap you?"

"What?"

"I've always wanted to slap a man, but the right situation's never come up. This seems like the perfect situation, doesn't it?" she said as she moved in closer to Julian.

"That's not how it works. You don't ask permission," Julian said.

Her hand came up quickly and slapped him in the face, catching him completely off guard.

"Fuck, that felt good," Lourdes said with a big smile. She turned around to Dan. "Did you see that? How's my form?" Dan gave her a thumbs up.

"Still swear like a sailor," Julian said. Lourdes gave him a funny look. "You know I love your potty mouth," he added.

"So what brings you down here, Jules?"

"I really need to talk to you. Is there someplace more private where we can go?"

"What's wrong with right here?"

"I'm sure he doesn't want to hear us air our dirty laundry," Julian said as he gestured toward Dan.

"Him? He'd probably love to hear us air out our shit-stained skivvies."

"This is serious," he said.

Lourdes could see the sincerity on Julian's face. "Okay," she told him. She turned to her assistant. "Dandelion, could you take those folders down to my office?" she asked him as she pointed to a stack of files on a nearby table.

"Of course, Dr. Villegas." He picked up the folders and left the room.

"Dandelion?" Julian said.

"His parents were hippies. His driver's license says Dandelion, but he tells everyone his name is Dan."

"I can see why."

"We have an agreement. I let him smoke weed at work. He lets me call him by his legal name. So talk to me, Hamilton."

"On second thought, how 'bout we take a little walk?" Julian asked.

Julian and Lourdes took a stroll across the campus. They made small talk at first. He talked mostly about his reconnecting with his brother. He spoke a little about the Sundarbans, though he neglected to tell Lourdes the gruesome details of the more recent events. He was waiting for the right moment to lay that on her. She updated him on some work she had been doing. She was tenured at a remarkably young age and was getting a huge grant from a foundation.

"Oh, and I ran a personal best 10K last month. Can you believe it? I'm 33."

"Congratulations, grandma," Julian said before turning pensive.

They continued walking without talking. Julian tried to make Lourdes think his silence was a result of his great admiration for the campus. His eyes went everywhere.

"Do you think they'd let me back into this place?" Julian finally asked to break the silence that had begun to border on awkwardness.

"Is that what you were so desperate to talk to me about? You're thinking about going back to school?"

"I wasn't until now."

"Then what is it? I have a shit ton of work to do."

"You can't talk about what I tell or show you, not to anyone, ever," Julian said.

"Okay. I can keep a secret."

"The girl in the orange shirt. Do you see her?" Julian asked as he pointed at a girl sitting on the grass across the Main Quad.

"The one with the book?

"Yeah,"

"What about her?"

"Go tell her something. Anything. Talk about Albert Camus. Ask for directions. Whatever."

"What on earth for?"

"Just do it."

Lourdes walked over to the girl in the orange shirt. The girl smiled and motioned for Lourdes to sit down in the grass, which Lourdes did. They talked for a couple minutes.

"Did that really happen` or did you make it up?" Julian asked Lourdes when she finally returned.

"Did what really happen?"

"Did a squirrel steal a bagel out of your tote bag?"

"Last spring. It had poppy seeds. I mean the bagel had poppy seeds, not the squirrel," Lourdes said as she looked at Julian with an incredulous expression. "You really heard that?"

"I heard everything. I forgot what a great conversationalist you are."

"You heard everything, even the part about the clam chowder?"

"You didn't say anything about clam chowder. You complimented her on her orange shirt, and commented on the book she was reading."

"How did you know it was Camus?"

"You said you loved The Stranger and The Plague, but felt stupid because you didn't get The Fall, and of course you mentioned the poppy seeds, but nothing about clams or chowder."

"Astonishing."

Julian led Lourdes to a bench. He explained to her what he'd been experiencing with his running and with his vision, too. Lourdes was a scientist and she was trained to be a good listener and think rationally, but she didn't know what to make of Julian's confession. This was outside the scope of any science she knew.

"Maybe you picked up some exotic virus. I'm sure you've been exposed to a lot of weird shit we've never even heard of."

They continued their walk. As they passed Regenstein Library something caught Julian's eye. It was a white panel van with a University of Chicago Building Maintenance Department decal on the doors.

"Follow me," Julian told Lourdes. I'm gonna blow that Ph. D. mind of yours."

Julian walked right up to the van and looked around to see if anyone other than Lourdes was watching. The coast was clear. With one powerful, balletic leap Julian was on the roof of the van.

"Holy shit. How did you do that?"

"I don't know," Julian said, still standing on the roof of the van.

"Okay, you've proved your point. Now get down, tiger," she told him while checking to see if people had stopped to stare or if campus security had seen what Julian had just done. No one had stopped and security was nowhere to be seen.

He jumped to the ground and told Lourdes, "I've never done that before, never even tried."

"Why would you?"

"I just knew I could do it. Why would I ever think I could make a jump like that?"

"A good question for sure," she said. She paused to consider something. "Are you still rich?"

"Filthy."

"Great, you can buy me dinner. I missed lunch and I'm starving."

With a big plate of enchiladas and a legal pad in front of her, Lourdes enthusiastically asked Julian a battery of questions about all the places he had been for the past six months, what he had been eating, if he had experienced weight loss or weight gain. Had he been sick or had any dirty cuts? Vomiting? Diarrhea? Hookworm? High fever?

Julian answered no to every question except one. He told Lourdes he hadn't taken his temperature, but the fever he had in Kolkata a week earlier had been the hottest he had ever experienced and it was accompanied by intense, high-resolution hallucinations.

Lourdes made a note about the fever on her legal pad. "This is good. Is there anything else you can think of that I haven't asked you yet?" Lourdes said.

"You haven't asked me if I've been shot recently?"

"Were you?" Lourdes asked with excitement.

"Twice."

"Holy shit," she said with a level of enthusiasm just right for winning a new car on a game show.

"In the chest."

Her enthusiasm quickly disappeared.

"Would it make a difference if I said I got shot in the head?" Julian asked.

"Only if you took it in the frontal or occipital lobe." Lourdes said.

"Thanks for the sympathy," Julian said.

"Sorry. I got wrapped up in the excitement of the challenge. Can I see where you were shot?"

Julian unbuttoned the first couple of buttons on his shirt and pulled the collar back to show Lourdes the bullet holes below his clavicle. She slowly and gently ran her index finger across the wounds. She traced their circular shape. There was no need for her to be so delicate with the wounds. They had healed significantly. She wanted to touch Julian, wounds or no wounds, and Julian certainly wasn't going to stop her. He hadn't been this intimate with a woman in years. She pulled her finger away and quickly stepped back into her scientist persona.

"When did this happen?" she asked.

"About 10 days ago."

"No fucking way. They look much older than that."

"I think a tiger licked them, but I can't be sure."

"Come again?" Lourdes said.

Chapter Six

Bolo

"This place is a fucking shit hole," McCauliff said.

McCauliff and KP were stuffed into a noisy auto rickshaw, bumper to bumper on a broad street in Dhaka that was packed with cars, trucks, buses, bikes, people and dogs waiting for a slow-moving train to pass. Hundreds of men, women and children hung from the sides of the train or rode on the rusty, corroded roof. It was evening rush hour and everyone was trying to get home. The twenty passenger cars of the train were crammed full. There were even more on the outside of the train, either because there was no room inside or they didn't have the 30 Takas, about 35 cents, to pay the fare.

KP watched a man run along side the train desperately looking for a place, anyplace to jump on. Even if the man weren't holding a big woven bag under one arm it looked impossible

"Twenty bucks says he gets a ride," KP said.

"You're on," replied McCauliff.

The running man held out his one free hand and a man hanging from the train grabbed it. The running man jumped up. His feet desperately explored the side of the train for a hold. There was nothing but other feet and body parts. The man dangled off the side of the train until the other man could hold him no more. The man fell hard to the ground and rolled away from the tracks.

McCauliff laughed at the man and said, "Fork it over."

"Not so fast," KP said. He pointed to the man, who was back up and running for the train again. The man grabbed an offered hand and was pulled up. He squeezed one foot onto the rail and held on to the edge of a window with his finger tips. The man who pulled him up took the bag from him so he could secure his grip.

KP held out his hand, a gesture that meant "pay up."

"That's fucking unbelievable," McCauliff said.

"Never underestimate the power of community."

"What the fuck does that mean?"

"It means people with a shared struggle will always help each other. No man left behind."

"Spare me the special forces bullshit. The motherfucker just got lucky."

"I'd rather be that motherfucker than have to go home without that tiger," KP said.

"What choice did we have? We'd never have found that fucking tiger without him. The guy's dead."

"Did you see three bodies? I saw one body and Andre's arm. Until I see this Julian motherfucker's rotting corpse, I'm gonna' assume he's a threat."

"Come on. We were in that fucking village for a week and he never came back. The tiger got him."

"Probably. But even if the tiger did get him, I'd still like to put a bullet in his fucking skull."

"Fine, you can go back to the end of the earth to find his body, but I'm getting on a plane to Chicago tomorrow."

If KP put a bullet in Julian's head, it wouldn't have been a first. Eric "KP" Klaypool served in the U.S. Army for 15 and a half years, the last 10 of them as a member of the elite Delta Force. He stayed in six months too long. A deadly incident in Afghanistan that he was at the center of had caused international outrage and much embarrassment for the Unit, the U.S. Army, and the country. His Army appointed lawyer called the killing of an Afghan woman and her two daughters an accident precipitated by KP's previously undiagnosed Post Traumatic Stress Disorder. KP played along with the PTSD defense. Unfortunately, his lawyers were unable to keep out of evidence a photo KP took of the "accident." The two girls lying dead on a blood-stained dirt floor made a disturbing image. KP's history of taking photos of dead bodies was revealed to the world. He had also been accused of taking a piece of a dead Taliban fighter's ear as a trophy. It was an accusation that was never substantiated, however true it might have been. Needless to say, none of it went over well with the brass. He was court-martialed and dishonorably discharged. Somehow he managed to avoid serving any time in Leavenworth.

Feeling betrayed, he entered the mercenary market with a "fuck all" attitude. He wasn't ruthless, he just had a skewed understanding of antagonistic relationships. On the battlefield, if you weren't an ally you were an enemy. KP extended that attitude to client relationships as well. If you weren't a friend or ally of a paying client, you were an enemy. There was no neutral.

***

In the private confines of Lourdes's office, surrounded by stacks of papers and books with no prying eyes or ears, Julian felt comfortable confessing the horrid details he had left out while they were eating. He told her more about how he was shot. He told her about watching Amara kill and eat a man and how Amara had offered him a human arm as a meal. He gave her the few details he knew about the two dead men and said he knew nothing about the two other men, except one of them went by the name KP.

"Do you think they're still looking for you?"

"It doesn't matter. I'm going to find them. I don't know how I'm going to do it or how long it will take, but I'm going to find them, every last one of them."

"Are you sure that's a good idea? You seem pretty wound up about it."

"I can't explain it, just like the other things going on with me, but when I," Julian paused and prepared himself to say his next words. "When I had to shoot Amara, something lit up inside me. I hadn't felt anger like that since Lara was killed."

"Let me do some bloodwork. We'll see if that reveals anything."

"I want to keep this quiet."

"Just me. No phlebotomists, no lab assistants. I promise. You won't get a full panel of results, still, I'll do whatever I can."

Julian agreed.

"I'll have to steal a few items from a lab down the hall. Wait here," Lourdes said as she made her way to her office door.

While Lourdes was down the hall, Julian snooped around the office. There were two bookcases. One was full of books, mostly heavy reading on various topics in biology. The other case was jammed with stacks of folders. There didn't seem to be any order to them, though it was hardly what most people would consider messy. Various diplomas were displayed on the east wall. A couple pairs of New Balance running shoes sat in the corner by the door. There wasn't a single photograph of her alone or with anyone else. He knew she had married, but there was no evidence of any man in her life. The room was generic. The most interesting item in the room was a formal invitation on the desk that read in embossed type, "The Van de Weghe Foundation invites you to a gala celebrating this year's Brilliance Award winners: Ms. Barbara Le Conte and Dr. Lourdes Villegas, Ph.D."

When Lourdes returned with a cart full of blood-taking supplies, Julian was sitting in a chair with his shirt sleeve already rolled up. He didn't want to appear to have been snooping. Lourdes wrapped a latex band around his arm and looked for a good vein. She missed on the first three tries. With each miss came a four-letter word followed by an apology. The fourth try gave her three 10 ml collection tubes of blood. She untied the latex band and taped a piece of sterile gauze over the puncture. She apologized again for all the extra needle pokes she had to give him.

"Can't be an expert at everything," Julian said.

"I'm pretty good on rats," she replied as she labeled the tubes. "I'll take the cart back."

Lourdes had the cart halfway through her office door when Julian called to her. There was a vulnerability in the way he said her name that caught her off guard. He almost always called her Lou, but he had said Lourdes this time. She paused before she turned around.

"I'm sorry," Julian said.

"For what?"

"For giving up the way I did."

Lourdes didn't respond.

"It was cruel," Julian added.

Lourdes measured her words carefully before she said, "I thought I was more to you than that."

"You were everything to me. I just couldn't stop myself and I'm forever sorry."

Lourdes pulled the cart back inside her office and closed the door. She leaned against it and stared at her feet.

"We can do this later. I'm sure you want to get home to your husband," Julian said.

"I got a divorce, Jules." She was the only person who ever called him Jules. Not even his mother called him that. "I waited four years to finally admit I didn't love him. He already knew. He always knew I would never get over you."

Tears were tumbling down her cheeks. She sniffled and said, "God, this is fucking embarrassing." She left pushing the cart.

***

On paper, Olivia Van de Weghe's professional accomplishments sounded made up. They were all real. She was brilliant and relentlessly driven, a combination that helped her graduate from Yale when she was just 20. She earned her Ph.D. in molecular genetics from M.I.T. when she was 25 and an M.B.A. from Northwestern's renowned Kellogg School of Management when she was 30 and working full time. If she had gone to work for any other company but the one her father started, she would have been running it already.

Even when he was young, Edward Van de Weghe was a dinosaur. His values were outdated and old school. No matter how brilliant and talented his daughter was, she was still a woman, and he didn't want a woman running the company he founded in the 1960's and built into a multibillion-dollar behemoth. He never had a son. He gladly offered her a job. She took the son of a bitch's offer for two reasons. First, her father promised to let her create her own research unit with the freedom to be bold in her quest for innovation. No other company offered her such a long leash. Her running the show at VanPharm was a different story. She was named vice president for research and development when she was 31, but there was almost no chance she would ever make president. She learned that while interning for the company in high school. She never really wanted to be president, she thought she might even turn down the position if by some miracle it were ever offered to her. She'd turn it down just to spite her old man. Being named president of VanPharm was far more important than actually being president. The second reason she chose to work for her father was she was taking Sun Tzu and Michael Corleone's advice to keep her friends close and her enemies closer, except she didn't really have any friends.

If she wanted something, or someone, she harnessed her brilliance and drive. She could be charming or funny or mysterious. It was all an act. The social confidence was fake. Getting men to like her or getting them in bed was easy. Getting them to stay was a magic trick she could never pull off. She had moved back in with her father to care for him after he took ill during the Tribathalmate trials. Although she basically hated him, he was the closest thing to a man in her life.

The one thing Olivia really wanted, up until she pretty much gave up on it, was the one thing she could never make happen. She wanted a normal family life, though she never told anyone. What she had wanted for herself was a husband and a couple of kids, maybe a golden retriever or a Labradoodle. Olivia had several relationships as an adult. All ended badly, most of them when her current partner simply couldn't take her anymore. Her ex-lovers used words like pigheaded, inflexible and ice queen as they were walking out the door. There was no denying Olivia was stunningly beautiful from head to toe and she was adventurous in bed. As powerful a weapon as that was, it could only make them stay for so long. As they left she begged them to stay and promised them she could change. They never stayed and she never had to make good on her promises. With every failed relationship any possibility of actually being able to change became more unlikely.

Up until 11th grade, she was gawky. Her classmates at the private snobatorium her parents sent her to didn't understand her drive and her need to excel. Throughout her childhood, girls were mean to her, particularly the popular ones. Olivia had no interest in being part of their clique. She didn't like those girls. They gave her no reason to. Even more so, she didn't like being the subject of their cruel jokes and comments, particularly the ones about her spindly, awkward body. In third grade she was given the nickname Olivia Oyl and it stuck to her for years. She hated the comparison to the big-footed cartoon character and all the jokes about what it's like to fuck Popeye that came later. It wasn't just the jokes aimed directly at her that hurt, it was also stuff she overheard. The other girls didn't even try to be discreet. She once overheard one of the mean girls say to another "Why did god waste perfect skin on such a pathetic loser?" There was a backhanded compliment in there. Olivia chose to focus on the insult. The comment was somewhat prophetic, however. By the time she was 17, she had filled out her perfect skin to divine proportions. She was undeniably a beautiful young woman. Unfortunately, all those years of being ostracized had done permanent damage. She was bitter and had nearly used up all her empathy. Her sweet, understanding mother was her only friend.

When she got to college, she began to think she suffered from a variety of mental health issues. She could only put a name to one of the many ailments she thought she might have: obsessive-compulsive disorder. She started seeing a student health therapist. Although the therapist did not give her an OCD diagnosis, she did give her a name for her issue: perfectionism. Everything she did had to be perfect. The therapist helped her understand that there is no such thing as perfection. It became a mantra for Olivia, though its recitation had little effect on her behavior.

The therapist did diagnose social anxiety disorder, for which Olivia latched onto another mantra: fake it 'til you make it. This was a powerful and effective tool for her, particularly with men. She quickly learned how to use her anatomical assets around the opposite sex. She had that trick mastered. She could come off as confident in almost any situation if she worked at it. In the company of women she had to work extra hard and was often unwilling to put in the effort.

Olivia's time with the therapist lasted just over three months. Walking home from what would end up being her last appointment, she saw a young woman pedestrian hit by a speeding car that jumped the curb. Olivia was nearly hit herself. It was messy. The woman was dead on the sidewalk when Olivia reached her. Olivia stared at the body until another passerby laid a coat over the dead woman. Olivia had the urge to pull the coat off the woman so she could continue examining her. She felt nothing for the poor woman. She was more interested in the hole in the woman's back that offered a view of her crushed kidney. It was then that Olivia realized her constellation of mental health afflictions was beyond her therapist's, or any therapist's, expertise.

A typical work day for Olivia started with meetings at VanPharm's corporate headquarters on La Salle Street in the Field Building, a 45-story granite art deco landmark in the Loop. She considered it a privilege to have an office in the Field Building, one of Chicago's abundant architectural gems, even if most of her day was spent away from it. Before lunch she was at the company's enormous R and D facility northwest of downtown, where she also had an office. She preferred it there because she didn't care for many of the people in management. Anton Battaglia, sycophantic and unbearably arrogant at the same time, had been hand-picked by Edward Van de Weghe to be CEO of the pharmaceutical giant and was Edward's closest ally. Olivia and Anton tolerated each other. He knew her to be brilliant but difficult. She saw him as a competent manager. What he lacked was vision. Ironically, it was her father who said a woman could never properly run a company like VanPharm because women lacked the required vision. The lack of vision comment angered and motivated her more than most of the other stupid, sexist things he said to her.

She didn't respect Anton. In truth, she respected almost no one. She believed that the smartest person in the room should be allowed to make the most important decisions, and she was usually the smartest person in the room. Anton would agree Olivia had the edge in that department. He didn't agree with the part about making decisions. More importantly, neither did her father.

By 5:00 Olivia was eager to leave VanPharm's R and D headquarters and go to her own private facility, where she did her best and most important work.

***

When Julian woke it was already 4:00 in the afternoon. For years he had aimed for at least eight hours of sleep, whether his schedule dictated he do it at night or in the day. He dozed nearly double that for three nights in a row. The first thing he did after he became semi-lucid was call Lourdes to find out if she had any results from his blood tests. The call went straight to voicemail. He left her a rather desperate sounding message, which she returned a half hour later via a text that said, "Sorry. Have a deadline tomorrow. Will run labs after. Promise."

A little after 5:00, Simon called and said there was something he wanted to talk to Julian about and could they meet at Gibson's around 7:00. Over the phone, Julian couldn't tell if Simon wanted to share good news or bad. He was happy to go either way. Gibson's was his new favorite place to eat. He was pleasantly surprised when he arrived at the restaurant and saw Vanessa at the bar drinking a glass of Tempranillo. To Julian, Vanessa's presence suggested Simon had good news, but whatever it was Simon had to say, he didn't mention it during the meal.

Vanessa watched in awe as Julian ate the final scarlet chunk of what had been nearly two pounds of porterhouse just 15 minutes earlier. He dipped a piece of bread in the blood pooled on the plate.

"I remember Simon mentioning once that you're a vegetarian," Vanessa said.

"I was," Julian said. "But I've recently come to regret those years," Julian said as he set his fork down fully sated.

"You gave up meat after Lara died," Simon said.

"I pretty much gave up eating after Lara died.

"That was a bad year," Simon said.

"The worst," Julian added.

Vanessa reached out for Simon's hand. He gave it to her and she squeezed it firmly.

"How about we share some good news?" Vanessa said, trying to guide the conversation out of the muddy ditch it had just rolled into.

Simon announced that he and Vanessa were getting back together. They were taking Julian's suggestion and selling the house in Lake Forest. She was moving into the apartment. They made it clear Julian was welcome to stay with them as long as he wanted. Julian had already been thinking about the need to get his own place. It wasn't because he felt like he was imposing on his brother, not yet, at least. Simon's apartment was more than roomy enough, and Simon was at work most of the time anyway. The real reason he wanted his own place was his growing need for more privacy to conceal the puzzling physical changes he was experiencing. He was already noticing changes to his physique. He was no longer skinny. Firm muscles were filling out his frame more and more every day.

Simon hadn't been home any of the times Julian woke up in the middle of the afternoon, but sooner or later he or Vanessa was bound to find out that Julian was sleeping as much as a newborn baby. Maybe they'd also find out Julian could leap onto the top of a van or eavesdrop on their private conversations and lovemaking from 50 yards away.

The three walked from Gibson's to Water Tower Place, where they found Johnny putting an elderly woman with one leg into a cab.

Simon waved to the woman and said, "Good evening, Marion."

The woman looked at Simon then at Julian like she was seeing double and she wasn't sure which one of them had greeted her. She waved back but said nothing.

"She never remembers my name," Simon said.

"I bet she would if you only had one leg," replied Vanessa.

As the cab pulled away from the curb, Johnny hustled over to open the door.

"What's poppin', y'all?" Johnny said.

"Good news, Johnny. Vanessa is moving in permanently," Simon said.

"Foreals?"

Simon nodded.

"Flickin'," Johnny said. He gave Vanessa a little congratulatory punch on the arm. "Some peeps are just born to be together."

Simon and Vanessa shared a happy look.

"I'll see you two later," Julian said.

"Julian, it was sweet last time when you gave us privacy, but it's not necessary," said Vanessa.

"I'm not doing anything like that. I just want to walk some."

What Julian really meant was he had an urge to prowl. Although he may not have been able to identify the activity he wanted to do as prowling, that's exactly what it was. It was an urge that had accompanied the other changes he was experiencing. He said goodnight and watched Simon and Vanessa walk through the front door Johnny held open for them.

"See you in a while, Johnny," Julian said as he turned toward Michigan Avenue.

"Mr. Julian," Johnny called out. Julian turned back.

"Crime's way up this year. There's a nutso been terrorizing the Mile. Always threatenin' to cut people's noses off. I call him the Schnoz Chopper."

"Catchy name," Julian said.

"He's cut like four people already and a woman almost died. Think she's still in a coma. So BOLO when you out walkin'."

"BOLO?" Julian caught some of Johnny's slang, but he didn't know this one.

"Be on the lookout," Johnny said as he pointed to his eyes.

Julian showed his understanding with a nod. "Got it." He laughed silently.

"I can speak caucasian if you prefer. It's just that I feel like there's something different about you and I can be myself."

"I wouldn't want you to be anyone else."

It was a Friday night and the Mag Mile was crowded with locals and tourists leaving the district's restaurants or going for drinks at its taverns and lounges. Couples strolled hand-in-hand. A large group of rackety twenty-somethings hogged the sidewalk in front of the Nike Store between Erie and Huron. At the corner of Michigan and Grand, a doorman from the Intercontinental was shooing a homeless man wearing bright pink running tights. Julian slipped the man 20 bucks. He had met with his bankers and now had easy access to his money. He made a habit of discretely slipping twenties to those in need. Earlier that evening, as he walked to Gibson's to meet his brother, a bedraggled man in front of the Waldorf Hotel shouted at him, "Hey asshole, got any motherfuckin' change?"

Julian was so amused by the man's approach he handed the guy 40 bucks and said, "Next time you see me, call me Julian."

The man looked at the two twenty-dollar bills in his dirty hand, smiled and said, "You got it, asshole."

When Julian was halfway across the DuSable Bridge he stopped. He looked over the rail and down to the Chicago River, where the reflection of a crescent moon floated on glassy water. When he walked across the bridge as a kid he always had an inexplicable urge to jump off. He liked to think he would have done it if it weren't for the trouble he would get in with his mother, and maybe the police. He told himself that even from the upper deck it wouldn't be a particularly dangerous jump. It was hardly the Golden Gate. That was over 200 feet. The DuSable was something like 30 feet from the upper deck. The swim to shore would take no more than a minute.

Julian continued to walk and later found himself standing halfway up the stairs to the platform at Adams and Wabash. He looked over the railing he had vaulted a few days earlier. The jump was much higher than he remembered. He had no memory of having to clear the six inch sections of metal pickets that protruded above the railing. He was impressed by his jump and not at all uneasy about it. He was certain he could, and would, do it again if he needed to.

For the next hour and a half, Julian hung out at the bottom of the stairs. He wasn't looking for trouble or waiting for a crime to happen. He didn't want to be a vigilante or join a safety patrol like the Guardian Angels. How could he? The Guardian Angels actually rode the CTA trains. Julian couldn't even scrounge enough nerve to make it to the platform. He was there because something told him he had to be. He thought it might have been his sister. Whoever or whatever it was, he accepted that he should look out for people in need. That's all he was looking to do. Being a hero didn't interest him. He had his own shit to worry about.

If any curious or suspicious Chicagoan had asked him what he was doing, he would have stumbled over his answer. He certainly wouldn't say that he had hundreds of millions of dollars, didn't need a job and had nothing better to do. Deep in his mind he knew the real reason he was there. He was still acting somewhat subconsciously. Even if he couldn't vocalize it, the truth was Adams and Wabash was where his life derailed, so Adams and Wabash would be his beat, even if his job was as simple as making sure people coming down from the platform staring at their screens didn't have their cherished phones ripped off or they didn't trip and fall ass over teapot down the stairs. In the time he was there no one did. He couldn't take credit for it. It just didn't happen.

By the time he returned to Simon's apartment building it was 1:00 in the morning. Johnny was still on duty.

"I was worried about you, Mr. Hamilton," Johnny said when Julian entered the lobby.

"Sorry, my job got me used to having no boss and keeping late hours."

"And what job was that, if you don't mind me asking?"

"I studied tigers and tried to protect them from poachers."

"Not many tigers on the Mile."

"Not real ones anyway," Julian said.

"What brings you back to the Chi? Again, if you don't mind me asking."

"Unfinished business," Julian said.

The answer was vague. Its essence was true. He had been so distracted by all that was going on with him physically that he hadn't given much thought to the primary reason he had come home. It surprised him that he could so easily forget about being shot and left for dead in the Bangladeshi Sundarbans. He had vowed he would set things right. He needed to get started on that. He felt a sudden rush of energy when he thought about it. It wasn't like a rush you would get from a hefty dose of caffeine. It was more of a primal instinct of fight or flight.

"I'll call the elevator for you," Johnny said.

"I'll take the stairs," Julian replied.

"Did your brother move or does he still live on the 63rd floor?"

Julian just smiled back at Johnny as he opened the heavy metal door and disappeared into the stairwell. He bounded up the first twenty floors, mostly two, sometimes three steps at a time. He slowed near the 45th floor and held a steady pace all the way to the 63rd. He was soaked in sweat, exhausted and exhilarated. He had never felt better in his life. He still had no believable explanation for what had caused the extraordinary transformation he was experiencing. If this was what it was going to be like, he didn't care how it started. His only concern was it might stop.

Chapter Seven

The Lake That Looks Like An Ocean

As the Yellow cab pulled away from the white zone outside Terminal 5 at O'Hare, KP's cell phone rang. He looked at the caller ID and groaned. He pushed the lock button on his phone and dismissed the call. He had already told his boss the Hamilton guy was dead. It had been easier to lie than argue over the details. There really wasn't anything more to discuss now that he was back in Chicago.

Sitting next to him in the back seat was McCauliff, looking weary and disheveled from the long trip home from Bangladesh. They had missed their original Hong Kong to Chicago flight because the flight from Dhaka touched ground in Hong Kong three hours and seven minutes late, exactly eight minutes longer than their scheduled layover.

They both suspected they wouldn't make it in time. They sprinted through the long international transit corridors anyway. The Cathay Pacific Airbus A350 bound for Chicago had already pulled away from the jetway when they made it to the gate sweaty and out of breath. An attendant in a gray vest and red striped tie apologized graciously after he told them the flight had already left. He apologized just as graciously when he told them there was only one daily Cathay flight to Chicago. The attendant was checking flights on other airlines when KP let loose on him. There was nothing in the way the attendant had spoken or acted that would have provoked a normal-tempered person to explode the way KP did. He called the airline pathetic and assured the attendant that any other airline would have held the plane for him, which even KP knew wasn't true. The attendant kept his composure throughout KP's tirade, even when the insults turned personal and vulgar. KP called the attendant a "fucking little chink faggot." The attendant simply shrugged politely, but his coworker had already called security.

McCauliff put his hand on KP's shoulder and tried to gently guide KP away from the counter and further conflict. KP knocked away McCauliff's hand with an aggressive swing of his arm. He stormed off and violently kicked a metal garbage can into the newsstand across from the gate, tumbling a stack of copies of the South China Morning Post. By the time the clanging garbage can had come to rest, security arrived, their hands resting on their sidearms.

KP's tantrum at the gate did not get him arrested. Spitting on one of the security guards did. He spent three nights in a Hong Kong holding cell before he was released. McCauliff spent the time in an over-priced hotel room that was so small he had to walk on his luggage to get to the bathroom.

McCauliff, who didn't have KP's Delta Force pedigree, let KP push him around to a certain degree. He figured it would cause him fewer headaches than if he was constantly confronting him. On a few occasions, McCauliff did push back, even punching KP in the nose in a hotel bar in Mumbai. KP was so drunk at the time, when he woke up the next morning he couldn't remember how he broke his nose. McCauliff told him he had fallen and hit it on a barstool. KP had no reason not to believe him. On a battlefield KP held the advantage. In a bar or in the company of drunken soldiers McCauliff could hold his own.

Declan McCauliff was a second generation Irish-American who grew up on the same block in Oak Lawn as the O'Brien brothers. It was McCauliff who got Aidan and Cill O'Brien the jobs that eventually got them mauled and eaten by a Bengal tiger. McCauliff was a hard worker turned violent lawbreaker. His father had always been quick to whip out his belt when any of his four sons stepped out of line or failed to pull his weight around the house. Fear of the belt instilled in young Declan a strong work ethic and a contrasting combination of both respect and contempt for authority. His mother was in an auto accident and lost the use of her legs when Declan was eight. Her disability put an extra strain on the family's finances and everyone was expected to contribute. McCauliff never minded a hard day's work, though a hard day's work was never enough to keep the family out of financial trouble. He took a second job robbing liquor stores and pawn shops, crime's entry-level position. It wasn't long before he became living proof that crime did pay. He turned out to be good at criminal activity, or at least he was pretty good at not getting caught doing it. He stepped it up, getting increasingly violent as he did so. In more than twenty years of robbery, assault, and eventually murder, he was never arrested or even questioned by the cops. Even after giving up so-called "honest" work and turning to crime full time, he stayed completely off the radar. He told himself it was a skill, but he knew it was really just one long stretch of good luck that would end some day.

McCauliff had always been in it for the money. He had acquired expensive tastes that needed constant funding. If he could get paid for it, he'd do it. He once put a bullet in a woman's leg for 75 bucks.

KP had different motivations. He liked to add notches to his gun belt. It gave him a sense of accomplishment when he took a photo of a kill. He had wanted to be the one to take out Julian, but knew his disfiguring facial scar would cause suspicion on the job in Bangladesh. The scar could make him look sinister and he accepted it would be better if he acted as a backup. Knowing the O'Brien brothers had failed made him furious. His current employer had little tolerance for failure. The O'Brien brothers were dead and KP was likely to take a lot of blowback. McCauliff was okay with KP taking the heat. He had never met the boss. He didn't even know the boss's name.

**

There were far more uncertainties than certainties surrounding the attempt on his life in a forest halfway around the world. There was a definite Chicago connection. Julian didn't know if it was significant. The O'Brien brothers were born in a Chicago suburb. One of them had a Cubs hat. Their satellite phone received a call from a Chicago number, but that call could have been placed by a kid in Mozambique and still say Chicago on the caller ID.

Julian didn't have a Facebook account and didn't want one. He had borrowed Simon's computer several times and the browser opened his Facebook page with every new tab. After an extensive examination of every Aidan O'Brien on Facebook, Julian was pretty certain that none of them was the Aidan O'Brien he knew. His brother was easier to find. Cill O'Brien's Facebook page was nearly blank, but his privacy settings were lax. His profile photo didn't show his face, just some greasy fingers wrapped around a half-empty bottle of Jameson Irish whiskey. There were, however, a couple of photos posted by others that clearly showed Cill's green eyes. They were the same color as the Jameson bottle. He hadn't written any original posts since the first week he signed up. Most of what he did post were shared stories about the Cubs. Sometimes he just posted the team's logo, as if he had to remind everyone that he was a Cubs fan. There were a couple of other nuggets of information that were helpful. Under education it said Oak Lawn Community High School. In the likes section, Cill had liked just three things: The Chicago Cubs, of course, Unicorn Darts, and Egan's Four Leaf Tavern.

If Julian was going to go to Oak Lawn, he would need to borrow Simon's car. Although Simon had a thing for Italian cars and motorcycles, his everyday car was German, a Mercedes S-Class sedan he kept in his building's parking garage. At the house in Lake Forest he kept a couple of old Ducati motorcycles and a 1960 Maserati 3500 GT Spyder convertible, his pride and joy in red. Julian wouldn't think of asking to borrow the Maserati, nor was it practical to, however he didn't hesitate calling Simon at work to ask if he could borrow the Mercedes for a little errand.

The first place he went was the Oak Lawn public library to see if he could find a high school year book. Julian couldn't remember Cill O'Brien's exact date of birth, though he did remember he was born in January of 1985, which meant he would have graduated from high school in 2003. He asked a bearded librarian if he had a 2001 yearbook for Oak Lawn Community High School, thinking there was a good chance a goon like Cill O'Brien had dropped out by 2003. The librarian nodded and gestured for Julian to follow him.

The librarian stopped at a shelf and dragged his finger along the spines of six decades of Oak Lawn Community High School yearbooks, finally stopping on one, which he pulled out and handed to Julian. The cover said "Shield 2001."

"The year I graduated," the librarian said.

"Here in Oak Lawn?" Julian asked him eagerly.

"Oh, no. Shorewood High School, Milwaukee, Wisconsin. Go Greyhounds," he said with a sarcastic little pump of his fist.

Julian took the yearbook to a cushioned red chair and started going through it.

In the second row, third from the left in the group photo of the class of 2003 stood a skinny kid named Cillian O'Brien. His face was expressionless, blank, like he was practicing for his mug shot. The photo was black and white, so Cill's green eyes didn't show. He was still easy to recognize. His face didn't look all that different than the last time Julian saw it, although there were no maggots in his nostrils in the high school photo. To his left stood a pimply-faced kid named Bruno

Guercini. To his right was a kid who wore a Blink-182 T-shirt and flashed peace signs in front of his face with both hands, making it difficult for even his mother to recognize him. The yearbook said the peace sign kid was named Declan McCauliff. The name was no more significant to Julian than Bruno Guercini.

There were no Cill or Aidan O'Briens in the phone book. Julian knew phone books were no longer as helpful as they used to be. He doubted hired thugs like the O'Brien brothers lived in households that required a land line. He decided to follow up on his other lead.

Egan's Four Leaf Tavern wasn't the sort of place that tried to look like a pub in Dublin. The owners didn't hire one of those Irish pub-in-a-box design firms. There was no dark walnut wainscoting on the walls and there were no dark walnut bar stools. There was nothing dark walnut at all, though the lighting was so dim in some corners of the place that you couldn't tell if you'd pulled a ten or a twenty out of your wallet. The stools were metal. The long bar was covered in formica with a black padded vinyl arm rail. The floor was concrete. The selection of distilled spirits was mostly limited to the well. The beers on tap were American-made lagers like Old Style and PBR. No doppelbocks or fruit lambics at this place. There was nothing Irish about it except for the name. You couldn't even buy Guinness in a can. The Leaf, as all the regular customers called it, was old-school corner tavern. You didn't go for ambience. You didn't go for food. Except for pickled pigs feet and mixed nuts, there was no food. You went to The Leaf to drink, bitch about your boss or your old lady, and, most importantly, throw darts. If it wasn't out of order, you could drop a couple of quarters in the jukebox to hear some Joan Jett or Def Leppard.

Julian was a native Chicagoan, but he left for Asia before he reached the legal drinking age. He never had the opportunity to become a regular at any particular bar or tavern. People with hundreds of millions of dollars didn't normally hang out at places like The Leaf. Julian was different from other super-wealthy 30-somethings. When he walked into the place he felt like he could make a habit of it. It was the kind of place where the bartender had to be as good at breaking up fights and listening to customers unload their problems as he was at making drinks. Julian was carrying a lot of baggage. He knew how it felt to be incomplete. Had he not run off to chase tigers in Asia he might have spent a lot of time in a place like The Leaf. Maybe he would have drunk more than he already did, which was too much. On the other hand, maybe he would have talked about his unresolved personal issues.

"Don't think I've seen you in here before," said the bartender, a bear of a man whose barrel chest and handlebar mustache made him look like an old-time circus strongman. "You from around here?"

"Nah. I came to look at a car I found on Craig's List, but I really needed a beer first," Julian said. He hadn't thought of an excuse for coming in, so he was impressed it had come to him so quickly. He had always been good at coming up with what he called "sincere bullshit," a skill he had used frequently when he had to talk his way out of a jam with park rangers in India or visa officials in Bangladesh.

"What can I get you?"

"PBR me," Julian said.

The bartender pulled the tap handle and poured a beer. "Cheers," he said as he set the beer in front of Julian.

"I was born and raised in Chicago and I don't think I've ever been to Oak Lawn before."

"Doesn't surprise me. Not much here."

"I did sit next to a guy at a Cubs game a couple years ago. Said he was from here. What was his name? O'Brien I think. I can't remember his first name, though I'd probably know it if I heard it."

"Lots of O'Briens in this town," the bartender said.

"I'm sure that's true. This guy had brilliant green eyes. And he chewed gum. I remember him chewing a shitload of gum."

"Cill. Comes in pretty regular. Has a brother named Aidan and five or six sisters."

"That's it, Cill O'Brien. Said if I ever made it to Oak Lawn I should go to Egan's Four Leaf Tavern. Also said he'd set me up with one of his sisters. He was drunk so I didn't take him seriously about his sisters."

"No one takes him seriously. Kind of a knucklehead, but he doesn't dare cause any trouble in here."

"Why's that?"

"He know's I'd knock his block off."

"Good to know. He still around?" Julian asked.

"Come to think of it, I haven't seen him—or his brother—in a couple a months. Probably got into some trouble with Declan or KP. Those two are no good."

"Hmm. Don't know them," said Julian. He finished his beer and used the empty glass to hold down a twenty on the bar. "Feeling flush today. Keep the change."

"Thanks for comin' in, bud. I'm Gabe," the bartender said as he reached to shake Julian's hand.

"Nice to meet you Gabe. I'm Luther. You the owner?"

"Nah, just work here. Owner's a retired firefighter who lives upstairs, but he don't come down much these days. He's 62 but looks 92. Can't breathe without an oxygen tank."

"Bummer," Julian said.

"That's what you get when you can't even take a shower without a cigarette. The only time he ever leaves the building is to go to the doctor."

Julian had seen KP before, but he wasn't lying when he told Gabe he didn't know Declan, though the name did ring a bell. Julian couldn't remember the last name, but he knew where to find it.

Julian went directly to the library shelf with the 2001 yearbook. After finding Declan's last name, he found the same phone book he used earlier and looked up McCauliff. There was only one in Oak Lawn. The listing was for D. McCauliff.

Julian parked the Mercedes around the corner and out of sight from McCauliff's simple mid-century ranch home. The lawn looked neglected, though it was still in far better condition than the one next to it. The house and the rest of the property was neat and appeared as well cared for as any on his side of the block. The other side of the street was all train tracks.

Julian walked closer to the house, trying to determine if anyone was home. Something about it was familiar. It wasn't a déjà vu sensation. He was certain he had never been there before. He thought it could have been a smell. In any case, it made him uncomfortable, edgy.

A middle-aged woman wearing a tattered yellow housecoat and slippers exited the house two doors down and approached Julian. He forced a smile.

"He's not home. Been gone for a couple of weeks or more," the woman said.

"Do you know when he'll be back?" Julian asked as he walked closer to the woman.

"Never, I hope. Who's asking?"

Like when he was talking with the bartender at The Leaf, Julian couldn't afford to leave his real name with this woman. Even though she appeared to have no affection for her neighbor, she might mention to Declan that he had a visitor. He didn't want anyone who thought he might be dead to find out he was alive and in Chicago. His sincere bullshit instinct kicked in immediately.

"My name is Luther. I'm spending this beautiful day talking to people about accepting Jesus Christ as Lord and Savior."

"Oh yeah? How's that going?"

"It's always a struggle, but one worth undertaking."

"Son, let me save you some time," the woman said. "The man who lives in that house ain't worth saving. You're better off for showing up when he wasn't home. He'd have chased you off with a baseball bat if he was here."

"Thanks for the warning. And what about you? Do you have a relationship with Christ?" Julian asked the woman, trying to make his evangelist act look authentic."

"Tried it for a while. Didn't really fit my lifestyle. I like playing the ponies too much."

"You're not alone. Have a good day," Julian said as he began to walk away.

"That's all you got?" the woman asked.

"I'm not pushy."

"You'd never make it as a Jehovah."

Julian smiled and again said good day to the lady in the housecoat, who kept her eyes on him as he walked down the block. At the same time Julian rounded the corner, an old white Cadillac crossed the intersection. The driver got a brief look at Julian. For a second he thought he knew him, but convinced himself he didn't. The Cadillac pulled into Declan's driveway. The lady in the housecoat knew the car well and was in no mood for a conversation with its driver. She hustled inside her house.

To get home from Oak Lawn, Julian took the Dan Ryan Expressway north. Traffic was terrible. When he had made it as far as Roosevelt, it felt like he was going in reverse. He just needed to get as far as the Circle Interchange, the worst traffic clusterfuck in the country. As he was pulling off, a Nissan Pathfinder cut in front of him. The Pathfinder would have hit him if Julian hadn't pumped the brakes and let the asshole go in front of him. Julian's eyes went to the Pathfinder's license plate frame. The frame said "Autoworld of Evanston."

Julian had been in Chicago for a good while now and he still hadn't been to Evanston to see his old house and neighborhood. He had told Simon and Vanessa that he could never live there again. Taking a little trip up there was different. He thought he might as well make the trip while he had his brother's car. He took Lake Shore Drive all the way up to Edgewater where it continued on as Sheridan Road. Just seeing the street sign for Sheridan made him sentimental. When he was a kid Julian thought Sheridan Road, which followed the shoreline of Lake Michigan all the way into southern Wisconsin, had to be the most beautiful road in America. He felt extremely lucky to have grown up on Sheridan, just across the street from a small park and Lake Michigan. His childhood bedroom had a view of what as a kid he called "the lake that looks like an ocean."

He parked down the road from his old house and walked through the park to the lake. He threw rocks in the water as he made his way up the shore until he was even with his old house. The sun was going down and many of the houses on the block were lit. His old house was completely dark. He walked closer. There was a for sale sign in the yard with a bright red sold sign attached to the top of the post. There were no cars or bikes in the driveway and no toys in the yard. The residents of this stretch of Sheridan Road kept their homes and yards tidy. You would rarely see even a single small dead branch in a front yard tree. If there was a garbage can visible from the street, it wasn't there long. In this neighborhood, from the exterior there was rarely anything that suggested anyone actually lived in the multi-million-dollar houses. Even the rare empty house was usually perfectly maintained. Still, with his old house completely dark he could tell from the street no one was living there. There was no furniture on the porch and no curtains hung in the front windows. When he lived there, his mother often kept the sheer curtains closed in the front of the house. They let light in, but were opaque enough to stop the prying eyes of gawkers. The neighborhood attracted a lot of gawkers.

Julian walked up to the north side of the house where there was a tall, thick hedge. With his superb night vision he could see clearly. He peeked into the dining room window. He saw no furniture. He walked further back and peeked into the kitchen. It, too, was empty. He kept going to the back yard enclosed by a tall wooden fence. He knew the fence well. His parents had it built when Julian and Lara turned six and got a Labrador puppy they named Ginger. Julian easily jumped up, put one hand on the top of the fence and vaulted over. He went all the way to the back section of fence that marked the property line. He stopped at the trunk of the big black cherry tree that he, his sister and his brother had loved to climb. In summertime they spent hours at a time in that black cherry tree. There was no need for a tree house. They simply climbed into the tree with a book, found a thick branch to sit on and read until it was too dark to see. Julian sat on the ground, put his back against the flaky, black bark of the tree's trunk and closed his eyes. He pulled the black queen out of his front pocket and rubbed it with his thumb.

Chapter Eight

Sex On The Beach

From the hallway Julian could clearly hear an unpleasant whirring sound coming from Lourdes's lab. He knocked on the door. There was no response. He knocked again. Still nothing. He cracked it a few inches. Lourdes was standing behind a workbench. In front of her sat a small machine that looked like the base of a blender. Julian opened the door a bit more and she saw him. She waved him in and pointed to a chair. A digital timer on the machine counted down the last 47 seconds of whatever function it was performing. Lourdes silently stared at the timer.

"What is that thing?" asked Julian.

Lourdes held up a finger, signaling Julian to wait. She tapped the timer, which now read 33 seconds. When the timer hit zero, the whirring stopped.

"It's a microhematocrit centrifuge. Pretty loud little fucker for a brushless motor," Lourdes said.

"Louder than any microhematocrit centrifuge I've ever heard, brush or no brush."

"Pretty familiar with them, are you?"

"Actually it's been a while since I've worked with one. Remind me what they do."

"I'll show you."

She flipped open the top of the machine. Inside was a metal lid with a knob that she used to loosen the lid. She pulled out a glass tube the length of her middle finger and no thicker than a strand of spaghetti. Almost half the tube was red, the rest was filled with a honey-colored liquid.

"The red part is made up of your blood cells. The other is your plasma. The centrifuge separates them so we can see your proportion of red blood cells. It's also called a PCV test, for packed-cell volume."

She held the tube against a chart with red lines all over it. She slid the tube along the chart until the colors on the tube and the chart lined up.

"Hmm," she mumbled.

"What is it?"

"Hematocrit is little low, but not unusually. I already tested your testosterone and it's on the high side. Hemoglobin was low-normal. Iron and leukocytes were normal. Nothing stands out."

From a drawer she pulled out a bright yellow plastic device that looked like a some sort of toy ray gun. She aimed it directly at Julian and squeezed the trigger. Two red dots quickly appeared on Julian's forehead and just as quickly disappeared. She looked at the devices digital display with surprise.

"Do you feel warm?" Lourdes asked.

"Not particularly."

"You're temperature is 99.5. Do you normally run this high?"

Julian shrugged.

"I want you to take and record your temperature every day for the next two weeks. Twice a day. Historically, human body temperatures are lower than they were when Wunderlich declared 98.6 normal. That was 170 years ago. Today, whatever normal means, it's closer to 97.5."

Julian interrupted with, "You're rambling and clearly I'm not normal."

"Well, 99.5 is normal for a tiger. That's low compared to a domestic cat, which typically has a body temperature of 100.6. And cheetahs, they're all the way up at 102.2. I'm sure thermoregulation is just a tiny part of this. What we need is a test of your genetic similarity to a tiger and I'm not set up to run genome sequencing. Though I do have a friend who might be able to help."

"I'd like to keep this between us for now," Julian said.

She nodded and kept rambling, more to herself than to Julian. The little gears in her head were turning faster and faster. She walked to a desk with a computer and called Julian over with a wave. She typed something and a Google results page opened. She scanned it and clicked. As she read from her computer screen, every once in a while she said aloud chunks of what she was reading. "Unraveled." "Nine-year-old male." "South Korea." "Genomic data."

She looked up from her computer screen and directly at Julian. "We'll need a control sample. Can you swab your brother?"

"Stop, please," Julian said.

"Sorry, I get a little carried away with this scientific mystery stuff."

"It's okay. It's just that I don't really want to know what's wrong with me anymore."

"You don't? Because this shit really turns me on."

"Do you mean in a scientific sense, or is it sexual?" Julian asked.

"A bit of both."

"Or maybe you're just curious about what other biological changes I might be going through."

"Definitely," Lourdes said. "Strictly in a clinical sense, of course."

"Of course," Julian said.

"Oh, the files," she said, leaving that non sequitur dangling as she walked across the lab. "Walk with me," she said before stopping at a storage closet door.

The closet was just big enough to park a compact car. The walls were lined floor to ceiling with sturdy metal shelves. Towers of cardboard banker's boxes overflowing with papers took up every inch of shelving except for a small space on one shelf that had a laundry basket with some folded clothes in it. Another basket contained a collection of shoes that ranged from well-worn running shoes to sleek Italian stilettos. On the floor was a simple twin mattress with a white fitted sheet. A red plaid fleece blanket and a pillow were heaped in the middle. She walked on top of the mattress to reach the back of the closet, where she pulled a box off a shelf.

"Let me guess, your ex-husband got the house," Julian said.

"I let him have it."

"His loss. I really like what you've done with the place. Nice blend of minimalism and clutter."

She carried the box out of the closet and set it on a nearby workbench.

"I have a little place in Bucktown, but I'm so tied to my work that most nights I sleep in the closet."

She walked toward the desk with the computer she had used earlier, leaving the box on the workbench.

"Do you want me to bring this?" Julian asked, referring to the box of files.

"No. That's for Dandelion."

"Oh. I thought it was something to do with me."

"Nope. I just realized I had forgotten to set it out for him."

Julian followed her to the computer desk.

"I have a favor to ask of you," she said.

"Okay."

"Um, I got a grant from this foundation and they're having this, uh, this gala or whatever you want to call it," she said stumbling over her words nervously.

"And?"

"Well, it's kind of a big deal for me and I thought maybe I should get someone to, like, go with me."

"Are you trying to say you need a date?"

"Yes, but," she said, trailing off in hopes he could finish her sentence for her.

"But you don't want me to get the wrong idea.

"Exactly."

"God, I've never seen you so nervous before," Julian said. "I would be honored to be your date. When is it?"

"Saturday night."

"You mean three days from now?"

She made some calculations in her head. "Yeah, I guess Saturday is three days from now. Oh, and I can introduce you to my geneticist friend."

"Probably not a good idea. I'm not ready to be a science experiment yet. And I don't think I need to be."

"This is just starting for you. You have no idea what changes you could go through even a day from now. We have to figure this shit out before something bad happens."

"After I find out who did this to me."

"You need to be careful, Jules. I'm worried."

"There's no need to worry, Lou," he said as he put his hand on her shoulder and squeezed affectionately. "I've got this."

***

The carmine red Porsche was going 60 miles per hour when Olivia pulled the handbrake and whipped the wheel hard to the left. The 21-inch tires squealed and smoked until the car was sideways across the road. She released the handbrake and floored it, threading the car between the stone columns at the end of her father's driveway. She sped toward the tennis court, where her father, dressed in tennis whites, was hitting balls fired at him by a machine. As she raced past, he flipped her the middle finger. She cursed him under her breath and slammed on the brakes. She backed up, got out of the car walked toward the tennis court.

Edward pushed a button on a remote control device clipped to his waistband and the ball machine stopped launching the fuzzy yellow balls over the net. The old man gestured to Letty, who was watching from a bench on the opposite side of the court. Letty stood up quickly and started to collect the balls, most of which were still on Edward's side of the court. Edward eyed Letty's firm bottom appreciatively as she bent over to pick up a ball. He walked to the bench and drank mineral water from a green glass bottle. Olivia was staring at him incredulously.

"You really need an advanced directive if you're going to drive like an asshole," Edward said as he lowered the water bottle.

"Oh, please."

"Really. I'd feel a lot better if I knew you had a man in your life who was willing to take care of a quadriplegic, because I'm far too old to do it."

"Couldn't it be a woman?" Olivia asked.

"Only if she were your nurse."

"Then I don't think you'd approve of my date for the foundation gala."

"It's not a joke, Olivia. There's no reason you can't find a proper man. You're beautiful, brilliant and you're rich," he said as if wealth were her greatest attribute. "What are people going to say?"

"Have you ever known me to care about what people say?"

"Never," Edward said with disappointment. He slid his racket into a bag and sat down on the passenger seat of the golf cart parked next to the tennis court. He whistled to get Letty's attention.

"If it weren't for me, you'd be ogling Letty's tight Guatemalan ass from a wheelchair."

"And I thank you for that gift every day. What's gotten into you?"

Olivia knew this was a precipitous path. She rarely lost her temper with her father and he had no idea of her true feelings for him. In fact, he assumed she worshipped him. She was good at pretending and she was good at making it look like she was joking when she really wasn't. However, when he brought up her unmarried status, which he did frequently, she sometimes struggled to tamp down her anger.

"I'm sorry. I had a rough day at work. The migraine trials are giving me an awful headache."

This made Edward smile. She had him back where she wanted him.

"I was thinking I would skip the gala," Olivia said.

"You picked one of the grantees this year. You have to go. I'll be your date if you can't get one."

"Maybe I'll take Letty," Olivia said in a way that made it unclear if she was joking or not.

"I was thinking, maybe we could experiment again with a higher dose," Edward said.

"Absolutely not. You were insufferable."

"I felt fantastic."

"No way."

Edward protested with a huff. He turned to admire Letty's ass. He sighed longingly.

"You're going to need a lot more than a higher dose to make that happen," Olivia said, the comment coming out a little more scornful than she had intended.

He harrumphed and said, "You sound like your goddamn mother."

Inside, Olivia's anger boiled. She fought hard to not let it show. "I'll see you later," she said flatly.

Olivia walked back to her car, got in and sped off toward the house. She pulled the car into the garage and closed the door behind her. She gripped the steering wheel tightly with both hands and rattled it aggressively. She snarled. From her pocket she pulled out one of the little vials filled with her bright orange liquid. After staring at it for a minute, she unscrewed the top and threw it back. She made the same sour face her father made every morning and her body heaved when it hit her belly. She thought he had been exaggerating. Now she knew he wasn't. The stuff was repulsive. It was also potent, particularly on someone young and healthy like her. She could feel it go to work inside her almost immediately.

***

"I'm eager to move in. Ask them how much they want for it furnished," Julian said as he stared out at the lake from a 69th floor apartment in Water Tower Place.

"I'll ask if we could work out a rental arrangement until the deal closes. The owner is at her place in the Canary Islands and doesn't have any immediate plans to come back," Tomasina, the real estate broker said.

The apartment Julian was about to buy was a 2,700-square foot, three bedroom with a professional chef's kitchen, two fireplaces and a voice-activated system for lights, blinds and music that Julian predicted he would end up disabling after weeks of frustrating attempts to figure out.

The owner of the apartment, a widow in her 50's, had spent several hundreds of thousands of dollars renovating it two years earlier when she bought it with her husband. She had spent just a few weeks there since. Her husband died a couple of months after the renovation was completed and the woman, who went to the Canaries seeking a quiet place to grieve, had fallen in love with the island of Lanzarote and was content to spend the rest of her life hiking across the volcanic landscapes, producing mediocre paintings and practicing yoga. She agreed to the rental arrangement and accepted Julian's offer to purchase it furnished.

Julian didn't have any strong opinions of the apartment's mid-century furnishings. He thought the finish on the wood plank floors was a bit dark, though he really didn't care about any of that stuff. He had few needs and one was simply having his own place. He didn't want to go through the freakish transformation he was experiencing in his brother's place. He wanted a quiet bedroom where he could sleep into the late afternoon, something to sit on when he ate or read, and he wanted to be able to do simple things like find a can opener if he needed one. He didn't need to spend $2.5 million for that, but Julian had always loved the lake. Like Johnny the doorman said, what's the point of having coin if you're not going to spend it? If a little bit of it went into Johnny's pocket, all the better. Furthermore, trudging around the city shopping for apartments was the last thing he wanted to spend time doing. Wrongdoings needed to be avenged and he had made little progress on that front.

***

Saturday night Julian sent a Town Car to bring Lourdes to his new apartment. When she arrived—dressed in a stunning short black sequined dress—she was wowed by the space that had just become Julian's only a day earlier. Julian was equally impressed with the way she wore that dress. He put his hand on her bare shoulder and gave her a kiss on her cheek. He couldn't help himself.

"You look beautiful," he said as he quickly pulled back from her personal space.

Lourdes was delighted to see Simon and Vanessa sitting at the marble-topped kitchen island drinking Pinot Grigio and eating oysters and seared tuna appetizers. Simon had gotten to know her when she and Julian dated. Julian and Lourdes had been inseparable and she spent a lot of time at the family's home in Evanston, where they frequently played vicious games of Scrabble. Lara, who was usually in Palo Alto at school, knew her well enough to know she adored her. Simon was happy his brother had found a girl he was madly in love with. Simon had run into Lourdes a few times over the years since Julian had fled the country, but they traveled in different circles and Chicago was too big to run into anyone with any frequency. It was Simon's suggestion that his brother and Lourdes start their evening in Julian's new place, where she could also meet Vanessa, the woman he was ecstatic to be living with again. He told her he was happier than he had been in years.

"Why would the effects of climate change on thermoregulation in mammals interest the Van de Weghe Foundation? Aren't they mostly into haughty violinists and authors?" Vanessa asked after Lourdes explained what the foundation was recognizing.

"I have no idea and I was afraid to ask. But the old man's daughter isn't so interested in that artsy shit. She's the one who found me. We got together over coffee. Between sips she dangled a million dollars in front of me and that was that," answered Lourdes. "At first I thought she was crazy, then I thought she might have a self-serving interest. I've gotten to know her a little and I don't think that's what it is. She's just a science nerd."

"Just like you," Julian said.

"And she's fucking gorgeous."

"Also just like you," said Julian, a comment that elicited a drawn-out "aww" from Vanessa as she affectionately draped her arm around Simon.

The little gathering marked a major turn in both Julian's and Simon's lives. Simon and Vanessa were happy together and kicking themselves for not being able to figure out the house in Lake Forest had strained their previously blissful marriage. The fix was so simple, but they both knew it had required Julian's presence and objectivity. As for Julian, just being in Chicago was a huge change. And even if it wasn't a real date, it still felt great to be standing in his new place next to the woman he had never stopped loving. She looked magnificent in her black sequined dress and she didn't hate him. He had expected her to, but she didn't.

***

Edward Van de Weghe sat in the passenger seat of the carmine red Porsche Taycan admiring the lapels of his Stefano Ricci tuxedo. The driver's door opened and Olivia slid into the seat. Edward stared as her legs slithered out of a jewel-embellished Tom Ford mini-dress, the hem of which was stuck on one of the contours of the leather seat. Until she freed the hem, the little dress didn't cover even an eighth of her lithe, creamy thighs. The top of the dress was open to an inch above her navel and nearly half of her breasts were exposed. There was little fabric for such an expensive dress. It had cost her $15,000, but she looked like a million bucks in it.

Edward caught himself surveying the wide expanses of Olivia's velvety skin. "Christ on a pony. She's my fucking daughter," he thought, then he took another look.

Olivia had caught his stare. It wasn't the first time. It was creepy, but she knew the man inside and out. It was always in her better interest to let it slide. "You look nice, too," she said.

"Thanks for the tux. You're right. It does look good on me."

"I knew it would."

She lied. Olivia never thought about how good it would look on him when she bought the thing. She bought it because it was the most expensive one in the store. She thought spending his money on something as pointless as an outrageously expensive tuxedo he would wear once or twice was a way of getting back at him, one little chip at a time. Ditto for her dress.

She kept the red Porsche just under the speed limit all the way to downtown, where traffic slowed her even more. Edward was comfortable and relaxed in the passenger seat as they rolled up

Michigan Avenue past Pearson Street. He stared at a woman on the sidewalk in a black dress. His foundation had just given Dr. Lourdes Villegas a million bucks, but he had never met her and, of course, he didn't recognize her as the woman he was ogling.

As it had done every year for the last 15, the Van de Weghe Foundation had booked the Grand Ballroom at the Drake Hotel for its annual gala. The Drake was just a few blocks from Julian's place and he and Lourdes walked to the party. Lourdes, who was accustomed to spending most of her days in running shoes, had to take off her heels for the last couple of blocks. Julian's feet didn't feel so great either. He had borrowed the shoes from his brother whose foot was a full size smaller than his. The tuxedo he borrowed from him fit remarkably well.

When they were close enough to get a good look at the entrance to the hotel and the line of limos waiting to drop off their black-tie passengers at the red carpet, Julian stopped in his tracks.

"Holy shit. All this is for you?" Julian asked.

"Not exactly. There are two of us," replied Lourdes, who was no less astonished by the spectacle.

"I've been living in the bush for over a decade. I'm not sure I'm ready for the black-tied aristocracy."

"You'll be fine. You're not a complete stranger to civilization."

"I don't want to have to re-introduce myself to some old friend of my parents and have them say, 'It's a shame about what happened to your sister,' or 'It's a shame what happened to your father.' And then there's my mother. I'm not ready for all that shame."

"Just pretend you're someone else."

"Hmm. An alias. I can do that. What's your mother's father's name?"

"Santos."

They both knew that name would never work.

"Bushrod," said Julian.

"Bushrod?"

"Bushrod Washington. George's nephew. Supreme Court justice. You know, Bushrod."

"You've got to be kidding."

"Yeah, you're right. Name an unimportant 19th century president."

"Millard. Chester. Grover."

"Rutherford," suggested Julian.

"Nah. You don't have the beard to pull off Rutherford."

"What about Ike? I like Ike," Julian said with confidence.

"You said 19th century, but okay, Ike."

"And I'm in real estate."

She made a loud snoring noise with a whistling exhale.

"Yeah, I guess you're right. I'll work on it."

Julian already felt more comfortable. The conversation reminded him of the old days when the two of them could talk about the silliest things for hours and hours.

The gala marked the 40th anniversary of the Van de Weghe Foundation. In keeping with the gemstone tradition of anniversaries, the decor in the grand ballroom focused on ruby red. Floral arrangements featured roses, of course, and ruby-colored hydrangeas, columbine and tickseed. Flutes for the traditional champagne given to all guests upon arrival were made of ruby glass. The Neons, a 1980's cover band, gladly took the extra $1,000 incentive offered to them to wear ruby colored neckties while they played hits by Tears for Fears, The Police and Huey Lewis and the News.

A young, uniformed server handed Lourdes and Julian champagne when they entered the ballroom.

"To thermoregulation," Lourdes said as she and Julian clinked their glasses.

She was overwhelmed. She thought she was prepared for the amount of attention she was going to receive. She quickly realized she wasn't. Ten seconds after crossing the threshold into the ballroom a photographer aggressively pushed in close and took photos of Lourdes, shouldering Julian out of the way as he worked his way around her looking for different camera angles. Maribel Kravitz, the diminutive executive director of the foundation appeared out of nowhere and told the photographer to take photos of her with Lourdes. Other pompous guests did the same.

Julian felt alone as he watched her get mobbed. He was prepared for that. It was the biggest night of her life and he wasn't going to ruin it by being a needy date. He had been lonely more often than not over the past decade, and if there was a bar close by when he was lonely, he went straight to it. In the Drake Grand Ballroom the bar was just 30 feet away. He finished his champagne cocktail with one big chug and started walking.

Three bartenders worked the long, well-stocked and busy bar. A couple hundred guests were already in attendance at the gala and many of them had cued up for drinks. Julian got in line. Standing one position ahead of him was a tall, gorgeous woman in a tiny dress that commanded Julian and every other heterosexual male at the party to stare at her legs. Julian was well aware he was staring. The woman with the glorious gams had her back to him and couldn't see where his eyes were pointed, so he stared a little longer, looking up at the same moment she turned around.

Remembering his father's solid advice for meeting women, Julian started a conversation simply by saying hello and introducing himself, ignoring only one small detail—the truth. "Hello, I'm Ike," he said.

Olivia took a long approving look at Julian. She introduced herself and said, "Nice to meet you, Ike."

Julian was pretty sure she said her name was Olivia, though he couldn't be absolutely certain. His mind momentarily went blank when he saw her tongue press into her top row of pearly teeth to pronounce the second syllable. Just a half hour ago he was pinching himself because he was so thrilled that Lourdes was back in his life despite his callous treatment of her years ago. At the moment, all he could think about was what it would be like to fuck this woman in his 69th floor livingroom with the killer view of the lake that looks like an ocean.

"God, please don't ask me what I do for a living?" Julian thought, hoping to have to tell as few lies as possible.

"What's your poison?" Olivia asked the man she knew only as Ike when she made it to the front of the line.

"Any and all of 'em, but Bourbon rocks if they've got it."

One of the bartenders heard Julian so there was no need for Olivia to relay the message. She held up two fingers and the bartender got busy. She felt a rush of confidence wash over her. She didn't have to fake it with Ike. She knew she could be anyone or anything she wanted.

She didn't know how she knew, but she knew. It could be her special juice kicking in, she thought. She had been taking it for a few days and had never felt better.

"I got in line wanting a fruity, girly drink, like a sex on the beach, but I'm always up for something different," Olivia said.

Her comment came off as playful and flirtatious, but he knew she wasn't playing games. She wanted to mate. He could smell it on her. There was a pheromonal mist filling the air between them and it was making his eyes water. He hadn't had sex in years and he had been fine with it, until the last minute or so. He had an overpowering desire to make it with this Olivia creature. He wanted to sleep with Lourdes, too. Maybe, he dared to think, he could take Olivia into a closet somewhere in the hotel and finish his escapades at home with Lourdes. If he played his cards right he might get them both at the same time some day.

Reason regained control. Why would he ever try to pull off a stupid stunt like that? His renewed relationship with Lourdes, now just a few days old, would never go the next level if he started fucking a woman he met at a party Lourdes had taken him to. He realized he only had partial control over himself. His human instincts told him to get away from Olivia, not because of something she might do, but because of something he was certain he would do, or try to do.

"My date might have something to say about that," Julian said.

Olivia handed him his bourbon. She clinked her glass to his. "My date wouldn't care. He'd be thrilled. He's been trying to marry me off for years," she said.

"Who's that, dear old Dad?"

113

"Old? Very. Dear? Not so much. But, yes, I'm here with my father."

Julian didn't know how to respond other than to laugh politely. Out of the corner of his left eye he saw Lourdes heading straight for him. He smiled at her as she approached. She walked past him and into Olivia's arms. The two women hugged like old friends.

"Oh my god, I can't believe this is really happening. Thank you, thank you, thank you," Lourdes said to Olivia as she held her in a tight embrace.

"You are so welcome. Your work is worth every penny," Olivia said.

The women let go of the hug. They offered each other compliments on their dresses. To show off hers, Olivia spun around on her toes and the dress twirled up just far enough for Julian to get a quick glimpse of the lower curve of her ass peeking out from under white lace panties. The view was so erotically taunting he had to bite his bottom lip. Both women were too focused on their girly chatter to notice his coup d'oeil. Julian considered walking away from them and was about to when both women turned to him.

"Do you know Ike?" Olivia asked Lourdes.

"We met in front of the hotel a few minutes ago," Lourdes said as she extended her hand to Julian in a way suggestive of something more intimate than a handshake. He took her hand and she put her other hand over his. She pulled him close and planted a slow, wet kiss on his lips.

"Nice to see you again, Ike," Lourdes said. She gave a sly look to Olivia, who quickly figured out her little joke. "Sorry. Just having a little fun. He's my date."

"Really? Last time we talked you didn't have one," said Olivia.

"I asked him a couple of days ago."

"Her father was busy," Julian said, which drew a laugh from Olivia and a confused look from Lourdes. "That was our first kiss, believe it or not," Julian added.

"I don't. Not a steamer like that."

Julian was being charming as a way to break up what he saw as an awkward situation. Too much charm could get him in trouble if he wasn't careful. The sudden appearance of Edward Van de Weghe bailed him out. The old man grabbed Olivia above the elbow, said, "Liv, there's a gentleman I'd like you to meet," and pulled her away as only an arrogant asshole in an $8,000 tuxedo could do. He made no attempt to excuse himself or even acknowledge the presence of Lourdes, the guest of honor.

The next hour went by pleasantly. By sticking close to Lourdes's side, Julian was reasonably confident she would be the focus of most conversations they had with other guests. He was right. Millie, the wife of an ear, nose and throat specialist from Hinsdale was the only person who asked Julian what he did for a living. Julian was comfortable using his alias. He wasn't so comfortable with the bit about being a real estate broker. That idea had popped into his head because of his recent dealings with Tomasina. He really didn't know anything about real estate, and he didn't care to. With a pancetta-wrapped peach slice in his left hand and his third glass of bourbon in his right, he told the ear, nose and throat guy's wife that he, like Lourdes, was a biologist. He even mentioned some of the papers he had authored.

Lourdes stuck to bubbly mineral water with lemon because she had a speech to give later. Julian suggested a little nip of something stronger might relax her nerves. She claimed not to be nervous and said she needed a clear head to be able to promote her work's importance with the clarity and cogency it deserved in language laypeople could understand.

"Isn't it as simple as saying you're trying to figure out how long it will take for climate change to obliterate the human race and the rest of Earth's mammals?"

"It's a bit more nuanced than that, Ike."

"You're not going to tell this crowd that life on Earth is the jackpot of an enormous cosmic lottery, are you?"

"Immense cosmic lottery," Lourdes said, correcting him. "And I don't know yet."

Fifteen minutes before she had to give her speech, her nervousness peaked. Her hands quivered. There were tiny beads of perspiration on her brow. Julian offered her a cocktail napkin with no explanation. She took the napkin and wiped her forehead. She exchanged the soiled napkin for Julian's glass of bourbon, which she emptied.

"I should have had a fucking drink an hour ago," Lourdes said.

"You'll be fine. Just watch the language."

Maribel Kravitz stood on the stage and introduced Barbara Le Conte. The precocious Canadian novelist, who was also being awarded an obscene amount of money, acknowledged the applause and launched into her acceptance speech. Le Conte's most recent novel, Life in Grayscale, which Edward Van de Weghe had read several times, put her onto his list of favorite writers, which included masculine giants such as John Steinbeck, Wallace Stegner and Cormac McCarthy. Barbara Le Conte, who had just turned 26, was the only woman on his favorites list, because, as Edward said, she knew "how to write like a man."

Edward saw himself as a sort of literary impresario and enjoyed thinking he had something to do with the success of some of his favorite young writers. All he was really doing was throwing money at them. There was a press release and a small amount of press coverage about Barbara Le Conte's recognition by the Van de Weghe Foundation, though it wasn't the sort of attention she couldn't create on her own, or hadn't already.

As Barbara Le Conte gave her speech, Lourdes waited in the wings. Maribel Kravitz was going to introduce her shortly. Julian stood in the middle of the crowd gathered around the stage. Olivia found him there and whispered in his ear, "Help me."

Julian's whole body tingled. He looked at her with surprised curiosity. "With what?" he asked.

"Grainger."

"Who's Grainger?"

"The bankruptcy attorney my father is trying to set me up with. The guy came with a date, but he won't leave me alone. He accidentally," she made air quotes with her fingers, "touched my ass. So I told him I was with you. I hope you don't mind. I didn't know what to do."

"Maybe you should make it look like we're together," Julian told her before he could stop himself.

"Great idea. Thank you," Olivia said as she cozied up to his side and put her arm on his shoulder. She whispered out of the side of her mouth, "He's heading this way. Be careful. He's kind of drunk."

Warning signals clanged in Julian's head. The charade of pretending to be Ike pretending to be Olivia's date could easily backfire. What were the odds Grainger hadn't seen Lourdes and Julian together? She had kissed him at the bar, but he knew Grainger wasn't close at the time because Edward had dragged Olivia across the room to meet him. That was over an hour earlier. He and Lourdes had been joined at the hip ever since.

Olivia wrapped her arm around the small of his back and rested her hand low on the fleshy part of his hip. His recently supercharged libido took complete control when he was around her. He had an erection that threatened to rip his tuxedo pants.

Grainger Reynolds worked at downtown law firm. He had an Ivy League education, a full head of floppy hair and a golf swing envied by both friends and enemies. He was, however, slightly less interesting than a soup spoon. At least that's what Olivia had determined over the course of their painfully long conversation about the differences between Wisconsin's and Illinois' bankruptcy exemptions. When it came to her looks, Olivia didn't bother with false modesty. She knew men and women thought she was beautiful. She was well aware that her legs were her greatest physical asset. It's why she wore the Tom Ford mini-dress. The dress was as empowering as Superman's cape. Her father had walked up to Grainger and said, in so many words, "I want you to meet my brilliant and gorgeous daughter, who, by the way, is single." Any man, drunk or sober, who would waste such a gift talking about bankruptcy exemptions was either gay or an idiot or both. Neither fulfilled her wants or needs.

Barbara Le Conte finished her speech to bright applause. As the applause dimmed, Grainger, ice cubes sloshing, left hand in his pants pocket, shambled over like a drunk prep school douche. He cleared his floppy hair out of his eyes and tried to make it look like he was just passing by. His act was thoroughly unconvincing, unlike the small but slow kiss Olivia planted on Julian's cheek.

Chapter Nine

Whump

"There you are," Grainger said to Olivia, who was just pulling her lips away from Julian's cheek. There was a detectable slur in his speech.

"Ike MacTavish," Julian said as he preemptively offered his hand to Grainger. He had never given Olivia a last name, real or fake, and he wanted a little control over the lies he might have to tell.

"Grainger Reynolds. What's your game, Ike?"

"Real Estate, mostly commercial, although I just sold an apartment at Water Tower Place," Julian said. Lying was easier than he thought it would be, still he wanted out of this conversation as soon as possible. His out came quickly when Maribel Kravitz returned to the stage.

"Quiet, she's going to introduce Lourdes," Olivia interjected.

"Who?" Julian said, mostly as a joke, but it played into the game nicely.

The three listened to Lourdes's speech, which Julian thought went better than either he or Lourdes had thought it would. She was confident, spoke clearly and showed no sign of nerves. She did not compare life on Earth to a jackpot in an immense cosmic lottery, nor did she start with a corny joke only a biologist would find funny, like the one she thought about using that says biology is the only science in which multiplication and division are the same thing. She did, however, make it clear that thermoregulation would play an important role in the survival of mammals, a class which included "almost everyone in the room." The line got a big laugh. She thanked Olivia Van de Weghe for her vision and her appreciation of the importance of the work she was doing.

Olivia excused herself to greet Lourdes as she left the stage. Julian saw Olivia whisper in her ear. Lourdes smiled and nodded. He assumed Olivia was letting her in on the charade she had concocted. Grainer was prattling on about a draw he hit with his seven iron when Olivia and Lourdes showed up arm-in-arm.

"Ike, Grainger, I'd like you to meet Dr. Lourdes Villegas," Olivia said.

Lourdes greeted Julian with the same unfamiliarity she showed Grainger, who had no clue he was the victim of a ruse which now included Lourdes as a third perpetrator. Both men offered Lourdes their congratulations. Olivia told them she needed to introduce Lourdes to her father and led her away. She actually had no intention of introducing Lourdes to her father. It was a way to rid herself of

Grainger. He was Julian's problem now, which Julian was okay with. Grainger's golf blather was certain to kill his erection.

Two minutes into his yarn about playing behind Phil Mickelson on the Old Course at St. Andrew's, Grainger took an abrupt turn when he interrupted himself and asked Julian, "Can you keep a secret?"

"As good as the next guy," Julian said.

"I hate my fucking job."

"Is that so?"

"Yup," Grainger said with a sigh that displayed a real sadness. Julian gave him a sympathetic look. "I never wanted to be a lawyer. That was my dad's thing. He kinda' forced me into it."

"Mine wouldn't let me be a lawyer. He said it would shame the family," Julian said. Grainger wasn't listening.

"The fucker died three days ago. I'm quitting on Monday. Woo hoo!" He rattled the ice cubes in his glass like a bell and slurped the rest of his drink.

Julian thought about asking Grainger what he would do next, but even if his opinion of Grainger had softened significantly, he didn't want to extend the conversation. He was about to wish him best of luck when Grainger saved him the trouble.

"I'm going to the bar and I think I'll stay there for a while." Grainger said and tottered off.

Julian found himself tapping his feet to the Neons' version of Bon Jovi's "You Give Love a Bad Name." As much as he wanted to spend time with Lourdes, he didn't seek her out. She was likely with Olivia and he wanted to avoid that pickle. His hearing was razor sharp, so he entertained himself by eavesdropping on a few conversations. Two elderly couples were all in agreement that the members of the band were fine musicians and the music they played was loud and terrible. Barbara Le Conte was in a deep discussion with Edward Van de Weghe on the subject of Margaret Atwood. Le Conte called Atwood an inspiration for both Canadian and women writers. Edward found her feminism heavy-handed, particularly for a woman who claimed not to be a feminist. Le Conte looked bored.

The most interesting thing he heard was the curt exchange between Grainger and a woman with cropped brown hair and a long red dress who was surely the date he had been ignoring. He was wobbling near the bar when she approached him. She reached into his coat pocket and pulled out a set of keys. She jingled them in front of his face.

"Fuck you," the woman in red whispered into his ear.

Grainger slurred "Love you, too, honey," as she showed him her back and walked away. She walked under the bright red exit sign, turned on her heels, flipped Grainger double birds and left the room. Next to Lourdes's speech it was the highlight of the evening. Julian would have been fine with going home at that point, but Lourdes had warned him she planned on staying at the party until the end. She felt it would be bad form to leave early, considering how much money they were giving her. He was having a good time, so he didn't mind. He worked his way around the room doing his best to steer clear of Olivia. He had no reason not to like her. He didn't even know her. He just didn't trust himself around her. He still loved Lourdes and he wanted Lourdes to love him back. When they were together in college, neither Julian's mind nor his eyes wandered. Lourdes was all he needed. Now his newly increased appetite had him floundering. It had to be related to the other changes taking place inside him, and if they were here to stay he would have to learn how to control them.

He knew he would have to deal with Olivia at the end of the night. He couldn't just take Lourdes and split without saying goodbye to the woman who had championed her work so vigorously. He needed a strategy for when the time came to say goodnight to Olivia. The plan he came up with was to hold onto Lourdes tightly. Feeling her body against his gave him focus. It gave him control. He got the sense that he could make this work. His new strength and speed were easy to manage. He could tune in his enhanced hearing when he wanted it and turn it off when he didn't. Night vision was still thrilling and not at all distracting. His libido had given him the biggest challenge and he was already exercising some control over it. And really, how often was he going to have to deal with someone as physically tantalizing as Olivia? He could go years without interacting with another woman with her combination of body, looks and je ne sais quoi. After tonight, he would probably never see her again. Yes, she had become friendly with Lourdes, though he doubted they would travel in the same social circles often, if ever. Their relationship seemed limited to a "Let's get a cup of coffee" kind of thing. Of course, relationships grow and change. Anything could happen, even the impossible. He knew that better than anyone.

At 12:30 the bartenders made their last call and a good number of the remaining guests headed to the bar. Though the party was still officially going on, it had lost most of its steam. Many guests from the older generations were long gone. Edward Van de Weghe had retired to the suite upstairs he had booked for the night. The Neons had nearly finished breaking down. All that remained was a couple of drums, an amplifier and a microphone stand. The crowd that was still there was made up of younger people and those who wanted to get as much alcohol as they could from the open bar. Julian, who had become a nocturnal creature, was still feeling fresh. It was Lourdes who was exhausted. She had met more people in one night that she usually did in a year. She felt like she had just run a marathon, a feeling she was familiar with. She ran the Chicago Marathon every October and tried to get to Boston at least every other April.

Julian was relieved when Lourdes made her goodbye to Olivia brief. She was too tired for anything more. Olivia, who still didn't know any better, referred to Julian as Ike when she said goodnight and gave him a polite hug. She held her body to his for no more than a second, but it was long enough to for him to draw in a potent blend of shampoo, perfume and estrus.

"I'll call you later this week to check on you," Olivia said to Lourdes as Julian led her out of the hotel lobby. Lourdes raised her hand in acknowledgement. Julian turned round to sneak one last peek at Olivia. She caught his look. All he could think to do was smile.

The Town Car Julian had arranged for Lourdes was parked at the curb. He had hoped she would spend the night in his guest room, but she had an 8:00 a.m. conference call. She chose to spend the night in her storage closet so she could be close to her office, where she needed to be to take the call. Julian passed on the offer of a ride, choosing a head-clearing walk home instead.

She slid into the back seat of the Town Car and closed her eyes. Julian reminded the driver of the address, passed him a hundy as a tip, and tapped the roof a couple of times to let him know it was safe to pull away. Julian took in a deep breath of spring air and held it in his lungs for several seconds. He let it all out and smiled.

The stores on Michigan Avenue were lit up, but the sidewalks looked deserted. "Where is everyone?" he thought, forgetting that it was after 1:00 in the morning.

As he walked across the intersection at Walton, Julian could see a faceless man in black jeans and a black T-shirt holding another man at knifepoint in front of the building now called 875 North Michigan Avenue but what will be forever thought of as the John Hancock Building.

From a block away, Julian could hear the assailant growl, "Give it up or I'll cut your fuckin' nose off!"

The victim didn't cooperate. The Schnoz Chopper punched him in the head and he fell to the ground.

"Hey!" Julian yelled, and took off running. The Chopper looked up and saw Julian far down the block. Not knowing how fast Julian could run, he assumed he had more time to complete his assault. He kicked his victim in the head several times. The man he kicked was strong and defiant. He covered his head with one arm. With the other he protected his jacket pocket. Julian covered the distance in a few seconds, which gave him just enough time to size up his target. When Julian got to the scene, the Chopper had his knife at the ready as he tried to pull the victim's head back to reveal his nose. Julian reached around the Chopper's throat with his left hand and stuck his right arm through the Chopper's legs and grabbed him by the crotch. He lifted the Chopper off his feet. He hissed in Chopper's face and heaved him. He had tried to throw him into the railing that rimmed the sunken plaza in front of the Hancock, hoping to incapacitate him. Unaccustomed to his new strength, Julian threw him too hard and too high. The son of a bitch, arms flailing like a flightless bird desperately trying to fly, soared over the thick metal railing and plunged another 15 feet to the plaza below. He landed on the concrete near the bottom of the stairs with an audible and messy whump.

Julian ran to the rail and looked down. "Oh, fuck," he muttered when he saw the Schnoz Chopper's limbs positioned in geometric patterns not even the freakiest circus performer could replicate. As Julian watched the blood puddle beside the Chopper's head he felt calm return.

His first thought was to get out of there. He could call 911 when he was around the corner. The desperate moans coming from the assaulted man changed his mind. He looked over at him and could now tell the suit was a tuxedo and the unlucky bastard wearing it was his new, golf-loving, job-hating buddy Grainger Reynolds.

Julian helped Grainger sit up and rest against the low wall that supported the railing that was supposed to incapacitate Grainger's attacker. Grainger's face was striped by blood, which was still streaming out of a deep gash under his left eye.

"Is that you, Wes?" Grainger struggled to ask. "That bitch Jennifer took my car."

The combination of all the drinking he had done and the beatdown he had just taken had turned Grainger's brain into scrambled eggs. He would have been better off if he just let the guy take his wallet. Julian was impressed by Grainger's tenacity. He wasn't sure if he should give his real name, his new Ike alias or stick with Wes, whoever the hell he was.

"Yeah, it's me. It's Wes," he said, having decided it would be easier on Grainger and better for him if his real name, and Ike's, wasn't mentioned.

"Thanks for scaring him off, Wes ol' buddy."

Not exactly what had happened, but Julian didn't correct him.

"Is my nose still there? The guy said he was going to cut it off."

"Yeah it's still there, right in the middle of your face." Julian said with a comforting tone.

Julian looked around. There was still no one on the sidewalk on either side of Michigan Avenue. Had no one else witnessed Grainger take that vicious beating? If no one had, there was a good chance no one saw him throw the Chopper over the rail like a bale of hay. He thought about taking off, and again he dismissed the idea. He reached into his pocket to take out his cell phone to call 911. He stopped when he saw a minivan taxi coming toward him from the south.

Julian waved his arms over his head to get the attention of the driver. He turned back to Grainger when he saw the cab was slowing down. He didn't want to be seen if he didn't have to be. The taxi rolled up to the curb and and the driver lowered the passenger window.

"Is everything all right?" the driver asked.

"He got mugged and there's a lot of blood coming out of his head. He's in pretty bad shape. Call 911."

"Okay, I'll make the call, but I gotta roll. I've got a fare waiting at the Ambassador and I'm already late. Dispatch is on my ass," the driver said.

Julian thanked him and the driver pushed the three numbers on his phone and drove off with the phone to his ear. Julian questioned the logic of staying. He had no clue how he would explain the contorted, bloody mess at the bottom of the plaza steps. Maybe the cops wouldn't even see the body, or better yet, they wouldn't even come. Just the paramedics would show up. Maybe the fucker wasn't even dead and he'd get up and run away. Or maybe they'd give him a medal for taking out the notorious Schnoz Chopper. Lots of maybes and only one certainty: If the cops came, he had some serious explaining to do.

"Help's on the way. Just hold on a little while longer," Julian told Grainger.

The sirens came from the northwest. They were still quite far away, but Julian could easily hear them. He lightly patted Grainger on the shoulder, assuring him things would be all right. Julian vaulted over the same rail he had thrown the Schnoz Chopper over, grabbed a branch of one of the trees in the plaza below and dropped to the ground as assuredly as a cat. He took off running south across the plaza and up the stairs to the sidewalk on Chestnut. From there he headed east and away from Michigan Avenue. He was reasonably confident no one had seen him and absolutely certain the cops hadn't. He didn't want to run into Johnny so he skipped the front door and entered through the parking garage. Being seen in the elevator was also a risk. He took the stairs to the 69th floor.

As he keyed open the door to his new apartment he thought about how glad he was to have his own place. He wanted to keep his brother and Vanessa out of any trouble he might get in. He took a moment to acknowledge he had killed a man without remorse. He wasn't happy about it, but he had to admit that, in a general sense, he felt great. He knew tonight's incident was just the beginning. The Schnoz Chopper was an accident. The others wouldn't be.

Chapter Ten

His Fucking Neck Exploded

Lourdes was in her lab analyzing data in a thick report when her cell phone rang. On the other end of the line was Olivia, who was seated in her Porsche in her indoor parking spot at her private research facility. It was late afternoon the Tuesday after the foundation's gala.

"I just wanted to check in with you," Olivia said.

"Still trying to catch up on my sleep, but really, I couldn't be better. I can't thank you enough," replied Lourdes.

"My pleasure. So, tell me about Ike. Is it serious?"

"Ike?" Lourdes asked, forgetting for a moment that Julian had used an alias at the party.

"Your date the other night."

"Oh, I should explain. That was Julian."

"The guy in Bangladesh or wherever? The one you wrote that paper with?"

"Yeah. We should have told you. He's got some issues with the society crowd and thought it would be easier to pretend to be some dork named Ike."

"Is he just visiting or is he back to stay?"

"I'm not sure what his longterm plans are, probably to stay for a while. He just bought a gorgeous apartment at Water Tower Place. You should see the view."

"So is it serious between you two?"

"No, just friends. But who knows?"

"Really? You'll have to tell me more. But I gotta run now."

Olivia hung up the phone. She bent over and rested her head on the steering wheel. There she sat motionless for a couple of minutes. She took a deep, cleansing breath, got out of her car and entered her lab. In the corner of the a well-equipped laboratory was an insulated box the size of a refrigerator. A digital thermometer on the front of the box displayed the temperature inside: 41.38 degrees Celsius. The temperature always read 41.38 Celsius. A change of even a tenth of a degree could ruin what Olivia considered her most important work, the juice that had snatched her frail, arthritic father from death's clutch, reversed the complete erectile dysfunction Edward viewed as a fate worse than death, and re-birthed him as an 89-year-old, ass-ogling tennis nut. Edward's recovery was astounding. It was more dramatic than she had predicted. In a clinical sense, Olivia was proud of the work, though she regretted her success had made her father an even more cocksure son of a bitch. She had to remind herself that he was really no more than a lab rat.

In addition to being what Olivia characterized as a sexist pig, albeit a brilliant one, Edward Van de Weghe was a tireless philanderer. While married to his first wife, Edward had fucked every woman who had said yes and plenty who hadn't. It didn't stop after he married Olivia's mother, who was twenty-five years his junior. His company manufactured the antibiotic he used to treat his gonorrhea, which he got from a high-priced but infected whore on a business trip to Johannesburg. The antibiotic worked, but not soon enough for Olivia's mother. She caught it, too. Gonorrhea stopped his philandering, but only temporarily.

Infidelity and infections weren't the worst of what Edward gave Olivia's mother. Mental abuse, particularly belittling jabs, were incessant and corrosive, right up to the night she climbed into the back seat of his BMW and slit her wrists. Edward found her as he looked in the rearview mirror while backing out of the garage. She'd ruined the seat leather.

Olivia was a 22-year-old Ph.D. candidate in Boston when her mother's late-night phone call woke her. She had called to say goodbye.

"Be strong and don't let your father do to you what he did to me," her mother told her. Olivia begged her mother not to do something foolish. She begged her to stay on the phone. The line went dead. Olivia immediately called her back, but no one answered. She tried the house phone. Nothing. Something in her brain broke. It was like the synapse that accessed what little empathy she had left had snapped. That part of her brain was cut off forever. She had never been fond of her father. After that phone call, she hated him. Much about Edward was detestable. What he did to her mother was unforgivable.

From the hotbox, Olivia took out five two-liter vials, put them on a cart and wheeled them to the next room. The centerpiece of her private facility was an enormous star-shaped centrifuge with a circumference that barely fit inside half a basketball court. It looked like a terrifying carnival ride. The walls of the room contained four feet of soundproofing to muffle the deafening whir when it spun. If her neighbors had been able to hear it, they would have called the police. The centrifuge spun at such an extraordinary speed that it created wind strong enough to blow Olivia's hair straight back. If she had ever let anyone witness the centrifuge in action, that person would no doubt have been terrified. Olivia, on the other hand, found it mesmerizing. She was a hybrid of mad scientist and adrenaline junkie, and could spend hours staring at it spin ferociously. There was no other centrifuge like it in the world. It was fabricated in sections by different suppliers and she assembled much of it herself.

At the end of each of the five points of the star-shaped centrifuge was a compartment. In each of the five compartments she put one of the large vials. Once all the vials were secured Olivia made her way to the control console. She slipped on a pair of black over-the-head ear protectors. She flipped the power switch on the console, turned the key, and pushed the big green button. An alarm sounded three times and the centrifuge started to spin slowly. For a minute it spun increasingly faster until it reached the terrifying optimal speed. She sat in a swivel chair by the console and watched her monstrous creation spin for forty minutes. An odd, dark thought had been occupying her mind recently when she watched the centrifuge. She wondered what would happen if she threw herself at the giant whirling contraption. Would she be splattered against the wall, or would the centrifuge suck her in and spin her to death? It was gruesome to think about, still she found the thought intriguing, at least from a Newtonian mechanics perspective.

She turned the centrifuge off and it continued to spin for an additional three minutes. When it finally came to a stop, Olivia opened one of the compartments in the centrifuge and removed the vial. Ninety percent of the liquid in the vial was cloudy gray, the remaining 10 was the same bright orange as the liquid her father drank every morning. The smile on her face revealed her satisfaction with the result. She removed the four other vials from their compartments. All of them had the same ratio of bright orange to cloudy grey. For each of the five larger vials, she poured off the orange liquid into five smaller ones. A total of twenty-four small vials went into a refrigerator in the laboratory. The twenty-fifth she took with her to her desk. She sat in her chair, opened the vial and drank its contents. When the disgusting liquid had settled inside her and her body had stopped shuddering, she opened a drawer and pulled out a bottle of tequila. She opened the bottle, put it to her lips and drank from it as if it were a fountain she had stumbled onto in the middle of the Sahara.

***

The Water Tower Place apartments were easy to stake out. There was a grassy park and a playground across the street. McCauliff and KP could easily watch the building from the park without being spotted. The Ritz-Carlton Hotel that occupied the lower floors of the high-rise made alternating shifts convenient. While one was in the park, the other was in the bar or hotel room they had booked for three nights. McCauliff, with his fondness for comfort and style, liked the room at the Ritz-Carlton a lot better than the straw hut in the Sundarbans. KP didn't prefer one over the other. His military career had hardened him. He was the kind of guy who could survive a month in the woods eating grubs and drinking his own piss. Room service at a posh Chicago hotel didn't do much for him. He had a conditioned ability to turn off his brain to the elements and all irrelevant activity. He could keep his eyes focused on the front door of the building for hours and have no sense of how much time had passed.

They arrived at 3:45 in the afternoon the first day. Immediately after checking into the room, KP took the first watch. McCauliff went to the bar. They switched after an hour. Just a few minutes into his shift McCauliff got lucky. His eyes were on the front door of the residences when Julian exited, gave a fist bump to the young black doorman who had just come on duty, and went inside the cafe next door. Julian looked familiar to McCauliff, who checked the blurry photo KP had shared with him via text. He was reasonably sure it was Julian, but he wanted a second look before he told KP. Three minutes later Julian came out of the cafe holding a paper bag and a couple of coffee cups. He handed one of the cups to the doorman and disappeared back inside the residences.

As McCauliff returned to the hotel, he intentionally walked past Johnny, who had just finished a satisfying first sip of coffee with an audible "Ahh."

"Must be good coffee," McCauliff said.

"Free is always good."

"Lucky you."

"Lucky me is right. My man brings me one same time everyday. Great way to start a shift."

McCauliff smiled at Johnny and went into the hotel. He checked the time. It was 5:04. He went to the bar to tell KP. Neither of them came out for hours.

McCauliff was supposed to take the first shift the following morning. He woke at 7:00, stumbled into the bathroom to take a piss and went back to sleep. At 8:00 KP used his belt to wake him up.

KP was on duty when Julian exited the building at the exact time he did the day before. He watched Julian go into the cafe and come out with a bag and two coffee cups. He handed one of the cups to the doorman and went back inside the building at 5:04. Everything was the same as what McCauliff had told him.

In their hotel room McCauliff and KP discussed the best way to kill Julian. After going over every possible scenario and outcome, they chose to snipe him on his way to get coffee. The door to the residences was close enough to the corner that KP, an expert marksman, could take him out from the backseat of a car and simply drive out of sight. They would be heading north on Lake Shore Drive in less than a minute. If the timing didn't work out on the first attempt, they would try again the following day.

McCauliff drove KP to a car rental agency where they rented a Hyundai Elantra. McCauliff's white 1970 Cadillac was way too conspicuous for this job. KP gave the clerk at the agency a driver's license and a credit card that identified him as Rexford Carrol, one of the aliases he used when conducting illicit business activity, and the real name of a fellow Delta Force operator killed in action in Iraq. KP followed McCauliff to a parking lot in Lincoln Park where no cameras would capture KP quickly transfer two cases from the trunk of the Cadillac to the trunk of the Elantra. In each case was a sniper rifle. One was a McMillan TAC-50, the same model sniper rifle he had used to kill a Taliban fighter in Afghanistan from over 2,100 meters away. It was a kill shot KP was proud of, though it was far from a record distance. For this simple job in front of an apartment building, the TAC-50 was overkill. The Sig SSG 3000 was the obvious choice for a shot from the backseat of a Hyundai Elantra at a range of about 60 meters. The Sig had an 18-inch barrel, 11 inches shorter than the TAC-50, and it was half the weight of the bigger gun.

KP followed McCauliff to a parking garage where McCauliff parked the Caddie for the night. They parked the Elantra in a different lot and walked to the hotel, where they would eat a nice meal and have several drinks without discussing the hit job they had planned for the next afternoon.

An hour later Julian left his 69th floor apartment to go to his post at Adams and Wabash. He walked past the front door of the Ritz-Carlton half a minute before McCauliff, already into his third bourbon and limoncello, stumbled outside to roll and smoke a cigarette. Most nights Julian was at Adams and Wabash watching out for people. If KP and McCauliff hadn't spent so much time in the bar, they might have known that.

Since that time when he ran down the purse snatcher, he had done nothing but stand around and try not to look suspicious. Occasionally he discretely handed out twenty dollar bills to people who looked in need or asked for spare change. He didn't make a routine of it for fear he would be labeled an easy mark. Giving away money wasn't his goal. He was there to help in other ways. Not once did anybody scream, shout or even ask politely for directions. Not a single declaration of a stolen smartphone. No one so much as took a misstep down the platform stairs. Since the purse snatching he witnessed his second day home, the only other crime he saw anywhere in the city was when Grainger was attacked by the Schnoz Chopper. A couple days after that incident, it came out in the news that the man police say was responsible for a number of knife attacks had fallen to his death at 875 North Michigan Avenue. Police suspected it was accidental and happened as the deceased fled an attack on an unidentified victim. No suspects named Ike or Wes, or anything else were ever mentioned.

Julian had killed a man. He knew he should have stayed and talked to the police, but he hadn't done anything wrong. It really was an accident. It didn't happen the way the police suspected it had, though it was an accident all the same. Furthermore, the Schnoz Chopper had terrorized Chicago for weeks and the woman whom the scumbag had put in a coma died the same night he did.

Sometime after midnight, Julian passed Cloudgate on his walk home. He noticed a couple of lowlifes following him. He had seen these same two young men, no more than 19 years old, on a previous night. He had given them each $20. They had seen Julian hand a twenty to a woman carrying her worldly possessions in a bright blue Ikea shopping bag. He suspected they weren't homeless, though it was possible they needed the money. That didn't mean they deserved it

139

when they asked Julian for some. He gave it to them as a way to get them to go away without robbing anyone, particularly the woman with the Ikea bag. He could have handled them if they tried anything, but he wanted to avoid having to do that. This time he had no intention of giving them anything. Their presence gave him an uncomfortable tingle, like hundreds of tiny pinpricks.

"Hey look, Wayne. It's Santa Claus," the more alpha of the two said to his buddy as they walked toward him.

"What you got for us, Santa?" Wayne asked in a threatening tone.

"You guys oughta know I keep a list of who's been naughty and who's been nice. Run along now. Better luck next year," Julian said as he made a shooing gesture with his hand. As the words came out of his mouth, Julian didn't recognize them as his own. He hadn't meant to say it like that. He wasn't trying to be supercilious. He did want them to go away, but he knew the way he had said it made them more likely to stay than leave. They continued walking toward him.

"Touch me and I'll break your fucking hand," Julian said

"Then just give us the money," Wayne said.

"Give us all of it and we won't have to come back," Alpha threatened.

"Go away," Julian said. There wasn't a trace of nervousness in his voice. He felt bold and confident. He hadn't had his new powers long, but he had an innate sense of what they could do, as if he had had them his whole life.

Alpha reached for Julian, which only made it easier for Julian to grab him by the arm. Julian twisted his arm and forced Alpha to his knees.

"You don't follow instruction too well," Julian said.

"Fuck off. Get him, Wayne."

Wayne lunged at Julian, who easily parried Wayne's attack with his forearm. Wayne landed on his ass. Alpha threw an awkward left at Julian's nuts with little effect but pissing him off even more. Julian yanked at Alpha's arm. He sank his teeth into the meaty part of his hand, thrashed it back and forth like a pit bull and tore off a thick chunk. He pushed the chunk to the back of his mouth to chew on it. When he realized what he was about to do he spit out the flesh in a spray of crimson. Julian dropped the bloody hand like it had stung him. He took off running and didn't stop until he was deep under the cold waters of Lake Michigan.

***

At 4:45 the following afternoon, KP and McCauliff watched the entrance to the Water Tower Place residences from their rented Elantra. KP pulled the bolt on the Sig. Sight lines were clear. Traffic was light. He slowed his breathing and heart to the rate of corpse and still managed to grin with pleasure. He thought about how long it had been since he had killed a man. It had been all tigers for the past couple of years.

The door at the residences opened at 4:58. Their target and a six-foot-tall blond woman stepped onto the sidewalk and walked to a waiting taxi. The doorman followed them pulling a wheeled suitcase.

"What the fuck is this?" KP asked.

"I don't know, but that's him," McCauliff answered.

"And who the fuck is she?"

"Who cares? Just do it."

As it turned out, the unexpected companion gave KP more time. The man opened the taxi door and held it for the woman. Pearson Street is oneway heading east, so as he held the taxi door, his back was to KP, giving him a clear shot at his medulla oblongata. A direct apricot shot, as snipers call it, is as close as you can get to instant death.

"That's it, motherfucker. Just stand still for me," KP said.

KP squeezed the trigger just as a horn from a nearby car sounded, causing the target to move his head slightly. KP kept his eye to the sight. He saw flesh and blood explode from the neck. The body went limp. McCauliff stepped on the gas, not hard, just enough to take off inconspicuously, and they were out of sight completely.

"Kill shot?" McCauliff asked.

"I missed the apricot, but I got his carotid. His fucking neck exploded," KP said through a grin.

***

The bullet hit Simon's neck below his right ear. He fell to the gutter between the taxi and the curb. Streams of blood spurted from his neck in staccato bursts and sprayed the interior and exterior of the taxi and Vanessa's white jeans. She hadn't heard a gun. No one else was near. Nothing made sense. She screamed Simon's name.

"Shit, shit, shit," moaned the taxi driver as he fought the urge to get sick.

"Call 9-1-1," Vanessa ordered. Johnny already had his phone out and was dialing.

Both of Vanessa's parents were doctors. She had watched her mother perform heart surgery a number of times. She was no stranger to blood. She pulled her shit together and went to work. She ripped off her cotton T-shirt and wrapped it tightly around Simon's neck. She knew Simon wasn't dead yet. His eyes were moving as he scanned her blood-stained face and teary eyes.

"Hold on, baby! Don't go!" Vanessa begged just as Julian exited the building and walked into bloody chaos.

Of all the locations in Chicago to get shot in the neck, this was the place to do it. Paramedics were on the scene in literally less than a minute. The home station for the Chicago Fire Department's engine number 98 and ambulance number 11 was on the other side of the park across the street. Northwestern Memorial was only three blocks away. Barely five minutes after getting shot, Simon was in an operating room surrounded by a team of surgeons and nurses. If either the fire station or the hospital had been a few blocks further, Simon would have been DOA. If Vanessa, who had made last minute plans to visit her parents in Newport Beach, had freaked out instead of jumping into action, he would have bled out in the gutter.

Chapter Eleven

A Room With A View

Lourdes's cell phone buzzed as she tried to feed a wrinkly dollar bill into a vending machine at Northwestern Memorial Hospital. She, Vanessa and Julian were waiting nervously as Simon's second surgery entered its third hour. The first one had lasted twice that. The first procedure had appeared to go well, but at 5:00 in the morning he was rushed back into surgery. Lourdes hadn't eaten anything and was desperate enough to drop three bucks on a small bag of cheddar and jalapeño potato chips. She had made a lot of calls that day and didn't want to answer her phone anymore. When she saw it was Olivia Van de Weghe calling she tapped the green button on her phone's screen.

"Liv, I can't talk now. I've been at Northwestern Memorial all night," she said into her phone.

"Is everything all right?" Olivia asked.

"No. Everything's fucked up. I'll call you later." She hung up the phone before Olivia could say anything else. The vending machine finally accepted the wrinkly dollar and she pushed the two buttons that made the potato chips fall into the slot. When she went back into the waiting room, Vanessa was thanking one of the surgeons who had just finished operating on Simon.

"What's next?" Julian asked the exhausted surgeon as he gave Vanessa a reassuring side hug.

"I'll know more in the next hour, but I'm pretty sure we got it. He'll be okay, but the recovery will be long."

The surgeon excused himself and left the room. Vanessa, emotionally and physically exhausted, collapsed into a chair. The tears she'd been holding back all day finally let loose. Lourdes sat in the chair beside her and offered her hand in comfort. Vanessa took it and gripped it tightly. The two women had only met once, but had felt an immediate bond. The tragedy brought them even closer.

"I need some air," Julian said. He left the room and went outside where he found a shady tree to lean against. He felt sick with guilt. His brother getting shot was his fault. He closed his eyes and took in three deep cleansing breaths. Even with his eyes closed he knew Olivia Van de Weghe was nearby. He had taken in her piquant scent. He took another deep breath, this time through his mouth. He could taste her. He opened his eyes and saw her approaching the hospital entrance. The gorgeous body that her tiny dress had revealed so much of at the gala was now sheathed in a dark blue suit. Still, he couldn't take his eyes off her. He watched her glide toward the door. She hadn't noticed him. Just as she was about to walk inside, something, nothing in particular, just a feeling or maybe a smell, made her stop and turn.

"Hello, Olivia," Julian said.

"Hey there," Olivia said with enough surprise to appear confused.

"It's Julian."

"I thought it was Ike," she said, having regained her footing.

"It's Julian. I apologize for the deception."

"What's going on? I got the impression from Lourdes that something awful had happened."

"It was my brother. He got shot in the neck."

"Oh my god, your brother? He's still alive?"

"Barely. He just got out of his second surgery."

"Who would do such a thing?"

"I don't know," Julian said. He lied. Julian did know who would do such a thing as shoot his brother. He also knew they got the wrong guy. He cursed himself for not realizing that buying an apartment in the same building hadn't distanced Simon and Vanessa from danger at all. It was stupid to put them in jeopardy that way. Stupid and selfish. He bought the place because it was easy and he didn't want to deal with the hassle of looking around. He didn't think they would find him before he found them.

"Is Lourdes inside?" Olivia asked.

"She's in there with Vanessa, my brother's wife,"

"I'll go in to give my regards. I'm so sorry."

"Thanks. Maybe I'll see you inside."

"I hope so," she said.

By noon, the potato chips Lourdes bought from the vending machine were long gone and she needed food. She, Julian and Olivia, who had been with them in the lobby for the past hour, went across the street to a place that sold chicken and donuts. Vanessa chose to stay at the hospital. They took a table on the patio and ate their chicken sandwiches and an assortment of donuts in relative quiet. The day had been emotionally exhausting for everyone. Olivia excused herself to go to the restroom.

"Do you think they know they got the wrong guy?" Lourdes asked when Olivia was out of earshot.

"I don't know, but I shouldn't go home. It's probably not safe."

"What about Vanessa? What's she going to do?" Lourdes asked.

"I think she'll be all right. She's of no interest to them. It's me they want."

"You could stay at my place in Bucktown."

"No. I'll get a hotel room somewhere."

"Promise me you'll be careful."

Julian leaned across the table and gave her a kiss on the cheek, a gesture she welcomed. "I'll be careful. I promise."

When Olivia returned to the table Lourdes said she needed to get back to her lab. Julian hailed a taxi, gave the driver a hundred bucks and told him where to take her.

"Say goodbye to Vanessa for me," Lourdes told Julian. Olivia gave her a big hug and said goodbye. Lourdes got into the taxi and it took off.

"What are you going to do now?" Olivia asked Julian.

"I was thinking I'd go back to the hospital for a while. After that I don't know what I'll do.

"Walk me to my car?" Olivia asked.

Julian and Olivia walked up one block to a parking garage on Huron Street behind the hospital. They rode the elevator to the sixth level. Olivia's Porsche was parked at the far end of the structure.

"Nice ride," Julian said.

"Get in. I'll take you for a spin."

"I should be a good brother and go back to the hospital."

"Fine, I'll take you."

Julian slid into the passenger seat and buckled up. Olivia drove the car slowly and carefully down the ramp to street level. As Olivia payed her ticket, Julian inhaled deeply. Her scent coursed through his body.

"Okay, take me for a ride," he said as the boom gate lifted.

Olivia didn't hesitate. She stomped on the accelerator and rocketed into a right turn onto Huron. Julian was thrown back into his seat so firmly he could barely move. Olivia wove through traffic for a block and a half and turned hard right onto Michigan, where she slid her Porsche into spaces between cars that most people couldn't even see. She ran a red light at Chestnut and it was clear all the way to North Lake Shore Drive, where the dense traffic finally forced her to slow down. After half a mile she accelerated down the exit ramp and into a parking lot near North Avenue Beach. The Porsche came to a screeching halt in an open space. She shoved the transmission into park, and let out a satisfied exhale.

"Was it good for you, too?" she asked.

"If being terrified is good, then yeah, it was fucking great."

She turned in her seat so she was looking directly at Julian. She paused to make sure she had his full attention. "I'm gonna lay it all out on the table for you, Julian. I'm 35 years old, I have a doctorate and a Masters, an important job and more money than I could ever spend. But you'd be wrong if you thought I had it all. I live in a giant museum of a house with my fucking father, who's old enough to be my grandfather and barely tolerable on his best days. The only person I ever really talk to is his Guatemalan housemaid who knows about 50 English words. I'm painfully lonely. I don't beat around the bush. I don't have time for it. When I want something I usually just come out with it. Sometimes it works. Sometimes it blows up in my face. But right now I find myself in unfamiliar territory."

"In what way?"

"Since I've never had any real friends, I've never had to worry about going around their backs. But recently I've come to consider Lourdes a friend. My only friend."

"I find it hard to believe that you only have one friend."

"Let's just say I can be hard to get along with."

Julian had already figured that out. He wanted her to get right to the point and he was pretty sure what it would be. "Don't worry about Lourdes. We're just friends."

"I know, but I get the feeling she might want to be more."

"You're beating around the bush. Tell me what you want," he said.

"I want to drive out to South Barrington and show you my father's stables."

"His stables? That doesn't sound like such a big deal," Julian said.

"Then I want to throw you in the dirt, tear your clothes off and fuck you like a wild animal."

"How far is it to South Barrington?"

"In this traffic forty-five minutes. With me driving, half an hour."

"I don't think I can wait that long."

"You could take me right here, but the back seat is pretty tight."

Julian looked at the back seat, which was smaller than he expected. "Yeah, you're right," he conceded.

"Don't you live around here?" she asked him.

If it had been any other woman, Julian would have suggested they get a hotel room, but he had never wanted anyone as much as he wanted Olivia, and from the moment he had first seen her he wanted to have her in his new living room with the view of the lake that looks like an ocean.

On the way to Julian's apartment, Olivia kept it at or under the speed limit and didn't run any red lights. With just her left hand, it was hard for her to drive the way she had earlier. Her right hand was busy massaging Julian's erection.

"I think I've been hard every second I've spent with you. How is that possible?"

She knew he wasn't expecting an answer. She just smiled and massaged away.

Olivia parked the Porsche in Julian's parking space. He took her through the back way, hoping not to be seen by anyone. His hands shook as he tried to tap the button to call the elevator. The display showed the closest was on the 48th floor. It might as well have been the 148th floor for how long the damn thing took to show up. They stood side-by-side without talking or looking at each other. His heart raced. Her scent was stronger than it had ever been. It was so thick and damp he nearly choked on it. The elevator doors finally opened and an elderly couple Julian had never seen before slowly stepped out. The woman had little trouble. The old man stumbled when the tip of his cane lodged in the gap between the floor and the elevator. Julian politely offered to free the cane, but the old man insisted he could do it himself. Julian remained calm and patient when what he really wanted to do was grab the old man and his cane and throw them both into the lobby.

When the old man was finally out of the way, Julian politely gestured for Olivia to enter the elevator.

"What floor?" she asked in a way that suggested they didn't know each other.

"Sixty-nine," he said. She responded by raising her eyebrows and flashing a knowing and juvenile grin. The elevator door was half-way closed when an arm reached through and stopped it. The door reversed directions and a short man in a suit and tie entered. There were beads of sweat on his forehead. He was out of breath.

"What floor?" Olivia said with the same detached tone she used when she asked Julian.

"Thirty-seven, thanks. Howard Erlacher, apartment 372," the short man said as he looked at Olivia.

"Olivia Van de Weghe. Just visiting."

The short man looked over to Julian.

"Julian Hamilton, apartment 691."

"Oh, you're Simon's brother," Howard said.

Julian nodded an affirmation.

"You guys look alike."

"That's what everybody says."

"How's he doing?" Howard said in a way that clearly indicated he had no knowledge of what had happened to Simon.

"Not so good, actually. He was shot in the neck this morning."

"That was him?" Howard said with a terrified surprise.

"Afraid so."

"Holy shit. Wait, is he still alive?"

"He got out of surgery a few hours ago."

"That's good news. I heard he was a goner."

The elevator stopped at the 37th floor and the door opened. Olivia held it for Howard, who wasn't ready to leave just yet.

"Please, give him my best wishes."

"I'll do that," Julian said.

"Nice to meet you, Howard," Olivia added.

"Likewise," Howard said as he stepped out of the elevator, still dazed by the news of Simon's shooting.

When the doors closed Julian grabbed Olivia and pressed his lips to hers. He slipped his hand between the buttons of her shirt and caressed her breasts over her soft, silky bra. Her nipples were hard as stones. She moved her hand down his body and stopped when she found his erection.

"Still there," she whispered in his ear. She nibbled his lobe.

"It feels like days."

"You deserve a medal."

Once inside his apartment, he led her across the living room. She kicked off her shoes as she walked. Off came her jacket, her shirt and the soft, silky bra. By the time Julian stopped walking she had nothing on. She tore off Julian's pants. He lifted her off the ground and she wrapped her legs around his waist. She ripped open his shirt and sent its buttons flying. He pressed her bare back against the cool glass of the large window that looked out at the lake.

"Nice view," she said as Julian pushed himself inside her.

Later, as they lay on the hard plank floor, naked, sweaty and exhausted, she ran her fingers across his chest. His body now had long, smooth muscles like an Olympic swimmer. Her fingers stopped at his weeks-old bullet scars.

"What are these?" she asked.

"Just some old scars."

"They don't feel that old. They're still bumpy."

"I'm a slow healer."

"You have other, more rewarding skills."

"Such as?"

"Such as that was the greatest fuck of my life."

"Mine, too. But I think I can do better."

"You're certainly welcome to try, but it can't be today."

"Why not?"

"I've got to get back to work."

"Wait a minute. You mean you would have driven all the way to South Barrington for one fuck and gone all the way back to work?"

"I would have driven all the way to Milwaukee if I knew you were going to fuck me like that."

***

Olivia Van de Weghe re-entered the living room fully dressed in her blue suit and heels. Her face was lit up with sexual afterglow. She had never looked more beautiful. She sat on the side of the couch where Julian was now lying, only partially covered by a throw pillow.

"I'm off to work," she said.

"I'm not."

"One question. What do we do about Lourdes?"

"Nothing. What she doesn't know won't hurt her," Julian said so matter of factly it was almost cold.

"Okay. I can live with that."

It wasn't until a few minutes after Olivia left that her intoxicating scent dissipated enough for Julian to regain control of his senses and faculties. It was almost as if he had woken up from a dream. Olivia's magic over him was gone. He cursed himself for having sex with her, no matter how good it had been. He had already figured out that he had no control around her, but he let himself get sucked in anyway. He never should have got in the damn car.

Julian hurriedly stuffed his backpack with some essential items and clothing and left his new apartment not knowing when or if he would ever be back. He didn't even know where he was going. On the elevator ride down he thought about going to the Drake because it was just a few blocks away. He quickly nixed the idea. He had met Olivia at the Drake. He needed a place where she would be completely off his mind.

With his backpack slung over his shoulder, Julian walked south along Michigan Avenue. When he got to the river he espied the London Guarantee and Accident building at the far end of the Du

Sable bridge. The Beaux Arts building was one of the most well known of Chicago's many architectural treasures. When he left for Asia there was no hotel in the building. Now LondonHouse was the building's principal tenant. He had always admired the building, and it had the advantage of being more or less equidistant from the platform at Adams and Wabash, where his sister lost her life, and Northwestern Memorial Hospital, where his brother's life had just been saved. And, most importantly, at least at the moment, his brother had told him the hotel had a great rooftop bar. He needed a stiff drink, maybe a half dozen of them.

It was 8:00 in the evening by the time he had a bourbon on the rocks in his hand. The sun had dipped below the horizon and twilight was still brighter than the artificial lights of the city. The day had been stressful, to say the least. The total combined stress over 12 years in the bush didn't even come close to the past 12 hours. He had had the greatest sex of his life, which should have relaxed him, but it had put him more on edge. Finally, the sound of ice cubes jingling against glass and the warm burn of bourbon sliding down his throat brought him peace. No matter how goddamn beautiful she was, no matter how magnificently she fucked, he vowed—again—to stay away from Olivia Van de Weghe. Nothing good could come from seeing her. He considered the option of going back to Asia to study tigers as soon as his business in Chicago was taken care of. It was as good an option as any he had at the moment. As much as he enjoyed being with Lourdes, as much as he hoped to spend more time with the brother he almost lost, and as much as he appreciated the wealth his brother had managed so well for him, he craved a less complicated existence. As he took in the incomparable view of the river and up the Mag Mile, he knew he would miss his hometown, but if there were going to be more days like today he might just have to let it all go.

Earlier he had talked to Vanessa, who told him Simon was in stable condition. He had called Lourdes to let her know he was all right. For her own safety, he didn't tell her where he was and she understood why. Neither of them wanted her to be burdened by the knowledge. There was still a lot to do to reach closure for Lara's death and exact vengeance from those who had tried to kill him. But right now the only thing he needed to do was drink his bourbon.

***

As she watched her giant centrifuge spin, Olivia thought about the man she originally knew as Ike MacTavish. When she first met him she felt an immediate animal and emotional attraction, one absolutely worth pursuing. Finding out his real name was Julian Hamilton didn't change that, but it did complicate things. She had been told Julian Hamilton was dead—twice.

Chapter Twelve

Bones

Olivia's cell phone vibrated in her pocket, startling her out of her thoughts of Julian Hamilton. Ordinarily she wouldn't answer her phone when the centrifuge was spinning, but this was a call she needed to take. She went into the laboratory where she could actually hear before she answered the phone with a simple "Hello." She never said more than that until she was absolutely certain whom she was talking to. She never sent texts.

"You called." KP said on the other end of the line.

"Four hours ago." She was brusque.

"Sorry. Been out celebrating a bit."

"Celebrating what, shooting the wrong fucking guy?"

"What do you mean?" KP said, irritated.

"You shot his brother and he survived. How could you have fucked this up so badly?"

"You never said anything about him having a brother," KP said defensively.

"I can't know everything. Part of what I pay you is for doing a little fucking research."

"Yes, ma'am. I realize that," KP said, suddenly contrite.

"Do you have any idea how frustrating it is to think this guy is dead and then run into him at a party, and then have it happen a second time?"

"We'll get him."

"Where?"

"The hospital."

"Christ, he's not stupid."

"What about your friend?"

"What about her?"

"Get her to tell you where he is."

"Again? I can't keep tricking her into telling me how to find him. She'll get suspicious."

"We'll get him. I promise."

"Just lay low for a while. I'll let you know if I hear anything," Olivia said with an uncharacteristically forgiving tone. It was true that she was frustrated. It was also true that she had enjoyed her most recent encounter with Julian. She couldn't imagine how he could possibly improve on his past performance, but she was more than willing to take him up on his offer to try. She might even give him several chances, if she could find him.

She locked up the lab and went to her Porsche. She had two dozen vials of magic juice in her pocket. She was toying with the idea of stopping her father's regimen and keeping all of it for personal use. He would never let her, of course. He would demand she give it to him. Her juice had given him a new lease on life. She knew he had it in his mind to start screwing around again. She knew he was capable of it. He made little attempt to the conceal the tent in his pajama pants he had most mornings. Olivia was sure he would eventually try something stupid with Letty, something that might get him sued. She was more likely to make it with Letty than he was. She'd thought about it before. She, too, admired Letty's tight Guatemalan ass. She'd been with women, but she was into men, at the moment one man in particular. The whole ride home Julian was on her mind. It was a maddening quandary to desperately want to fuck the man she'd paid to have killed. She wasn't sure why he had come home. She had to assume it was to get revenge.

***

Julian's first four bourbons had little intoxicating effect on him. The fifth one put him over the edge. Elena, the charming cocktail waitress he had been flirting with all night, who barely looked 21, knew she shouldn't have given him the fifth drink. She only did because Julian had been paying as he drank and he left an extra twenty on her tray every time she brought him a bourbon. She finally cut him off when he tried to order a sixth.

"How about I serve it to you tomorrow night?" Elena said.

Julian liked to drink and he'd been cut off plenty of times, though never with such a combination of eloquence and coquettishness as this.

He wasn't sure if it was just a line she used on all her customers when she needed to, or if it really was an invitation.

Elena intrigued him. He could tell she wasn't originally from the U.S., but he wasn't sure where she was from. Her accent was slight, almost unnoticeable. She was beautiful without being distinct. Her hair was long, thick and brown. She wasn't light skinned. She wasn't dark. She could have been from almost anywhere. His best guess was South America. Paraguay maybe. He couldn't get any closer than that. The more time he spent with her, the less he thought about where she was from. It was her scent that grabbed him. Her scent was different than Olivia's and it wasn't nearly as strong, but there was no denying its potency.

Julian had observed the mating habits of tigers for years and knew all about male and female behavior. He knew that just before they entered estrus, females would mark their territory with their distinctive urine. During estrus the females vocally called out males to attract them, kind of like the way Olivia called him out. Based on her scent, what she said and how she said it, he thought Elena might have been making a similar attempt.

"Sounds like a good plan," Julian said. "I should go down to my room now anyway. It's been a rough day." She gave him a sweet smile and thanked him for being so understanding.

***

Julian had been just sober enough to hang the do not disturb sign on his door as he tottered in at 1:30 a.m. His room at the LondonHouse was in the new glassy structure squeezed into the slender space between the equally slender Mather Tower and the original London

Guarantee building. The facade of the new building created a stark contrast to the stone of the older one. The rooms in the new building were bigger and had floor to ceiling windows that looked out at the river.

It was 2:30 in the afternoon when Julian woke. The first thing he did was check his phone for news of the shooting. Halfway down the Trib's homepage was an item with a headline "Mag Mile Man Shot in Neck." The article quoted a doctor who called Simon's survival a "miracle." It also said that police had identified no suspects in the shooting.

Julian called Vanessa to find out how Simon was doing. He wanted to see his brother, but he knew going to the hospital could be dangerous. He asked Vanessa if he could meet her for a cup of coffee somewhere close to the hospital. He had something important to discuss with her and he didn't want to do it at the hospital.

"Wait, wait. That bullet was meant for you?" Vanessa asked, nearly spitting out French-roasted Sumatran after she heard his explanation. He nodded. "Why on earth would someone want to kill you?"

"I don't know. I mean I have theories, but the less you know the better."

"Julian, you gotta give me more than that."

"I took on some clients in Bangladesh that I shouldn't have and now I'm caught up in something I had nothing to do with. You guys are safe. You don't have to worry about going back home. I won't be there and if these guys can read a newspaper they must know by now they got the wrong guy."

"Have you talked to the police?" Vanessa asked.

"Not yet. But I plan to."

"When?"

"Soon."

"How soon is soon?"

"Today," Julian said. "And I'll be the point person for the police so you don't have to deal with them." Of course, that was a lie. Julian had no intention of ever going to the police. He quickly changed the subject. "Did Simon mention to you what I want to do on June 11th?"

"He did."

"Do you think he'll be able to go?"

"I really don't know. I doubt it."

What Julian was referring to was a little ceremony he was putting together on the platform of the Adams and Wabash station to mark the 13th anniversary of Lara's death. Julian had told Simon of his plans just a couple of days before he was shot. It was going to be simple with only four guests: Julian, Lourdes, Simon and Vanessa, who had never met Lara, but she was Simon's wife and of course she would be there. They would each say a few words and leave some flowers on the platform, peonies, if they could find any. They were Lara's favorite.

The ceremony was as much for Julian as it was for Lara. He still hadn't been able to go all the way up to the platform despite spending many nights on the stairs and the street below. The ceremony was extra incentive to get him up there. He hoped to give it a few more tries in the time he had left. He wanted and needed his brother to be there with him. Even if Simon couldn't go on the 11th, Julian would go alone to mark the occasion and return when his brother was able to join him.

"I know how important this is, but Simon not being able to go is nothing compared to having people out to kill you. Do you know these people?" Vanessa asked.

"Not really, I've only seen them from a distance," Julian said, telling her only half of a lie. "Please don't tell Simon any of this. I'll come to visit if I can. Maybe you could tell him I stopped by while he was sleeping."

"For Simon's benefit I'll keep my mouth shut about people trying to kill you and I'll even lie for you about visiting, but only if you promise me you'll talk to the police. There must be something you can tell them about who tried to kill your brother." Julian could hear resentment in her voice, like he was letting Simon down. He was.

"I'll talk to them today."

Repeating such a brazen lie to his brother's wife should have been difficult. It wasn't. What was he supposed to tell her? He couldn't tell her that even though his brother came within a millimeter of his life, he wasn't going to call the police because he was going to kill the people who did it. That wouldn't go over well. Vanessa might even call the police on him, and she'd be right to do so.

***

KP didn't like being told to lay low. Julian had done nothing but avoid being killed, yet he had become a jagged thorn in his boot. KP wasn't used to that sort of frustration. He had an empty page in his book all ready for Julian. He had even written in his name, an attempt at manifesting his death.

When he was growing up in South Philly, KP was one of just a few white kids living in Southwark Plaza, one of the city's crime-ridden

163

public housing towers. The day after he graduated from South Philadelphia High School in 1995, a remarkable achievement for a kid who had a drug-addicted prostitute for a mother and essentially raised himself and his younger brother, he enlisted in the Army. Being in the service was the best thing that ever happened to him, until his court-martial, that is.

KP liked to tell his Army buddies that he saw or heard more people killed in his neighborhood when he was a kid than he did in all his tours of Afghanistan and Iraq. It started in his own home. He was lying in his bed on a freezing February night when he heard a gunshot ring out across the hall. He was five years old. He didn't jump out of bed to see what happened. There was no need. He knew his mother had finally shot the fucker. The countless scars and bruises on her body, including the deep, bloody gash over her left eye that he gave her minutes before she shot him, was enough for the authorities to make the decision to not file charges against her for killing the father of her children.

KP was 12 when he walked past a trio of police cars parked in front of his building. A brick thrown from high up on the tower hit the windshield of one of the police cars. Shards of auto glass hit KP in the eye. He was 16 when he got the scar that ran from his temple to his mouth from an errant bullet that grazed his face. The boy next to him wasn't so lucky. He took a bullet in the eye and died at KP's feet. That boy was his little brother. War wasn't much of a change.

KP had given the army six years of his life before he made his first kill, a Taliban fighter in Helmand Province, Afghanistan, in late 2001. Ending someone's life didn't affect him anymore than if he had flipped someone the bird for cutting him off on the highway. It wasn't traumatic, nor was it a perverse thrill. It just was. One thing he did think about was the level of control over death he had when he pulled the trigger himself. When he was just a witness he had none.

Shortly after his first kill he started his death book, a collection of notes, some more detailed than others, of the deaths he'd caused and the deaths he'd seen or heard, going all the way back to his mother shooting his father. He began adding photos after the introduction of decent cell phone cameras. The number of deaths he witnessed would always outnumber the deaths he caused, but that first entry he made in Afghanistan was joined by many more in the years that followed, both in and out of his service to the United States Army.

Olivia had read about KP's court-martial. Many people had. It got a lot of press, way more than the Army was comfortable with. It stuck in Olivia's mind when she first read about it. What really held her attention was a story she read years later about tiger poaching in an English language newspaper from Delhi. KP's name was mentioned because he had been hired by an Indian wildlife organization to help catch poachers. The article identified him as a former member of special forces in the U.S. Army now working as a "security contractor." The article never mentioned he had been at the center of an international controversy. Olivia didn't recognize the name, but the long facial scar made it easy to recognize the photo the Indian newspaper used. It was an official photo of KP in his green beret with the Delta flash and shield patch. U.S. papers had used it when he made news for killing an Afghan woman and her two young daughters.

Olivia reached out to the wildlife organization, made a sizable donation and lied her way into getting them to give her KP's contact info. It was similar to the method she later used to find Julian.

Olivia asked KP how much the organization was paying him. He gave her a number, which she knew he inflated. She offered to double it anyway. He said yes. He moved to Bridgeview, a southside community next to Oak Lawn. As her operation grew, KP brought on McCauliff, who played in the same darts league at The Leaf. McCauliff, in turn, recommended bringing on the O'Brien brothers, which he and KP now regretted.

KP was the only one of the four who had ever met Olivia. The others didn't even know they worked for a woman. As long as they got paid, they didn't care whose cash they stuffed into their pockets. It was the best gig any of them would ever get. They traveled to places they had never even heard of and stayed at top hotels, where they spent as much time in the bars as they did in the beds. Olivia paid for business class thinking it made her men, who were really no more than thugs, appear to be legitimate businessmen. They even wore suits when they traveled.

It was rare that the job called for violence on people. When Olivia paid them to kill Julian if necessary, and everyone thought it would be, it was the first time they had been given a human target. They had tried twice to kill him and they failed both times. KP had never failed her before.

***

Julian also laid low. He spent several lazy hours watching movies. He explored the hotel. At the spa he chatted with a woman about honey drizzle massages and lime oil scalp therapy. In the fitness center he discovered a couple of treadmills. He was curious to know how fast he could run. He jogged easily while he waited for the only other person in the room to leave. When he was finally alone he bumped the machine up to its steepest incline and fastest speed. He ran a half mile uphill in just under two minutes. He knew he was fast, but he had no idea it was world class speed. He could have run faster if the machine had been able to keep up with him.

It was all just killing time. He was putting off another call to Vanessa that would require him to lie again. When he couldn't put it off any longer the lie he told was that he had spoken with the police and they, for the sake of his and his brother's safety, told him not to go to the hospital. He hated lying to her, but he couldn't have it any other way. Getting them for attempted murder on his brother wasn't enough. As callous as that sounded, it was his truth. He wanted to punish them for trying to kill him in Bangladesh. What were Chicago cops going to do about something that happened in a forest on the other side of the world? Most importantly, he wanted to make them pay for forcing him to kill a tiger. Even a mercy killing was unacceptable.

Julian ate dinner at the restaurant on the 21st floor. To entertain himself he eavesdropped on several conversations. A middle aged couple was arguing over accommodations they had to make when her mother moved in with them in a month. She was willing to give up her sewing room, but he was definitely not eager to have his mother-in-law and her spoiled, furry Himalayan cat as housemates. Three men in suits discussed the bare-boned severance package they were going to offer the 25 employees they were terminating at their golf cart factory. A stilted conversation between a woman and a man in their mid-20's suggested they were on a first date. He mentioned something about Japanese anime and she lit up.

By 9:00 he was at the rooftop bar. It was more crowded than it was the night before and all the tables were taken. He took the one open stool at the bar. The perky blond bartender was shaking a cocktail. Julian scanned the space for Elena. He didn't see her. The bartender came over and took his order.

"Is Elena working tonight?" Julian asked the bartender as she set down his bourbon rocks.

"Elena hasn't worked Fridays in a few months."

"Oh, what a shame."

"She's special, isn't she?"

"Sure is," Julian said while trying to conceal his chagrin.

The bartender walked off to help another customer. With his reality put in check, Julian finished his drink in three sips, laid a twenty on the bar and left. He pushed the button to call the elevator. While he was waiting he was joined by three young couples. They were holding two equally loud conversations and Julian struggled to turn down the volume in his head. He recognized nothing. It was all word salad, disorienting static. He thought about moving out of line, but the elevator showed up before he could. He walked in first and hit the button for his floor. The group, still chatting away, packed in after him. The clatter of the two ongoing conversations bouncing off the walls of the small space gave Julian a headache. When the elevator reached Julian's floor no one moved aside to let him out. They were too busy blabbing. Julian asked one of the men to move. No response. Julian asked again. Nothing. He felt the pinpricks of anger and didn't want to ask again. He plowed through the group, accidentally knocking one of the women off her stilettos.

"What's your fucking problem, man?" one of the men shouted.

"Trust me, none of you want to find out," Julian replied and walked away.

***

Tribathalmate, VanPharm's disastrous arthritis medication, was in a class of drugs known as biologics. It was protein-based and hardly revolutionary. Similar medications used to treat severe arthritis, such as Enbrel and Humira, were already on the market. Iliviora, the trade name for Tribathalmate VanPharm pulled out of thin air, never made it to market. For the participants in the study, side effects like infections, nausea, diarrhea, rapid heartbeat and temporary blindness were the norm. Nine participants suffered an unpleasant medley of side effects then died. Lawsuits were filed and settled for undisclosed but substantial sums. Olivia had strongly opposed starting the trials. She insisted Tribathalmate wasn't ready, no matter what the company or the FDA said. It wasn't until Olivia's objections were tragically validated that VanPharm dropped the entire program, choosing not to develop any class of new arthritis medication. Olivia, however, wasn't ready to give up.

She researched every kind of non-pharmaceutical arthritis therapy, from frankincense to bee stings to gin-soaked raisins. After all her effort there was only one that intrigued her: tiger bone wine. One of her mentors at MIT had told her to "question everything, dismiss nothing." Her field of genetics was real, hard science and she spent many years studying it. Still, she never discounted any alternative or Eastern medicine like so many MD's who say if they didn't learn it in med school, it's not real.

The Chinese have been making tiger bone wine for more than 1,000 years and using it for rheumatism, arthritis, headaches and warding off ghosts. And, as is the case with so many concoctions in certain branches of traditional Chinese medicine, men drink tiger bone wine because they're desperate for something to make their dicks hard. In traditional tiger bone wine, the bones of tigers are crushed and macerated in a rice wine for several years—the longer, the better. Some tiger bone wine isn't made of tiger bones at all. The cheaper, more common variety uses the bones of dogs, horses and other animals. True tiger bone wine is usually made from tigers raised on farms for the specific purpose of making the peculiar, foul-tasting elixir. Some connoisseurs, however, insist that tiger bone wine made from wild tigers is superior. Enter the poachers.

Restoring her father's health wasn't Olivia's motivation to start her tiger bone wine project with the uninspired code name TB. She was driven by pure scientific curiosity. Her father was a convenient guinea pig she could easily monitor. In the two years he had been taking her TB formulas, the results were better than she hoped for. Had he not been so busy basking selfishly in his restored virility, he would have pressed her harder on possible FDA trials and how TB would help VanPharm's bottomline. He wouldn't have liked her answer. She hadn't developed it in VanPharm's labs and she did it on her own time. VanPharm had no claim to it, legal or otherwise.

In the earliest days of the program, Olivia sourced tiger bones from a farm in the province of Heilongjiang in northeast China. As she got further into it, she made the unfortunate but inevitable leap to buying bones from poached wild tigers. According to her science, it was true what they said about wild tigers. Their bones made better wine. Also according to her science, Bengal tigers produced a more potent product than Siberian, Sumatran or any other kind of tiger.

Using her genetic know-how, Olivia started her quest for a game-changing process using the genome editing tool CRISPR (clustered regularly interspaced short palindromic repeats) and Cas9 (CRISPR associated protein 9). Billions of dollars have been spent on genomic editing and CRISPR-Cas9 to create cutting edge medicines to, potentially, cure genetic disorders and other diseases. Olivia's approach was similar and at the same time radically different. She discovered that with CRISPR and Cas13 she could target the RNA in the tiger bones and catalyze an enzymatic reaction that, combined with the complex molecular separation performed by the centrifuge, made it super-concentrated. What she got was a tiger bone wine 1,000 times more potent than traditional tiger bone wine from a process that took less than three days as opposed to three years or more.

Ethics is one of the biggest hurdles for scientists working in genomic editing. Using CRISPR, for example, to customize human appearance, such as eye color, throws up a number of ethical red flags. Olivia didn't have to deal with that particular ethical quandary. Hers was an altogether different breach. She used bones from tigers killed illegally. She thought someday she might be able to use a single strand of tiger hair to make TB. Until her process became that sophisticated, killing tigers for their bones was, unfortunately, the only way. When she first started acquiring wild tigers, she bought them from poachers who were selling off every usable part of the tiger. Tigers are usually trapped by snares or spring-loaded traps. Even if a tiger manages to escape from the trap or take the trap with it to elude capture, its fate has already been sealed. Injuries caused by traps or snares that remain fettered to the tiger's leg make it impossible for the tiger to hunt and feed itself.

Over time, Olivia's operation became so singularly focused on bones that she simply sent KP and his crew to kill a tiger, carve it up, take its bones and leave the rest, like killing a buffalo for its tongue. She justified her barbaric practice by claiming it was all done in the name of alleviating human suffering.

Chapter Thirteen

Intoxication, Suicide And Jackassery

The afternoon after getting stood up by Elena, Julian strode across the University of Chicago campus with a sharpened focus and more realistic objectives. His olfactory instincts had proved unreliable. It worked with Olivia, but after being so wrong about Elena he knew that some day it would earn him a slap in the face, a kick in the balls, or worse, an indictment. There was really only one woman he wanted to be with and that was Dr. Lourdes Villegas. After the incident with Alpha and Wayne, Julian started questioning his ability to control himself. The recent incident in the elevator supported his suspicions. He was certain KP and McCauliff were in town and responsible for shooting his brother. He could have taken care of McCauliff at any time. He knew where the guy lived. But he also knew that once he went down that road there would be no room for a U-turn. His time with Lourdes would probably be over. He still had a way to go setting things right with her. Getting a little closure on Lara's death would also be jeopardized if he started killing people. He decided to give it until after the memorial on the 11th before he started meting out justice.

Rather than call Lourdes he had decided to make a surprise visit. He still had not told her, or anyone else, where he had been staying. Everyone in his life was better off not knowing where he was. In the taxi to the university he had called Vanessa to check up on his brother. If all went well Simon might be released the following afternoon. When Vanessa asked about progress with the police, he told her another lie and said the police still had no leads and even name-dropped the officer quoted in the Trib.

Lourdes wasn't in her office. Her research work gave her no time to teach. She could only be in her lab. When he knocked on the lab door, Dan answered. He reeked of weed.

"She's in the bathroom putting on makeup," Dan said.

"In the middle of the day? Lourdes Villegas, the woman who bathes with baby wipes so she won't miss 10 minutes of work?"

"The Van de Weghe Foundation is sending over someone to take photos. She's a little nervous."

"What's there to be nervous about? She's already got the money."

"That's what I told her."

"Typical," Julian said.

"Hey, I've been wondering," Dan said. "Whatever happened to that tiger you wrote about?"

Dan's question caught Julian off guard. It took him a while to come up with an answer. "I had to leave him in the forest."

It was true. He did leave Amara in the forest. He just didn't mention that the tiger was also six feet under it.

"That must have been hard for you," Dan said sympathetically.

"Harder than you could ever imagine."

Lourdes exited the bathroom wearing a bright white lab coat. She always wore lab coats, but by this time of day they were usually smudged with green goo or had multiple coffee stains. Her hair was tied up in an elegant wrap and her face looked like it had been made up by a Hollywood makeup artist. Julian wolf whistled.

"Stop it. This is the way I always dress," she said.

"No, you usually have ketchup or egg salad on your coat," said Dan.

"You look great," said Julian.

"Thanks. I didn't have a lot of time to prepare. Olivia just called this morning and asked if she could bring over a photographer to take some shots for the foundation's annual report. She should be here by now."

"Olivia's coming here?" Julian asked in a way that unintentionally conveyed his apprehension.

"Uh, yeah. Is that okay with you?"

"Why wouldn't it be?" Julian said, hoping to sound indifferent.

"I don't know. That's why I asked."

"Anyway, I came by to see if you wanted to get a cup of coffee. Obviously that won't work. Can I bring you one?" Julian offered.

"I'm fine, thanks," Lourdes replied.

"You'd probably spill it on you lab coat anyway," Dan said.

"What about you?" Julian asked Dan.

"Thanks, but I'm on a cleanse."

"Well, I guess I'll come back in a couple hours," Julian said. He certainly wasn't coming back while Olivia was there, even if Lourdes had accepted his offer of a coffee.

Lourdes followed Julian out. In the hallway she asked, "Have you been to the police yet?"

"I talked to them yesterday," Julian said.

"Did you tell them about what happened in Bangladesh?"

"Yes. They think it might help." So many lies, he thought.

***

The photoshoot took 30 minutes. The photographer took some headshots and some posed working shots of Lourdes wearing safety goggles and blue latex gloves while doing the standard science-related activities. There was a series of shots of her curiously examining a microscope slide she held up to the light. Another showed her carefully filling a pipet from a flask full of blue liquid, which was just water with a single drop of food coloring.

After the shoot, Lourdes and Olivia went to a campus coffee shop. On the table in front of them were two lattes and Olivia's laptop computer. She inserted the flash drive the photographer had given her into her laptop and pulled up the 100-plus images. They both immediately agreed on which headshot to use. They were split over the work shot. Lourdes preferred one of the shots of her as a curious scientist with a microscope slide. Olivia thought one of the pipet and flask shots was the best because she liked the way the bright blue liquid in the flask played off Lourdes's darker features. Lourdes said she was fine with either and let Olivia decide.

With the photo selection completed, the conversation fluttered from one insignificant topic to another until Olivia asked how Simon was doing.

"I talked to Vanessa this morning. He may get to go home tomorrow afternoon."

"That's promising. Do the police have any idea who did it?"

"Julian talked to them." She stopped herself. She didn't want to say anything that would violate her promise of discretion when talking about Julian's situation. She took a long sip of latte.

"And?" Olivia asked, coming very close to appearing too eager.

"They told him they've got nothing."

Olivia was relieved she didn't have to press her for more details. She paused intentionally, not wanting to rush through the mental script she was reciting. "And how's Julian doing with all this?" Olivia finally asked.

"I don't know. He seemed a bit off when he was here a little while ago, but we didn't get a chance to talk."

"He was here?" Olivia asked.

"He wanted to get a coffee, but I had the photo shoot and he said he didn't want to get in the way."

"He wouldn't have been in the way."

"Like I said, he seemed a bit off. Someone tried to kill his brother, so I guess he gets to be off."

The photo shoot with a professional photographer for the annual report that wouldn't come out for another six months was just a setup to give Olivia the context and opportunity to ask one particular question. Olivia finally asked it. "Does he have other family he can go to?"

"Just Simon. His dad died from cancer when Julian was in high school. His sister was killed by a train. That was horrible. I'm sure you heard about it. It was all over the news about 12 years ago.

"That's awful," Olivia said.

"Six months later his mom killed herself."

Olivia was silent, motionless. She looked numb.

"You okay, Liv?"

"Yeah. I'm okay. It's just so sad," Olivia said. She was being sincere. She found Julian's story tragic, and, at least where mothers were concerned, painfully familiar. A window into Julian's psyche just blew open.

***

Olivia had first heard about Julian Hamilton the same way she first heard about KP; she read about him. It was a short article on the Scientific American website that ran shortly after "The Man-Eating Tiger That Refuses to Die and Deserves to Live" piece ran in Frontiers in Zoology. She clicked the link to the original article written by Julian. A tiger that had a taste for man fascinated her. When she read the tiger had survived multiple shootings, prompting villagers to suggest it was immortal, Olivia knew she had to have that tiger. She understood why the author left out where the tiger lived, but she could find it if she tried. There weren't many tigers left in the world. It was a Bengal, which put it in the Indian subcontinent, still an enormous territory to search. A little more research led her to an article in Animal Behaviour he co-authored with a biologist from just across town at the University of Chicago.

A Google search of Dr. Lourdes Villegas brought up a several scientific papers in peer-reviewed journals. Her work in thermoregulation was definitely impressive, but it was to find Julian and his special tiger that Olivia dangled the possibility of a million-dollar brilliance grant from the Van de Weghe Foundation. It wasn't her money. What did she care? Of course, she told her there would be a rigorous interview process. That was just for show. The money was going to her no matter what. She didn't have to give it to her. If Lourdes told her what she wanted to know, she could have simply told her that the foundation decided to give the million dollars to someone else, but Olivia wanted her to have it. It was high time the foundation supported something other than her father's vain attempts to ingratiate himself with his favorite artists and writers. Lourdes was a worthy recipient and Olivia liked her.

Olivia submitted a list of Lourdes's colleagues she wanted to interview. She followed through on some of them, but there was only one name on the list that she had any real interest in. When Lourdes saw Julian's name, she laughed.

"What's so funny," Olivia asked.

"I think you'll have a hard time getting hold of Julian Hamilton," Lourdes said. She told Olivia she hadn't heard from him recently, but she knew he was deep in the Sundarbans and would not be reachable for several months.

"The Sundarbans. Wow. I've always wanted to go there," Olivia said. "Do you know where he is?"

"It's this tiny village. I think he said it was something like Nurnashmari, but I really can't remember what the fuck it's called," Lourdes said, making Olivia chuckle.

"Forget it. I don't need to talk to him that badly. There are plenty of other people on the list," Olivia said. His name was not brought up again.

Lourdes's memory was better than she thought. Olivia had to dive deep into Bangladeshi geography, but she turned up a village named Nurnashmari in the Shyamnagar region of the Sundarbans. Getting there would require a lot of planning. She had a deep pool of resources and was up for the challenge. That damn immortal, man-eating tiger would be hers even if it meant she had to kill the only person in the world who could help her find it. Julian had made it abundantly clear how far he would go to protect it. Not for a second did she think killing Julian would be going too far on her part.

Olivia had been so focused on getting Amara's bones that she didn't have a plan in place if the mission failed. She had wrongly assumed killing Julian would be the easy part. She had GPS coordinates for the village of Nurnashmari and a former Delta Force operator running her team. How hard could it be? Yet the mistakes were piling up.

Two of her mistakes were simply telling KP where Julian lived and then giving him an inadequate photo. They ended up shooting his brother because no one had looked into the possibility of family members living in the area. She lectured KP about it, but as her interest in Julian evolved she realized she was better off doing the research herself. She had already discovered things about him that meant more to her than they ever would to a heartless bastard like KP.

Online, Julian was a hard target. There was a Julian Hamilton on Facebook. He was from Vancouver and was black. The Julian Hamilton she was interested in had never written a shitty, one-star review of a Mexican restaurant on Trip Advisor. He hadn't tried to connect with other tiger researches through LinkedIn. He had been in the forests and jungles of southern Asia for years. He had no address, no registered phone number, car insurance or even a magazine subscription. All that came up were the few articles he had written or co-written, and she had already read those.

After the fiasco with Simon, Olivia did some of her own research into the brother KP almost killed. Finding information about Simon Hamilton was a lot easier than his brother. In the photos of Simon she found online she could see the striking similarity to Julian. Three residences came up in a deep search, one on the island of Mustique in the West Indies, one on Lake Road in Lake Forest and one on Pearson Street in Chicago. The combination of the physical similarities, Simon's Chicago address and the dearth of available information on Julian made it easy for Olivia to see how KP had shot the wrong guy. Anyone could have made the same mistake.

Her post-photoshoot conversation with Lourdes gave her a lead that hours and hours of online research hadn't been able to provide. After saying goodbye to Lourdes at the cafe, Olivia sat in her car and Googled "Hamilton train killed Chicago." Pages upon pages of results popped up, including news stories from major publications in Chicago and around the country. What happened on the platform at Adams and Wabash was truly horrible. Olivia did remember.

She found many other stories about people killed by trains in Chicago, New York and around the world. She learned that riding in trains was safer than driving or even walking on a sidewalk. Standing on a platform waiting for a train was far more dangerous than riding in one. A woman in Chicago was hit and killed when she jumped onto the Red Line tracks to retrieve her cell phone. A man fell, or maybe jumped, right in front of the Orange Line. Intoxication, suicide and jackassery were most often to blame. Lara's situation was different. She wasn't stupid, drunk or suicidal. Being an innocent victim made her tragedy stand out. As Olivia read about Lara, it wasn't the tragic victimhood that impressed Olivia most. It was the date it happened. The anniversary of Lara Hamilton's death was just days away.

Two attempts on Julian's life had failed. She doubted anyone who was twice the target of assassins would sit by idly. She had been intimate with Julian, but she didn't know him well. She couldn't get a good read on him. He had jumped at her offer to fuck like wild animals and he didn't seem bothered by hiding it from Lourdes. He was wealthy, yet he spent years in the bush. Was he a man who would get his hands dirty meting out justice personally or was he the type to blab to the cops? Lourdes said Julian had spoken with the police, though she had been halting and a bit vague. Maybe she knew something. Olivia couldn't know Julian had lied to Lourdes about going to the police. It wouldn't have mattered if she did know. Police or not, she could not risk it. Julian needed to be eliminated and she finally thought she knew where to find him.

***

The next morning Olivia kept to her routine at her father's estate in South Barrington, though the routine had recently been modified. When she opened her top dresser drawer to get her father's dose of TB-13, she got one for herself. Edward had been asking her to increase his dosage nearly every morning for the past couple of weeks. Every morning she gave him an emphatic no. She knew he stole a vial or two out of her dresser from time to time, but scientific curiosity kept her from calling him on it. If his practice of stealing extra doses worsened, she'd put an end to it. Maybe.

She arrived at the Field Building at 9:15 and parked her Porsche in her usual lot. Instead of going to her office, she took a stroll to the "L" platform at Adams and Wabash. She thought it an odd coincidence that Julian's sister was killed just a few blocks from her office. She knew the intersection of Adams and Wabash well. Her bank was on the corner. She took Adams to get there and it took her directly under the tracks. However, she had never been up on the platform. She rarely rode the trains. Having three work spaces spread across town made driving herself a necessity. Nothing about whatever was up there had interested her before. Now she had a good reason to go up.

She climbed the stairs, paid her fare and stepped onto the platform. She found a bench to sit on and watched a southbound Orange Line come in on the other side of the tracks. It was followed a few minutes later by a northbound Brown. She watched several more trains come and go. When she saw the northbound Green approaching, she walked out to the far edge of the blue rubber safety strip. She wanted to be as close to the train as she could when it went by her. She wanted to feel the train blow her hair back. She wanted to get the tiniest idea of what it might feel like to get crushed by a 170-ton train, or watch someone else get crushed.

Chapter Fourteen

Burn All The Liars

Lourdes was surprised to see Julian when he showed up in her lab. It was a work day and the lab was full of assistants, both old and new. She had stacks of data reports that she and Dan were sorting through. With the grant money from the Van de Weghe Foundation she had hired researchers around the world to collect data on various mammals and there were stacks upon stacks of it waiting to be analyzed.

She told him she was busy, but he insisted they talk. They went down to her office. He needed her to do some more work on him.

"How do I look?" he asked her.

"Like you need a bath."

"Okay, but otherwise do I seem normal to you?"

"As normal as you ever do. Why, am I missing something?"

"I don't like what's happening to me. I need to go to anger management."

"I told you something like this would happen," she said with the scorn of an angry mother. "Can we do the damn weekly check-ups like I suggested?"

"I think it might be too late for that."

Julian told her about pushing the man in the elevator at his hotel and other recent instances of being overly aggressive, whether he was provoked or not. He had snapped at a man at a coffee shop because the man was too busy looking at his phone and wasn't keeping up with the line. He laid into a bank teller who had starting counting off $500 in fifties when he insisted he had asked for twenties. He had to fight the urge to punch the guy. He did not say anything about tearing off a chunk of Alpha's hand with his teeth or the incident with the Schnoz Chopper other than he had done some potentially incriminating things and she was better off not knowing the details. His speed, strength, eyesight and hearing were all worth keeping. These new changes to his personality were unwelcome. His aggressive episodes were preceded by tingling pinpricks and followed by hours, even days of a foggy partial amnesia.

"Is your beard thicker? Got hair in places you never had it before?" she asked him.

"No."

"Acne? Headaches? Insomnia?"

"No."

"What about libido?"

"Through the roof."

"Hmm. Have you done anything to satisfy it?" This was both a scientific and personal question for Lourdes. As a scientist she wanted him to answer honestly. Personally she hoped he hadn't been with anyone recently.

"No. Nothing."

It would have been stupid and cruel to tell her that he had screwed Olivia Van de Weghe just hours after his brother nearly bled out in the gutter. A lie was not only the sensible thing to say, it was required. He had told so many lies recently and he was okay with almost all of them. More than anyone, Lourdes deserved honesty, but he just couldn't give it to her.

"Maybe you should," she said reluctantly.

"What do you mean?"

"You should find a way to satisfy those urges."

"You mean a woman?"

"Sorry. I hope you didn't think I meant me." She immediately regretted her phrasing. She was uncomfortable. "Maybe you could get one of those Japanese dolls."

"It's okay. I know what you meant."

"They're incredibly lifelike."

"Would you please stop?" Julian said, feeling the pinpricks start. He was dead serious, though Lourdes was too flustered to notice.

"Make sure you get one with a removable vagina. They're much easier to clean."

"Shut the fuck up already!" Julian growled. He stood up quickly, knocking his chair over. He kicked the chair across the small office. He caught her terrified look when he showed his teeth. He tried to reign in

187

his rage. He clenched his fists, crossed his arms and pulled them tight to his chest, straightjacketing himself. He fought to keep himself from crying.

"Jules, it's me. It's okay. I was just deflecting. I'm not sure what to do or say anymore." She walked toward him, her hand poised to gently caress his cheek. He turned away.

"I'm telling you I'm dangerous."

"Let me help you."

He had never directed this kind of anger at a woman before. It had always been male on male aggression. He was in uncharted territory. He could no longer trust himself around her.

"No. Stay away from me!" Julian yelled. He ran out of the room and out of the building. Lourdes chased and called after him without success.

***

On the morning of the anniversary of Lara's death, Simon was recovering at the house in Lake Forest and was unfit to attend the memorial. Simon and Vanessa were effusive in their regret, piling on unnecessary apologies, which made him feel even worse about almost getting his brother killed. He didn't want to speak to Lourdes. He was ashamed of his behavior in her office and frustrated by his inability to control it. He texted her that the memorial service was canceled. The truth was, even if Simon could have attended, Julian wouldn't have wanted him there. He didn't want anyone to be there. He wanted to go alone. For everyone's safety, he needed to go alone.

***

McCauliff drove a rented silver Ford Taurus slowly down the right lane of Wabash Avenue. KP was in the back seat, a position that allowed him to shoot from either side of the vehicle. He easily identified Julian, who was on the far side of the one-way street, standing at the bottom of the stairs to the "L" platform wearing a black hoody and jeans. Traffic kept them from changing lanes.

"There he is. Go around the block," KP ordered.

McCauliff took a right turn on Adams and another right on State. The plan was simple— make another pass in the left lane and do it gangster style. KP had lost patience for doing it any other way than a simple drive-by.

"Do you think he saw us?" asked McCauliff.

"Doubt it. It's too dark. Who cares anyway? He doesn't know us," KP said, still completely unaware Julian had observed them in Nurnashmari. And, of course, he knew nothing about Julian's keen night vision.

KP had a Glock 19 with a standard 15-round magazine. The handgun was just like the one Aidan used to shoot Julian. It didn't really matter how fast McCauliff drove. With the double action Glock, KP could empty the entire 15-round magazine in a few seconds. Even if KP were shit-faced drunk he would hit Julian with at least half of them. Tonight, he was stone sober and Julian had been standing there like a paper target.

They made a second pass. Julian was no longer at the bottom of the stairs. KP and McCauliff scanned the area. Julian was gone. The traffic light at Adams turned red. McCauliff stopped the car. KP slid across the backseat from window to window looking for Julian. The roof of the Taurus blocked his view into the unlit maze of metal beams and crossbars that supported the elevated tracks. It was the perfect place to hide.

Julian dropped from above and landed on the hood the Taurus with a heavy, deafening thud. He threw himself at the windshield. His eyes flashed bright blue flares from inside the dark hood he had pulled over his head. He bared his teeth. Freaked and panicked, McCauliff stomped the accelerator and sent the Taurus into the intersection. He swerved to evade a cross-traffic truck and crashed head-on into a metal post supporting the tracks on the other side of Adams. Julian jumped off the hood just before impact.

Julian ripped open the backdoor of the Taurus and leered inside. He growled and hissed at KP like a crazed demon. KP, confused and nervous, scrabbled backward toward the other door while he tried to aim the Glock. Julian grabbed KP's arm and wrenched. The Glock fell to the car floor. Julian yanked KP across the seat with astounding force, set his forearm against the roof rail and snapped bones. KP's arm folded like it had a joint between the elbow and wrist.

McCauliff was already running down Adams when Julian saw him. He chased and ran him down easily. He leapt onto McCauliff's back and rode him into a row of rental bikes. McCauliff's head snapped back as his throat slammed into a set of handlebars. McCauliff clutched his throat, coughed and gagged.

Julian turned around and saw KP holding his right arm in his left as he hobbled up the stairs to the platform. He knew KP was the one he should go after. He gave McCauliff an arresting kick to the head that made his writhing body go limp. Julian sprinted toward the stairs. Light traffic slowly criss-crossed the intersection. From the top, KP saw Julian jump over the hand rail and land halfway up the stairs as easily as if he had jumped a curb. KP stood dumbfounded. When he saw Julian coming at him four steps at a time, he bolted. Julian leapt over the turnstile effortlessly and ran onto the northbound platform. Of all the time he had spent around the platform in the past weeks, this was as far as he'd gone.

KP looked around for somewhere, anywhere to go. A Green Line train was 30 yards down the line, approaching the station from the south. It was slowing but still coming in with force. KP leapt down and onto the tracks and ran to the other side. Julian made it as far as the blue safety strip. He could have easily beaten the train. Instead, he fell to his knees and buried his face in his hands.

***

Night flashed to day. Darkness to light. Twenty-year-old Julian stood on a train platform next to his twin sister, who was wearing a white hoody, "Stanford Chess Club" printed across the chest. A Green Line train approached. Lara scrunched up her nose the way she always did before she sneezed. It made Julian laugh. She had just come home from Stanford the week before and they'd gone to the Art Institute to see a new exhibit. They were catching a train home. The urge to sneeze disappeared. She relaxed her nose.

A raggedy homeless man ran at them full speed, shouting "Burn all the liars" at the top of his lungs. He slammed into Lara and they both flew toward the tracks. The world slowed down for a half second, long enough for the twins to lock eyes. Her eyes showed sheer terror. The train hit Lara and the homeless man dead on. Their bodies bounced off the front of the train car and fell to the tracks. Four cars rolled over them before the train came to a stop. The homeless man's scraggly head was crushed like an over-ripe tomato. Lara was cut in half at the waist.

Chapter Fifteen

Appetite

The news of Lara's death was everywhere. It was inescapable. Papers around the world covered the story of the young college student killed by Jerome Scarborough, a homeless man well-known by Chicago police to be dangerous to himself and others. Because of his erratic and threatening behavior, Scarborough had been kicked out of every homeless shelter and soup kitchen in the city. He was 38 years old and had been homeless since the day he walked out on his 12th set of foster parents when he was 16. Activists called for more funding to help the mentally ill. The Chicago Police Department was attacked for letting a dangerous lunatic wander the city. Some even blamed the shelters that wouldn't serve him and the foster parents he walked out on. Everyone had an opinion about what was wrong with the city of

Chicago. Few offered solutions. Even fewer thought about the victim's family. Julian's world went to shit. He plummeted into a chasmic depression. The trauma was crippling. Nightmares and flashbacks woke him every night. He never went back to school.

Lourdes, who was home in California for part of the summer, called frequently, but each time she did, Julian had less to say. Many times he didn't even bother to answer her calls and texts. When she came back to school they hardly saw each other. She offered to come over to be with him. He always declined. He rarely left his bedroom. If someone had been able to tell him why Lara was killed, he might have found some solace. No one ever could. Simon told him it was because their sister was so beautiful. She stood out in a crowd no matter where she was, which made her an easy mark. Julian wanted to believe that. He had nothing else.

Julian's mother, Cassandra, sank into a deep depression like her younger son. She tried therapy and a cabinet full of medications prescribed by her doctor. Nothing worked. Six months after Lara was killed, Cassandra washed down a fistful of pills her doctor had not prescribed with a bottle of Swedish vodka.

Julian loved his mother. He loved her right up to the moment his brother told him he had found her cold, blue body partially submerged in a foot of bath water. His love split into equal parts contempt and hate. How dare she give up like that. If anyone had earned the right to commit suicide, it was Julian.

Unlike his mother and brother, therapy helped Simon. He threw himself into his work and was slowly able to piece his life back together, though Lara was never out of his thoughts.

A month after his mother killed herself, Julian left the country. For six months he had barely been able to venture beyond his front door. Then he simply took off for Asia with no plans but to be near tigers. It was a ridiculous, depression-induced delusion, but if Lara did come back as a tiger, he might find her. From the gate at O'Hare he sent a text to his brother telling him not to worry. He had to go away for a while. He would check in at least semi-regularly. To Lourdes he sent a different text. It read, "Lourdes, love of my life, I want to be the kind of man you deserve, but I can't be that man anymore. I am so sorry."

Everything about the text sounded off, like a horrible joke. Unless it was about tigers he was a shit writer. She once told him it was a good thing he wanted to be a biologist because he'd make a terrible poet. She knew he was sincere. It still made her sad. His inability, or worse, his unwillingness to share his feelings with her was devastating. More than anything, she was furious with Julian. For a year he called or emailed her just enough to stay on the center mark between her fury and her friendship. Over time, the contact became less frequent, though not because he felt bad or depressed. He still felt both, but like his brother, he focused on work. As a result, he was in the bush more and less able to reach out to her. Tiger therapy, as he called it, was moderately helpful. He had a preternatural feeling that he belonged with them. He had no idea how telling that feeling was.

***

Julian was on his knees in front of a train door when it opened. The few people who got off and on had to walk around him and the seeping pool of vomitus he had just spawned. One passenger cursed him. Another called him a disgusting bum. A man bumped him with his knee. Julian growled like a wild animal. The man quickly apologized and disappeared inside the train car.

Julian took off running to look for McCauliff. Halfway down the stairs he jumped over the handrail. The Taurus was still smashed up against the post, but McCauliff wasn't where Julian had left him gagging and clutching his throat.

A few curious people had gathered around the abandoned Taurus, though no police had shown up yet. Julian snarled at them through his hood. A nosey man was peeking into the car. Julian shoved him out of the way and got in the car. The keys were in the ignition and the car was running. He backed the car off the post, threw it in drive and sped south down Wabash.

***

The plastic front bumper of the rented Taurus scraped the street all the way to Oak Lawn. It fell off after Julian hit the curb pulling into McCauliff's driveway. He had one leg out of the car when he heard the ping of a cell phone. He looked at his own phone. No message. He searched the car floor, where he found an iPhone 11 under the seat. The screen showed a text had come in from KP. The text read, "U still alive? He swiped the screen. Face ID came up. He was locked out. He put the phone is his pocket. He walked around the back of the house and took a look through a window of the house next door to see if anyone was peeping. The house looked unoccupied. He kicked in McCauliff's back door and turned on the lights in the kitchen. It was remarkably tidy. A neatly folded rag laid next to the sink. In a cabinet small matching brown bottles of spices were lined up in alphabetical order. Even the drawer with the aluminum foil and plastic wrap was clean and organized. Rubber bands were tightly wrapped into a ball the size of his fist.

Next to the kitchen was the living room. It, too, was orderly. On a coffee table was an assortment of magazines, including a half dozen issues of Maxim fanned out to display a little taste of each covergirl's glistening breasts. He explored the rest of the house. In one of the two small bedrooms was a desk with a computer. The bookshelves held a variety of genres, from Stephen King's Pet Sematary to a copy of Charles Bukowski's The Most Beautiful Woman in Town with the receipt still sticking out of the pages.

In the second bedroom there was a collection of furniture and furnishings, but the only thing Julian focused on was a tiger-skin rug at the foot of the bed. Julian stumbled as he saw it and took a knee. He couldn't stand to look at it, nor could he look away. Many tiger rugs are fake. Julian knew immediately this one was real. Based on the size of the skin and the length of the tail, Julian guessed it had been a male. The coloring made him certain it was a Bengal. Julian looked in the mouth of the tiger and saw the four-inch fangs. Its vacant yellow eyes stared straight at him. Julian raged. He tossed the room. He flipped over the mattress and sent it crashing into a full-length mirror. He threw the dresser against the wall. The drawers fell open and spilled neatly folded briefs and socks. A piece of chain with an oval-shaped ring dangled from the halfway open bottom drawer. Julian grabbed the chain and pulled out a 10-inch steel jaw trap with large, vicious teeth. Trapped in the teeth was a second identical trap. The barbaric contraption was popular with tiger poachers until simple but equally cruel snares took over insidiously. Holding the traps in his hand nearly made him sick. He dropped them on the floor and returned to the living room to wait in darkness for McCauliff to stumble home.

Half an hour later the beams of car headlights swept across the wall of the living room. Julian looked out the window and saw a taxi in the driveway. The rear door opened and McCauliff exited. He looked over the rented Taurus as he walked gingerly to the front door. Julian felt the pinpricks poke deep into his skin.

McCauliff unlocked the door and hesitantly stuck his head into the room. "KP, is that you?" he called out in a voice that was croaky and strained. He got no answer. He rubbed his bruised throat. He pulled a gun out of his waistband, raised it and slowly entered the living room. The lights were on. The room was empty. He walked toward the kitchen, gun still drawn.

"Don't fuck with me, KP. Not tonight," he called out to the empty room.

He stepped slowly into the brightly lit kitchen. Out of the corner of his eye he saw Julian flying at him. He turned to shoot, but before he could get a shot off Julian slammed into him, sending him crashing into a table. The gun fell on the floor. Julian kicked it across the room. McCauliff tried to get up, but Julian put his foot on his neck. When McCauliff tried to squirm away, Julian stepped down harder.

"Why are you trying to kill me?" Julian said.

"Fuck you."

Julian picked McCauliff up and threw him at the stove 10 feet away. McCauliff bounced off it like a rock. Julian was right there to put his foot back on McCauliff's neck. McCauliff bled from his ear.

"I said why are you trying to kill me?" His rage ready to explode.

"And I said fuck you," McCauliff responded.

With one arm, Julian grabbed McCauliff by his shirt collar and lifted him off the ground. He glared at McCauliff. His breathing was deep and he exhaled heavily through his nose. He opened his mouth wide and hissed.

"Are you some kind of freak or what?" McCauliff said, suddenly nervous and not so cocky and truculent.

"Yeah, I'm a freak," Julian said in a threatening growl. "Now tell me who's running your little circus."

"I don't know. I've never met the boss."

"You expect me to believe that?" Julian asked as he grasped McCauliff's thumb with his other hand.

"It's true. I swear." McCauliff stuttered as he felt Julian squeeze his thumb harder. "Hey, come on, man. Not my right thumb. I throw darts with my right," McCauliff begged.

With one quick flick of his wrist, Julian snapped McCauliff's thumb.

"You fucker!" McCauliff snarled in pain. He tried to pull his hand away from Julian, who now held his index finger.

"All my orders come through KP. It's the god's honest truth," McCauliff said. He relaxed a bit as Julian let go of his finger. When Julian released the grip he had on McCauliff's collar, he fell to the floor in a heap.

"I'll talk to KP then."

"You'll never find him. But I can take you to him," McCauliff said as he crawled to his knees.

"I don't need you anymore. I have your phone."

"Lot of good it will do you."

"We'll see." Julian said. He grabbed him by the ears and broke his neck with a powerful, bone-grinding twist.

He propped McCauliff's body against the wall, his head flopping on his useless neck. Julian held his head in place while he took the iPhone he found in the rental car and swiped the screen. The Face ID message appeared. Julian held the phone in front of McCauliff's face until the screen unlocked.

He opened KP's recent text and studied their past conversations. McCauliff liked to abbreviate. KP couldn't spell for shit. Both of them favored the big thumbs up emoji. The initials JH were mentioned often, as was throwing darts at The Leaf. Julian responded to KP's text with a thumb's up emoji and "Mission accomplished pick me up at 9 tomorrow for darts," keeping with McCauliff's history of not using punctuation.

Half a minute later KP sent a response. "Going to hospital in morning. Arm fucked up. Can't throw but will need a fuckin drink."

Julian dragged McCauliff's body into his bedroom and flung it onto the tiger skin rug. He let loose a ferocious, inhuman sound that was part growl, part roar. Spit flew from his mouth. He got on all fours, ripped off McCauliff's shirt and sank his teeth into the dead man's shoulder. He tore off a bloody chunk of flesh and chewed. He swallowed. He took another bite. And another.

Chapter Sixteen

Pour Me Another

Julian fell into a deep sleep. He woke at noon and found himself on McCauliff's bedroom floor with only a vague idea of where he was. He sat up and rubbed the sleep out of his eyes. When his vision was clearly focused, he saw his blood-smeared hands. McCauliff's mangled body laid beside him on the tiger rug.

He stumbled into the bathroom. In the mirror he saw the blood and gristle that covered much of his face. He washed the blood off his hands and used them to clean his face. He picked at dried bits of flesh that were caked onto his bloody cheeks and licked them off his fingers. He couldn't help himself. His transformation had gone far beyond where he had feared it would go. His similarities to Amara now included the great Bengal tiger's appetite.

The lights in the kitchen and front bedroom were on, but Julian intentionally kept the rest of McCauliff's house as dark as possible. He needed it that way.

KP pulled into the driveway. He rang the door bell six times just to be an annoying prick. He opened the door hesitantly and slowly entered the dark room.

"How 'bout some light, you inconsiderate motherfucker?" KP shouted into the house.

Julian replied by making throat clearing noises and closing some drawers to make KP think McCauliff was in the bedroom. He listened as KP took a couple steps into the house. Then he heard exactly what he wanted: the metallic clank of a jaw trap biting into KP's ankle.

"Motherfucker!" KP screamed at the top of his lungs.

The lights flicked on. KP looked up and saw Julian across the room. Julian grinned with satisfaction. KP rushed at him. He made it just one foot before he was jerked backward, setting the teeth of the trap deeper into his ankle. The chain of the trap was screwed into the wooden planks of the floor. KP reached down to open the trap. With his broken arm in a splint, it was impossible.

"You motherfucker!" KP seethed at Julian as he grimaced in pain.

"That's quite a limited vocabulary you have," Julian said. KP responded with some angry growling noises he failed to make sound threatening. "My point exactly."

Julian walked into the dining room as KP watched him scornfully. He flipped over the solid hardwood dining table, sending placemats and candle holders flying. He grabbed one of the table legs, effortlessly snapped it off and tested its heft.

"I've always, excuse the pun, wanted to turn the tables on a cowardly tiger poacher like you," Julian said. "How's that trap feel on your ankle? I bet it hurts like a motherfucker."

Julian slammed the table leg into KP's shin, just above the trap.

"Motherfucker!" screamed KP.

"I had a feeling you'd say that," Julian said as he took a couple of slow practice swings. KP growled in defiance as he fell to his knees.

"Tell me who's paying you and I'll put you out of your misery with a one or two solid blows to your skull. Keep your mouth shut and it's going to take a while." Julian waited three seconds for an answer. When none came, he struck KP in the ribs. KP fell onto his chest. Julian hit him on the back of the thigh.

"I need a break. I didn't realize clubbing defenseless animals was such hard work," Julian said. He sat down on the couch and picked up an issue of American Rifleman. He glanced at the front and back cover. KP fought his way back up to his hands and knees. Julian was impressed. There was no denying KP was a tough motherfucker.

"What happened to my partner?" KP asked.

"Do you mean Aidan or Cill? Because they're both dead. A tiger ate them. It was an awesome thing to watch."

"You know who I mean."

"Oh, you must be talking about Declan. That was me. I gotta admit he tasted better than I thought he would."

"Very funny, asshole."

"You think I'm joking? His body's in the bedroom, at least what's left of it."

"I'm going to fucking kill you."

"Really? That would be quite a trick." Julian got up and started going through KP's pockets. He found an older Samsung Galaxy with a pattern lock. He would never get into the phone without KP's help.

Julian grabbed the back of KP's shirt collar, pulled back and said, "Tell me how to open your phone." KP didn't respond. Julian hit him on the back of the other thigh with the table leg. "I said tell me how to open your phone."

"I'll tell you when we're both dead."

Julian abruptly stood up and went back to the issue of American Rifleman. He looked at the address box on the cover. The magazine was addressed Mr. Eric Klaypool. The letters were curvy and distorted. Two of them, the K and the P were considerably clearer than the others and stood out. He looked at the address sticker on an issue of Maxim. It was addressed to Mr. Declan McCauliff, as was an issue of Saveur.

"Hey, Eric," Julian said to KP.

"I don't answer to Eric." KP said.

"You just did."

Julian stood up and gave KP, who was still on all fours, a solid blow to the middle of his back. KP fell flat on his face. As Julian circled him, KP rolled over onto his back and spit blood.

"Who's your boss?"

KP said nothing.

"Tell me and I'll put you out of your misery."

"Misery? I love this shit."

Julian hit him in the upper gut. The blow was harder than he had intended, a solid liver shot, which could have been fatal by itself. KP raised up both his fists a couple of inches and flipped Julian double birds. His hands fell limply to the floor. The display of insolence nearly killed him.

Julian got down on his knees so he could look KP straight in the eyes. "I admire your loyalty. But are you really willing to die for this guy?" Julian got no answer.

KP's chest rose and fell as he breathed, proving he was still alive. How much longer he would live, Julian didn't have any idea. He could last another two minutes or two days. With a tough bastard like KP, two days was more like it. If he did suffer for a while, Julian thought KP might be more willing to talk. In the meantime he had an errand to run.

Julian left the room and returned with a roll of duct tape that he used to gag KP.

"I'm going out for a while. Your friend in the other room is starting to stink."

To make sure KP wouldn't be able to free himself from the teeth of the jaw trap while he was gone, Julian took KP's left hand and spread it out on the floor. KP was in no position to resist. Julian stomped down hard on it with his heel. KP emitted a single muffled whimper. Julian foraged in KP's pockets until he pulled out a set of keys. He grabbed the issue of American Rifleman and left.

In McCauliff's driveway was a green Buick Riviera GS with sleek hideaway lights and a dual 4-barrel V8. Julian typed the address from the issue of American Rifleman into Google maps and fired up the

Riviera. KP lived in nearby Bridgeview, so it wouldn't take long to get there.

Julian stopped in front of a house set back far from the street. He confirmed the address and pulled into the driveway. He used the only other key on the keychain he had taken from KP to open the front door. With KP's car in the driveway it looked like he was home. Julian could turn on the lights and wander the home freely. The house had enough furniture for just three people to sit down at the same time. The kitchen table had one chair. In the living room there was a beat-up recliner and a footstool that doubled as a table. He checked the living room closet. It was empty. The kitchen cabinets and drawers had a tiny collection of mismatched plastic utensils that looked like they came from the free box at a garage sale. There were two bedrooms, one of which was completely empty except for an old Kirby vacuum clean. Nothing Julian saw provided any useful information.

In the other bedroom was an enormous four-poster bed that took up most of the room. In the drawer of the small bedside table were some ribbons and medals from KP's years in the army. On the shelf below the drawer was a book of The Far Side cartoons and a dogeared journal. Julian opened the journal and flipped through the front half of the book. It was filled with low-quality home printer photos of dead bodies and scribbled comments and dates. Many of the deceased wore black turbans or red and white checkered ghutras. In some of the photos there was no blood or obvious cause of death. At the other end of the spectrum there was a man whose face was so bloody and mottled with shards of bone and bits of brain that it looked like his skull had been turned inside out.

When Julian was three quarters of the way through the book, he flipped a page and saw a Siberian tiger lying dead on the ground, a snare tangled around its leg. The pinpricks hit him. He slammed the book shut. Nausea surged. His breathing was forced and racing. Of course, he had seen similar scenes up close and personal, but no matter how many dead tigers he saw it went straight to his gut. Seeing Amara lying dead on the ground after he put a bullet in his head was the second worst thing he had seen in his life, only because seeing his sister sliced in half by a train was the worst thing anyone could ever see.

There were many more pages in the journal he hadn't looked at. He knew what those pages contained. He didn't need to look at any more photos of dead tigers. Still, morbid curiosity took control and he opened the journal and went through every page. There were photos of dead tigers hanging from trees, secured to crude stretchers and tangled in all sorts of traps and makeshift snares. There were dead Bengal, Sumatran, and Siberian tigers. He contained his fury until the last entry of the book, a photo of KP on his knees posing for a trophy shot beside a large Bengal. With one hand KP held up the tiger's head. With his other hand KP flashed the shaka sign. The motherfucker was grinning.

Julian released his fury with a long, deep growl. He ripped off one of the bedposts and threw it at the wall, burying it six inches into the plaster. He wanted to kill someone, anyone. He wanted to torch the house, to burn it to the fucking ground. He knew he needed to check himself and bring his dangerous, unproductive rage under control. He paced around the house wringing the book in his hands. Killing tigers had always made him furious. He had always wanted every single poacher to spend the rest of his life in a squalid, third-world prison cell. Such a punishment was no longer sufficiently severe. After seeing the photos in the book, he wanted to kill—and eat—every motherfucker who had even looked at a tiger wrong. It wasn't just rage. It felt necessary, like self-preservation. He took deep, measured breaths and talked himself down until he was calm enough to walk out the front door, get in the Buick Riviera and drive to McCauliff's house to finish beating KP to death with a table leg.

***

On the way back to McCauliff's Julian drove past Egan's Four Leaf Tavern. He circled around and parked the Riviera in The Leaf's parking lot. It was almost 11:00 and he was surprised to see the place nearly half-full. The juke box was playing Van Halen's Panama. There were a couple of games of darts taking place and people were drinking and laughing. Julian soaked in the working class ambience as he made his way to the bar. He took a seat next to a couple of older men who were throwing dice. Gabe was on the other side of the bar.

"You look familiar," Gabe said, having to raise his voice just a bit to get over the sound of the small crowd. "It's Luther, isn't it?"

"Good memory, Gabe," replied Julian.

"Blue Ribbon for ya'?"

"It's after five. Make it a bourbon rocks."

Gabe poured the drink and set the glass down in front of Julian. He watched Julian take a long pull on the bourbon. Julian put the glass on the bar and voiced his satisfaction.

"Just what the doctor ordered, huh?" Gabe said.

"Got that right," replied Julian.

"If you're looking for Cill, I haven't seen him. Nobody has," Gabe said.

"That doesn't sound good," Julian said.

"Heard he and his brother went to Pakistan or India or someplace like that and no one's heard a word from them since."

"Strange."

"Something bad was bound to happen to those two sooner or later. Hey, did you get that car you were looking at?"

"Nah. The guy wanted too much." There was a single sip of bourbon left in his glass. "Pour me another, Gabe," he said. Gabe was way ahead of him. He set another bourbon and a bowl of nuts on the bar.

"Can't offer you much else in the way of food. Just have the pickled pigs feet, but I don't take you for a pickled pigs feet kind of guy."

"It's all right. I have dinner waiting for me at home."

Chapter Seventeen

The Red Thong

Olivia Van de Weghe was a news junkie. The first thing she did every morning after arriving at her office was browse the Chicago Tribune and Sun Times websites. Today was a slow news day with one violent exception, a crime so disturbing that even Chicagoans, a population desensitized to violence by constant reports of teen shootings and weekends with double-digit murders, were appalled. A woman in Oak Lawn, a relatively safe town compared to Chicago, called the police to report that from two houses away she could smell mothballs and rotting cabbage. A couple of Oak Lawn police officers did a welfare check and discovered two bodies that one of the officers described as looking like "partially eaten roadkill." One victim was wrapped in a tiger skin rug. The other had one jaw trap locked on his leg and another buried deep into his face.

The article did not identify the deceased. It didn't need to for Olivia to know who they were. Although she had never personally met McCauliff, she had him checked out. She knew he lived in Oak Lawn. The trap and tiger rug were dead giveaways. The night KP and McCauliff had gone for Julian at Adams and Wabash, KP had held off checking in with Olivia until he heard from McCauliff. When he was finally able to tell Olivia that McCauliff confirmed Julian was dead, he also told her about Julian's strange behavior and special gifts. He had jumped on the roof of the car, broken his arm like it was a toothpick and could run and leap like some sort of savage superman. For several days Olivia believed Julian was dead. She had mixed feelings about his death, but she knew it needed to happen. She was surprised by the pleasure she got from thinking he was still alive. If Julian could do all the things KP had told her about, there was no reason to think he couldn't handle KP and McCauliff. The jaw traps and cannibalism were an intriguing twist.

The moment Olivia first laid eyes on him at the foundation's gala she had recognized something feral about Julian. That feeling was more than confirmed the afternoon the two of them fucked ferociously in his high-rise apartment. She had no explanation for the extraordinary and implausible abilities KP had witnessed. She didn't have to understand how he got them to believe he had them. In some strange way it made sense. And now that Julian appeared to share Amara's taste for man, she was more fascinated by him than ever. She no longer had any interest in seeing him dead. Alive and well was far better. She had to be more careful around him now, even if she was no longer as worried about him getting her in trouble with the police. What she had on him was more damaging and scandalous than anything she had done.

***

Olivia found that Julian's cannibalistic behavior made for fascinating reading. Julian's reaction to the same story in the Trib was more like that of most Chicagoans. He was appalled and disgusted. As he sat on his comfy bed in his LondonHouse suite and read the story it was almost as if he were reading about someone else. Details were fuzzy, but he didn't have complete amnesia about those horrific couple of days at McCauliff's house. He could remember wiping down all his fingerprints after he had gotten his fill. He even went to KP's house to clean. He fell asleep on KP's floor with a rag in his hand. His conscious and meticulous attempt to hide his guilt scared him as much as anything.

His most recent trip to the platform at Adams and Wabash had been brutally painful, but he felt a purge of at least a few of his demons, as if they had been expelled when he vomited. Unfortunately, they had been almost immediately replaced by new ones. His thoughts went to Lourdes. Would she know it was him? Would she turn him in? He would have to wait a few more days to find out. She had gone to San Francisco for a conference. Odds were she knew nothing about the article in the Trib. She didn't read the news much. She was too wrapped up in her work. There was zero chance she would see a printed copy of the Trib while she was in San Francisco, though there was always a chance the story was shocking enough to make national news. She had every right to turn him in, and he would be okay with it if she did it after he found—and killed—whomever was behind the bizarre plan to kill him and Amara.

He was willing to go to prison for what he had done and what he still planned on doing. After thinking about being incarcerated for a while longer he came to the conclusion it would be hell. For a dangerous inmate like him prison could only mean solitary confinement. He would never leave his cell unshackled. He would never be put in the general population for fear he would kill and eat an inmate. He would be better off dead. He thought about jumping in front of a train. He could add himself to the list of tragedies of the cursed Hamilton clan from Evanston—pancreatic cancer, murder, attempted murder, suicide and cannibalism. He'd be dying proof that money can't buy happiness.

Time was no longer a luxury. If he wanted to complete his quest for vengeance he needed to act quickly. He was no closer to discovering who was in charge than he was when he was in the bowels of the Sundarbans. He could no longer afford to hide. If whoever was calling the shots still wanted him dead he would have to advertise to the world that it was open season.

The first thing to do was move back into his apartment. With Simon and Vanessa in Lake Forest, they were out of danger. Sitting in his apartment and staring out at the lake wasn't exactly broadcasting to the world his message of come and get me. He needed to publicly call attention to himself. He had plenty of money, more than he could ever spend. It wouldn't be too hard to buy a little attention.

Julian walked to Gibson's for dinner. After many meals there he had learned a bloody cut of beef had a calming effect on him. Along the way he passed the homeless man he frequently saw mingling around the Waldorf at the corner of Walton and Rush.

"Hey, Julian the asshole. Give me some motherfuckin' change," the homeless man said as Julian approached. The homeless man was smiling. In the man's eyes Julian could see a warm light of consciousness. Julian immediately smiled back at him.

"How 'bout I buy you a steak instead?" Julian asked.

"Throw in a couple glasses of wine and you've got a deal."

"Sold, but while we're there, just call me Julian. It's endearing, but you can drop the asshole thing."

"I can do that," the man said confidently. "That's really just an act."

"And verbally assaulting people works?"

"Worked on you, didn't it?"

"True," Julian said.

Suddenly, the homeless man's enthusiasm collapsed. "Maybe some other time."

"What? Why?"

"No place is going to let me in looking like this." The man tugged at his torn, stinky windbreaker with one hand and his grimy pants with the other."

Julian scanned the block for someplace he could get the man some clothes. "Let's go shopping for a new jacket and pants," Julian said as he nodded to the Versace store across the street.

"You all right, Julian?" asked the homeless man, whose name Julian would later find out was Marcus.

"Please. I need your help with something and I'd like to talk about it over a fat ribeye," Julian said.

"Fine, but I ain't gonna wear no crazy pink blazer from Versace."

Marcus took Julian to a store down the block where they picked out some jeans, a red plaid shirt and a waxed cotton jacket.

As they ate ribeye and drank merlot Julian asked Marcus a litany of questions about homelessness in Chicago. Where did he sleep? How often did he go hungry? How did he keep warm in the winter? How do romantic relationships on the street work? What mental health services were available for the homeless?

It turned out that Marcus was the right man to offer a steak dinner. He had loads of information and opinions on Chicago's homeless situation and he shared them freely. Over his nine years of homelessness he had met everyone from insincere high school grade-grubbers ladling soup for their college apps to the directors of some of the largest organizations in the city.

"Money," was Marcus' answer when Julian asked what was needed most. "Honestly, there are a lot of really good people trying to help. They just don't have the money. It's pretty simple. Money—and socks. Nothing better than a clean pair of socks."

The following afternoon, after a considerable amount of research into the organizations Marcus had recommended, Julian called his brother. It was really Vanessa he wanted to talk to. He wanted her help setting up what he wanted to call the Lara Hamilton Memorial Trust, a foundation dedicated to supporting those organizations that had already taken on the mission of ending homelessness in Chicago. She enthusiastically agreed and pledged a substantial donation from her and Simon.

"How much money are we talking about?" Vanessa finally asked Julian.

"I was thinking $100 million."

"Wow!" Vanessa said.

"Spread out over 10 years." Julian clarified.

"Still wow."

"What else would I do with it? Besides, this insures the money will go to the right people if something happens to me."

"Are you expecting something to happen to you?" she asked.

"In this family anything can happen. You've learned that by now, haven't you?"

***

The creation of the Lara Hamilton Memorial Trust was timed to give Julian the opportunity to get himself in the newspaper. Thanks to Vanessa, within 48 hours of eating ribeye with Marcus, Julian was talking to a female reporter from the Chicago Tribune in the living room of his 69th floor apartment.

Sarah Redstone received her Master's with high honors from Northwestern's Medill School of Journalism and had been working for the Tribune for almost two years. She was 25 years old, had a glorious mop of tiny curls on her head and an enormous chip on her shoulder. When her editor assigned her the story, she was upset. She viewed the story about a rich white prick trying to get his 15 minutes as just another piece of fluff in a never-ending line of un-newsworthy assignments. She wanted a crime beat. Her editor knew it, and for whatever reason, didn't care. Regarding this story, he didn't give her many details. All he said was the rich prick's donation was a significant one and it was all going to the homeless.

In the elevator up to the 69th floor she was still grumbling about having to meet this guy at his own apartment instead of a cafe somewhere because he probably wanted to flaunt his gaudy wealth. There was a reason they were meeting there. It wasn't because Julian wanted to show off. He did hope his apartment would make it into the story. He wanted his adversary, whoever that was, to know he wasn't hiding. He told Vanessa's friend who worked for the PR firm that helped set up the interview that he had a bad foot and preferred to do it at home. It was a lie, but it was such a harmless lie that Sarah Redstone would never know.

Sarah was a young woman from Chicago's South Side, across town and a world away. She was in no mood to play games with some rich white guy 69 floors above the Mag Mile. When Julian first let Sarah inside, her eyes were immediately drawn to the living room windows that looked out over the lake. She tried to appear uninterested. It didn't work.

"The view of the lake is the best thing about this place," Julian said.

"It's nice, but I prefer the ground floor where I can hear the waves hit concrete and sand. Reminds me of hot summer days when I was a kid." Sarah said.

"I'm sorry. I don't have much more to offer you than water or bourbon," Julian said as he gestured for Sarah to take a seat in an overstuffed chair.

"I'm fine. Let's get started," she replied. What she meant was, "Let's get this over with."

For the first five minutes of the interview Julian talked about about insuring the money went to the right place if something were ever to happen to him. He was doing with his money exactly what he wanted to do with it: giving it away to organizations providing food, shelter and mental health services to the homeless. When it came to helping the homeless, he wasn't trying to rewrite the playbook. It didn't need rewriting. It needed funding.

The conversation pivoted when Sarah wanted to know if he had a personal connection to homelessness and mental health issues.

"My sister was killed when a homeless man threw her and himself in front of a train. It took me a long time to stop blaming that one man for killing my sister. If he had gotten the help he needed, it might not have happened. They were both victims of societal apathy."

When Sarah heard this her interest was stirred. She scribbled notes at twice the speed as she had earlier. When she heard Julian say he had witnessed the tragedy from a few feet away, she locked up. The note taking stopped. She looked at Julian in silence. She opened her mouth to to ask another question. The words wouldn't come out.

"Are you okay, Ms. Redstone?" Julian asked.

"I'm sorry. My behavior is unprofessional," she said while straightening her posture.

"It's a difficult subject."

"I know. Believe me, I know." Sarah sniffled. She wiped a tear from her eye.

"I'm a good listener if you want to talk about it."

"I don't like to talk about it. And this isn't how our interview is supposed to go."

"Forget the interview and talk to me. It helps." Julian was great at giving counsel on this subject. He was terrible at taking it.

Sarah, like Julian, had witnessed a tragedy. And like Julian, she had locked it away for years. Around him, though, she felt strangely at ease.

"My sister ran into the street chasing a basketball. She was hit and killed by an ambulance. A fucking ambulance. Can you believe that?"

"How old was she?" Julian asked.

"Ten. I was 12."

"That was a long time ago."

"Not long enough, apparently."

"If you don't talk about it, it's like putting it on hold. It doesn't age. It doesn't get older. It just gets heavier."

"Yeah, it does. Especially the guilt."

"Because it was her and not you?"

"No, because I threw the ball so she wouldn't be able to catch it. I was just teasing. I didn't mean to. . ." She took a moment to wipe her tears and collect her thoughts. "I haven't been able to pick up a basketball since. I loved to play. I had dreams of playing in college."

"I've been going to Adams and Wabash almost every night for weeks, but I've only been up to the platform once, and it didn't go so well. Seems pretty stupid to live in the city and not be able to ride the damn train, doesn't it?"

"No, not at all."

"If I ride a train, will you play basketball?" Julian asked her. He regretted it when he saw Sarah's apprehension. "Sorry. That's none of my business. I don't even know you."

"You know something about me few people could ever understand. You have the right to at least ask."

"Thank you," Julian said.

"And yes. If you ride a train, I'll play basketball."

Sarah and Julian agreed to return to the conversation she was sent there to have. They talked for a long time. As Sarah got ready to leave, she handed Julian her business card."

"In case you think of anything else," she told him.

"Thanks."

"And if you get on a train."

"I'll do that," Julian said as he acknowledged the card clutched in his hand.

Sarah left happy. Although she still wanted the crime beat, she finally felt like she had something important to write about. Julian was confident he would get what he hoped for, both for the population his new foundation would benefit and for his ploy to draw out whomever still wanted him dead. The interview also reminded him of how little control he had over his life. His inability to come to terms with Lara's death was part of it. Mostly it was the polarity between being able to chat pleasantly and counsel a young woman reporter in the afternoon and the stark awareness that by midnight he could be picking bits of human flesh out of his teeth.

By 6:00 pm the next day Sarah Redstone's story had blown up. As Julian had hoped, she included details about what he did with his time and where he lived. The article was, however, much more than he could ever have hoped for. Sarah skillfully wove into the story the threads of the trauma of losing loved ones and the plague of homelessness in Chicago. Julian was impressed with how Sarah was able to put into words the thoughts that had whirled constantly in his head since the day his sister was killed. Sarah's story gave him much needed comfort. She had calmed his whirling thoughts, at least the ones about his sister. His concerns about killing and eating humans were anything but calm. He knew that if someone irked him, even just a little, he might not be able to control himself. If things could always be agreeable, he'd be fine. But in what world would that be possible?

Shortly after he finished reading the story his phone rang. Simon's name appeared on the caller ID. He expected it to be Vanessa. He was pleasantly surprised when he heard his brother's voice on the line. He said Vanessa had read the story to him and they had both cried. Simon also shared the news that he was able to stand and walk on his own. Julian expressed his relief. He assured him he had been watering the plants in their apartment and promised to come up to Lake Forest to visit soon.

Simon was the one hitch in the suicide option. He had not witnessed Lara's body severed by the train, though he had suffered, too. He was made of a stronger fabric than Julian and had a more effective coping mechanism. That was in no way cause for Julian to pile yet another family tragedy on this brother. Then again, if he were ever to get caught for killing and eating KP and McCauliff, the shame and stigmatization he would inflict on Simon might be worse than the sorrow caused by having a second sibling kill himself.

An hour later his phone rang again. Caller ID said it was Lourdes. Shit.

He answered the phone with a nervous "Hello."

"I made it home safely. The conference was a big success," Lourdes said.

"I'm glad."

"I saw the story in the Trib."

"Oh, yeah? What story?" Julian asked.

"The one about the foundation, dummy."

"You saw that already? It's only been online for a couple hours."

"Olivia called to tell me about it. It's wonderful."

"Olivia? How did she see it?"

"You're trending, Jules."

He didn't enjoy hearing the name Olivia. He had managed to keep her out of his thoughts recently. He had been too busy setting up his foundation and meting out vengeance to think of her. At least she hadn't mentioned reading the other article.

"About the other day in your office," Julian said.

"Yeah, that was kind of scary."

"It could get worse."

"Or maybe this whole thing will eventually just go away, wear off," she said hopefully.

He doubted that was true, though he didn't admit it to her. He didn't say anything for an unusually long time. It was almost as if the line had gone dead. There was one thing Julian really needed to say. He was having a hard time getting around to saying it.

"Jules, you still there?" she asked.

"Uh, yeah. I'm here."

"You're not okay, are you?"

"No." He took another long pause." Look, until I can figure something out, I think you should stay away from me. It's not safe for you to be around me."

"You can't hurt me through the phone, can you?"

"No, of course not. It's just not the same if I can't be with you."

"Well, this feels painfully familiar," she said.

Julian thought he could hear her crying. He wanted to say something comforting, but he resisted.

"I love you, Lourdes Villegas," Julian said and quickly hung up.

***

Edward Van de Weghe knew his forced retirement as CEO and Chairman of VanPharm was a medical necessity. The job had literally almost killed him. He was in a wheelchair for the first couple of months after he was released from the hospital. He spent most of his days convalescing, watching Fox News, reading and rereading Cormac McCarthy's Blood Meridian. Initially, he had three home healthcare nurses who each worked eight hour shifts. Two were men. The woman worked the graveyard shift. A service sent Letty as a replacement for his previous domestic aide, Lonna, who had moved to Des Moines to be closer to her mother. Not even Letty, with her beautiful brown eyes and glorious posterior, could make Edward smile in those first few difficult months of retirement.

Olivia moved in permanently after Edward's fourth month of what he referred to as being "a dying old fart" and started giving him TB-13's predecessors. It took only a couple of weeks for Edward to feel the positive effects. A month later he was well enough to dispatch with the home health care workers. He wanted to go back to work, such that it was. However, the board of his own company was unanimous in the decision to stick with his replacement, Anton Battaglia, Edward's designated successor. At least he could get back on the tennis court. Tennis had always been his favorite game. He had played since he was a child. By the time he was 70 his arthritic pain was so severe that just looking at a tennis racket made his joints hurt.

Even before he felt good enough to get back on the tennis court, Edward Van de Weghe was participating regularly in another beloved pastime: jerking off. He was thrilled by his renewed ability to get rock hard. Like so many men in China, the hardness of his erection was what he used to appraise his virility. He would lock himself in the bathroom, sit on the toilet and fantasize about fucking his Guatemalan maid in the pool house. Sometimes it was the stables or the tennis court. Sometimes he did it two or three times a day.

Now, after several months on TB-13—Amara's bones were supposed to be the base for TB-14—he started exhibiting behaviors of an addict. Of the four C's of addiction—craving, compulsion, consequences and control—the first two had a solid hold on him. The other two were lurking around the corner. The TB formulas had changed his world and he had come to rely on his daily hits. The small serving Olivia gave him every morning was no longer enough for Edward. He figured if he took twice as much he would feel twice as good.

While Olivia was at work and with Letty at the market stocking up on Grey Goose, Edward went into Olivia's bedroom to raid her stash.

He had always respected her privacy and stayed out of her room. Until recently, that is. He had easily figured out where she kept the stuff. Any time Olivia opened one of her dresser drawers, the heavy brass pull handles made a clanking noise. If both of their bedroom doors were open, he could hear the clank from his bedroom far down the hall. He usually heard it right before she came to his room in the morning to give him his vitamins and the special juice. How much of her privacy would he be violating if he knew exactly what he was looking for and exactly where to find it?

He had never stolen more than one vial from her dresser drawer before. Today, there were 40 vials, double the largest amount he had ever seen. Unless she took inventory, he convinced himself he could take as many as seven without her noticing. The number was a hopeful guess. He went back to his bedroom, popped the top off the first vial and forced the contents down his throat. The taste had gotten worse with each generation. He did the same with the remaining six. He capped the empties and set them on his bed. He looked at his clock. It was only noon, which meant much of his morning dose was still in his system, bringing the total number of doses to almost eight.

From the drawer of his bedside table he pulled out some red thong underwear he had taken from Letty's dirty laundry. He walked to the middle of his room and dropped his pants. He didn't even bother to close the door all the way. He imagined himself taking Letty from behind and fondling her bare ass. He snorted her thong while he pleasured himself. As he was about to cross the finish line a sharp bolt of pain hit his chest. He dropped his junk and clutched his heart. He stumbled over to his bed and tried to sit down. He was too dizzy. He fell on the mattress and rebounded in a comic pratfall onto the floor. The empty vials fell with him and rolled under the bed.

Letty's voice came from down the hall. "Señor Van de Weghe?" She said loudly as she reached the top of the stairs. "Tengo tu bodka."

Edward tried to call her. All he managed was a muffled gurgle.

"Señor Van de Weghe?" she called again as she walked toward his room. More gurgling and saliva oozed out. Letty knocked on the door as she slowly pushed it open. She saw him, flat on his back on the Persian rug. His pants and boxers were at his ankles and his 89-year-old little soldier was still at full attention. The red thong she thought lost was wrapped around his fingers.

"Señor Van de Weghe?" she repeated calmly. He was still alive, though non-responsive. She had always been indifferent to Edward. He tipped her well. Still, she thought if he was going to stare at her ass all day, he should give her more. Now that she had seen her thong in his hand, she didn't give a shit. She tried to pull it out of his clutched fingers but couldn't. He was holding them too tightly. She knew the old man was dead when he finally let go. She checked for a pulse. She expected to find nothing and that's what she found. The service that had given her the job had provided her some basic training for situations like this. Well, sort of like this. Death by masturbation wasn't covered.

Letty called Olivia, who said she would be right home. She was in no rush. Edward's dead body lay on his Persian rug for two hours before she showed up. His pants were at his ankles. His dick had flipped its light to off-duty. Letty had no interest in preserving her employer's dignity. She did, however, pocket her thong, not because she wanted to keep it. She planned to burn it.

While looking around her father's bedroom, Olivia saw a glint of light coming from under the bed. A ray of sun coming through one of the windows illuminated a column on the floor all the way to the bed. The sunlight was being reflected by one of the empty vials. She reached down to pick it up and saw the other six.

Olivia, who had long thought she didn't care whether her father lived or died, suddenly realized she did care, at least she cared about the timing of his death. One positive to come out of his death was she learned the consequences of taking too much TB-13. She had been taking it regularly and felt fantastic, but she had to be careful. This was a firm reminder to fix any addiction and overdose dangers. She was confident she could. For the most part, however, Edward Van de Weghe's sticky, undignified death had come at a bad time. His passing would certainly mean aunts, uncles, cousins, family friends and business associates would call or come around to pay their respects. She didn't have time for any of that postmortem protocol. She didn't know what Letty wanted to do. She would keep her on if Letty was willing. If she did choose to stay, Olivia could send her on a paid vacation to Guatemala for a month. She could delay reporting the death for a day or two. Turning the air-conditioning way down in her father's bedroom would help delay the stench. At the moment the least she could do for him was pull up his pants.

Chapter Eighteen

In The Dirt

Julian hoped they'd come for him at his post at Adams and Wabash. It gave him more control over the situation and would help minimize any potential collateral damage. He believed his brother was out of danger up in Lake Forest, though he still had a high-rise full of neighbors to think about, of whom he knew the names of just two: Howard Erlacher and Marion, the woman with one leg. And, of course, there was Johnny. He would never want anything to happen to him. If it happened at Adams and Wabash it would appear more random than if it happened at the same building where his brother was shot. He went to his post earlier and stayed later.

Olivia preferred to find Julian at or near his home. It would seem suspicious if she were to show up at the corner of Adams and Wabash at midnight. She still did not know how much he knew. He hadn't tried anything yet and she hoped that meant he didn't know about her. She had gone to great lengths to remain anonymous. Of the four men who worked for her, all of whom were now dead, only KP had ever met her or even knew her name, and he was the one person she was confident wouldn't give her up. Even though the United States Army had cast him aside, he had seen himself first and foremost as a Delta operator. Loyalty ran deep.

Olivia told her crew at the VanPharm research and development department she had been called out of town for a day. If it weren't for her father's dead body starting to melt on a $25,000 Persian rug, she would have told her team she would be gone for several days.

Her plan required careful preparation and some heavy lifting. A coincidental encounter with Julian was the ideal situation to set the plan in motion. She had no thoughts of taking him by force. She knew she wasn't capable of that and she wanted to assure he stayed alive. What she was confident in was her ability to seduce him. She was unaware of the pheromonal effects TB-13 gave her. She just knew he had little resolve around her. If he had any weakness, it was that.

She wandered around Michigan Avenue for an hour in the late afternoon, not really hoping to run into him, though she was prepared if she did. By 7:00 in the evening she had stationed herself in the park space next to the old Water Tower at the corner of Michigan and Pearson. From there she had a good sightline to where Julian would turn onto Michigan as he started his walk to Adams and Wabash. Olivia had read the article by Sarah Redstone in the Trib and made note of the part where Julian said he walked most everywhere because he enjoyed it, didn't own a car and hadn't been able get on a train since his sister died.

At 7:30 Olivia saw Julian make the turn onto Michigan Avenue and walk south. She followed him from the other side of the street for several blocks until she was reasonably sure he was headed to Adams and Wabash. That was all she needed to know. The second night he did the same thing, only he started fifteen minutes later. On the third night she positioned herself to run into him as she exited the Ritz-Carlton. She waited in the lobby until 8:30 and was ready to give up when she saw him on the sidewalk talking and laughing with Johnny. She exited the hotel just as he crossed in front of the entrance.

"Julian," she said with mock surprise. "How are you?"

His surprise was genuine. "Hanging in there," he said as he breathed her in. His senses were scrambled, as if he had huffed gasoline. He couldn't resist a schoolboy-like peek at her legs. Olivia's short skirt gave him a lot to see. He hoped his gawking wasn't obvious. It was, though Olivia didn't mind. She wanted him to look. She needed him to look.

She had a mental script of how she wanted the conversation to go. Next she would ask about Simon, Vanessa and Lourdes. If he asked her what she was doing in the neighborhood she would say she was supposed to meet a colleague at the rooftop bar of the Ritz-Carlton, but the woman had just canceled on her. She'd say something like she was all dressed up with nowhere to go.

Things went according to script. When Julian finished telling her he hadn't spoken with Lourdes in a while, she hit him with "I have to go feed my father's horses." She pressed her lips against his ear and whispered, "Do you want to come?"

The whisper made him quiver from his ear to his toes. It was if she had flipped a switch in his brain. He immediately ran through the possibilities, the pros and cons of taking her up on her offer. His future wasn't so shiny. Vengeance had proved hard to find. He had told Lourdes, whom he still loved, to stay away from him. He was either going to jail under the most scandalous circumstances imaginable or he was going to kill himself, perhaps spectacularly. A roll in the hay in Edward Van de Weghe's stables would make a good last hurrah. In fact, there seemed to be no reason not to. There would be no guilt, no self-loathing. He could relax and enjoy himself. They could make it a date. It wouldn't just be spending 45 minutes on the freeway to go fuck in the dirt. A date would be drinks and dinner, and then fucking in the dirt.

"Where's your car?" he asked.

It had sounded like a good idea when he thought of it. In the hermetic confines of the Porsche, Olivia's scent was telling him to skip drinks and dinner and get right down to business. He never brought it up and let Olivia drive with little distraction.

The interior of the Van de Weghe mansion was dark, as were the exterior and long driveway. Olivia pulled into the parking area in front of the stables where a lone floodlight beamed on a man getting into a pickup truck. On seeing Olivia, the man approached her opening window.

"Hi, Reggie. Everything all right in there?" she asked.

"That foal's a handful, Miss Olivia. So sorry about your father." Reggie said then nodded to Julian, who nodded back.

"Thank you. Let's get together soon to talk about horses."

"Sure thing. Have a good night." Reggie gave Julian another nod, climbed into his truck and drove off.

The inside of the stables was dark and smelled of manure. Olivia flipped one switch, illuminating a single empty stall. The chestnut mare in the next stall snorted. Except for the mare and her foal, Olivia and Julian were completely alone. There wasn't another soul on the entire estate. Letty had jumped at Olivia's offer of a free trip and was already in Guatemala. Reggie wouldn't be back until 10:00 in the morning. Olivia took Julian by the hand and led him to the empty stall. There was no urgency like there was the first time they got together. They both knew that this time they had all night. She flipped the latch on the gate to the stall and pulled the door open. She pushed Julian into the stall.

"Take off your clothes," Olivia told Julian. He immediately started undressing and tossed his clothes on the floor. She took a slow, deliberate survey of his athletic physique. She dragged her fingers over the ridges created by his prominent abdominal muscles. She undressed. It didn't take her long. She wasn't wearing much. They stood face-to-face.

"This time I'm in charge," she said.

"They're your stables."

Yes, they are. So down on the ground, boy. I'm going to take you for a ride."

Julian lay on his back in the dirt. Olivia climbed on. She slid onto his hips and straddled her legs around him. She could feel his erection pressed up against her ass and lower back as she rocked back and forth. Her eyes were closed and a lock of hair hung in front of them. She bit down on her lower lip. Her face was beautiful. Every inch of her was beautiful, beautiful and perfect, Julian thought.

She tilted her hips back, took him in her hand and guided him inside her. He explored her luscious flesh with his hands. The first time they fucked it had been fast and savage. This time it was slow. It was luxurious, even on the hard dirt floor. He thought of nothing but the pleasure her body was giving him. For the first time in a long time his mind was delightfully engrossed in that and only that moment.

When they finished Olivia went to the tack room and came back with three blankets. She laid one on the ground, made a pillow with the second and cocooned herself and Julian with the third. He spooned her. He put his hands on her breast and pushed himself inside her. They climaxed together. He stayed inside her until they were both asleep. He woke her in the middle of the night, climbed on top of her and they went at it again. His mind didn't wander to any other thoughts. He was perfectly content where he was. This woman, whom he thought was so dangerous, no longer felt that way. She was soft and caring. The curves of her lithe body fit with his perfectly, like die-cut puzzle pieces. She could be, he thought, his mate.

Julian and Olivia slept soundly for the rest of the night on the dirt floor of the horse stall. At 6:00 in the morning Julian was jolted awake when Olivia stabbed a 16-gauge hypodermic needle into his bare ass.

Chapter Nineteen

I Swear On My Sister's Grave

Olivia pushed the plunger and injected Julian with 2.5 ml of acepromazine. By the time he knew what was happening, Olivia was out of the stall and closing the door. Julian, the blissful lover, was now an enraged beast. He charged. Olivia engaged the lock just as Julian crashed his naked body into the door. He growled loudly. The mare and her foal whinnied and stomped. For a brief moment she was terrified and backed away. As soon as she knew the stall would hold him, her terror turned to curiosity. She stepped closer to observe him better. He pounded the walls of the stall. They were five feet high with metal bars running from the top of the walls to the ceiling. The stalls were built to keep pests and predators out, but they could just as easily be used to lock—or cage—someone in.

"What did you stick me with?" he demanded.

"An equine sedative. It's completely safe. Of course, you got nearly as much as we give a 1,000-pound horse. You'll be all right in a few hours, or days. I'm not sure."

"Why are you doing this? I mean last night was," he stopped mid-sentence.

"Last night was what? Perfect? Is that what you were going to say?"

"Yes," he admitted somewhat reluctantly.

"I agree. We can talk about our future when you wake up."

"What future?"

"Sweet dreams, tiger," she said as she walked away. She turned around and blew him a kiss.

Julian grabbed two of the metal bars and pulled himself up to the top of the wall. "Get back here!" he growled. Olivia ignored him and left the stables. He shook the bars. They didn't give. He jumped to the ground and ran to the back wall, which was solid all the way to the ceiling. He pounded the wall with his fists and ran back to the front of the stall. There was no escape. He was caged.

The acepromazine kicked in hard. Blurred vision. Dizziness. He hit the floor.

Olivia calmly drove to the house and let herself in. It was the first time since she moved back into her father's house that she had been truly alone. There was always someone there, whether it was Letty, her father or somebody cleaning or fixing something like the security system or the cooling unit in the wine cellar. The house was hers now. The first person she told about her father's death was his personal lawyer. He said he would make all the arrangements and told Olivia what she already knew: She was Edward Van de Weghe's sole heir.

***

Julian was groggy and still half asleep when he heard a tremendous whir. His eyes were blurry and with his cheek pressed against the floor the only things he saw were spinning flashes of light and blurry vertical stripes. The noise hurt his ears. It hurt his whole body. He tried unsuccessfully to sit up. He didn't even have the energy to pull his hands off the floor. He rested on all fours as he gathered strength. His head hung low. His guts tightened and his body convulsed. He puked on the floor. He rolled onto his back and focused on his breathing. His naked sinewy body was hot and slippery with sweat. The whirring and the spinning shadows were relentless. It was like riding the Tilt-A-Whirl with the hangover to end all hangovers. He faded out again.

When he woke an hour later the whirring and the spinning had stopped. He was better and terrible at the same time. His skin was clammy and cold, his mouth dry and dusty. He knew he was no longer in the stables. Other than that, he had no idea where he was.

"Take this. You look awful," a familiar voice said. A hot towel fell on his shoulder. He felt relief as he wiped his face and body with the towel.

"Put this on." Julian recognized Olivia's voice. A blue silk robe landed on the floor in front of him. He looked up and saw Olivia's vague form. She held a glass of water. He reached out with his hand for the glass and bumped against a metal bar. She put the glass in his hand. He took a drink. The water helped. His focus sharpened and he noticed lots of metal bars. He was in a cage. The cage was bolted to the floor. He wanted to lunge at Olivia, but he didn't have the energy.

"Where am I?" he asked her.

"In my private research facility. I won't tell you exactly where it is. What I can tell you is it's somewhere in the city."

"What was that awful noise I heard earlier? I thought my head was going to explode."

"That was my centrifuge. Impressive, isn't it?"

"Is it brushless?" Julian asked flippantly.

"Is it what?"

"Never mind. Inside joke."

"A funny one, I'm sure."

"Who the hell are you?"

"I admit I am hard to get to know. I have many secrets. But I know all about you, Julian Hamilton, AKA Ike MacTavish. I know about your sister and your mother. I know you spent years in Asia chasing tigers. I know you just pledged $100 million dollars to help the homeless. That was noble of you. It's a lot of money."

"So you can read a newspaper. Big deal. What do you want from me?"

"I want to be your your partner."

"What do you mean partner? I don't want a partner, especially one who drugs me with horse tranquilizer and locks me in a cage like an animal."

"You may not want a partner, but you need one."

"You're fucking crazy. What the hell are you talking about?"

"I can help you, Julian. I'm the only person in the world who can help you."

"Help me with what?"

"With your problem."

"And what problem would that be?"

"You eat human flesh."

Julian was stunned. He stared daggers into her eyes. "What do you know about that?"

"Those were my men, Sherlock. So were the two who died in the forest near Nurnashmari."

"You?" he blared at her. She gave him a guilty shrug. He charged the cage wall. He reached through the bars to grab her. She pulled back just in time and he missed. He took a bar in each hand and shook the cage. He hissed.

"Those bars are one-inch solid stainless. An elephant couldn't get out of there and neither can you, even with your enhanced abilities. And don't bother screaming. There's four feet of insulation in these walls. If a helicopter landed on the roof you wouldn't know it."

Julian went to the center of the cage and sat down defeated.

"Look, I know you've done some terrible things lately. I've done some terrible things, too. I'm doing a terrible thing to you right now. Unlike you, I do these things in the name of science, not because I'm hungry.

"I don't have any qualms about killing people who kill tigers," Julian said.

"But you ate them."

"I see it as karma."

"I don't believe in karma. I'm a scientist. And in the name of science, I want to study you. I want to find out what makes you run fast and jump high. I want to understand how you got this way, the science of it. You could help me revolutionize my already revolutionary process. In exchange, I fix your cannibalism problem.

"How could you possibly do that?" Julian said as walked to the front of the cage.

"I've done some groundbreaking genome editing with tiger DNA recently. There's a strong link between aggression and genetics and I noticed some interesting copy number variants in yours."

"Speak English," Julian said.

"I think I can snip out whatever it is that makes you aggressive and want to eat people. You'd get to keep all the good stuff, whatever it is you have. Do you have night vision? I'm really curious about that."

Olivia gave Julian the short version of the genesis of TB-13. She told him how much it had done for her father and how much potential it had. She had been taking it and never felt better. She didn't neglect the dark side of her operation, how she had assumed he had to die because she knew he would never let anyone kill his tiger. He was, unfortunately, something like collateral damage. Of course, he had heard of tiger bone wine before and it made him sick to think about it. He didn't want to have anything to do with that kind of traditional Chinese medicine.

"I'm out," he said.

"Really, you don't want super powers with no downside? I think you're lying."

"Believe me, it's not so great. And even if I did want it, which I don't, I'd rather not have you poking and prodding me like some sort of lab chimp."

"Too late. I already started sequencing your genome, and like I said, the CNV's are interesting. I'd say I'm off to a good start, and, of course, I'm brilliant. I do need to get some DNA from someone in your family for comparison. I'd ask your brother, but, you know, it would be kind of awkward," Olivia said.

"Because you tried to kill him, too."

"I didn't pull the trigger. I wasn't even there. Although I suppose I am partially to blame."

"Partially? Please. If it wasn't for you none of this would have ever happened."

"Fair enough."

"I'm not helping you. I'd rather die in here." Julian turned away from Olivia and walked to the back of the cage.

"If you work with me, you'd be saving tigers."

"How?" Julian asked, now a bit more interested in her proposal.

"If I can use your altered genetic material I won't have to kill any more tigers. I won't need them. This stuff is so potent I could dilute it a hundred times and it would still dominate the market in China. No one will want the old stuff, which could significantly slow down the poaching. I could do it without you. I took enough blood and tissue samples from you while you were knocked out to last a couple of years. Still, it would be useful to have you around to study and tweak things once in a while. And everything would be faster and easier if I had your brother's DNA. If you refuse to work with me you'll be nothing more than a footnote in my lab journal."

"This is too much for me right now. I need time to think."

"Fine, I have a funeral to go to. I'll come back tomorrow. While I'm gone ask yourself if the world is a safer place with you out there or in here."

Olivia left the room. Julian could hear the heavy door close behind her. All the lights went out. Julian was alone in his cage in total darkness and absolute silence. He had nothing to do but think about his current place in the world.

***

Olivia spread her arm across the panel of light switches and flipped all eight of them. The painfully bright burst assaulted Julian. He shielded his face with his hands while his dilated pupils contracted. He couldn't see her, but he could hear her footfalls as she approached the cage.

"Good morning, Julian. Or is it afternoon? I lost track of time. Did I tell you my father died the other day?" She didn't get an answer from Julian, who was still trying to adjust to the sudden change in lighting, nor did she expect one. "The obit I wrote said he died peacefully at home. The truth was he had a heart attack while jerking off. My father was 89 and could still stroke it twice a day."

"You must be so proud," Julian said.

"Actually, I am.

"Too bad he's not around to accept his lifetime achievement award."

"Make all the jokes you want. He went 15 years without an erection. My formulas gave him his jam back and cured his crippling arthritis.

Two years ago, his joints hurt so much he couldn't even hold his cock to pee. The day before he died he played tennis for two hours."

"How wonderful for him."

"It could be wonderful for so many millions of people, not just men. And you could be a part of it. You could help me give them their life back."

Julian thought about it. "No more tigers can die. Promise me that," he finally said.

"I can't make promises for other people."

"It starts with you."

"I promise I will not kill or pay anyone to kill tigers ever again."

"And you'll fight for their protection."

"I promise."

"All right."

"So you'll help me?" she said with the enthusiasm of a schoolgirl.

"I'll help you," he said, defeated.

"And you'll help me get a sample from your brother?"

"You don't need my brother," Julian said.

"Tell me how."

"You'll have to let me out. "

"That's not going to happen."

"Then forget the whole deal. Put a bullet in my head right here. I don't care," Julian asserted.

"How do I know you won't run off or worse? I can't take that risk."

"I swear on my sister's grave that I will not run away or do anything to hurt you. I'll go get it and come right back."

It was an iron-clad promise. Still, she needed more. "Fine, but I'm going with you."

Chapter Twenty

Is That Enough DNA For You?

"You can take off the blindfold now," Olivia said as she drove her Porsche out of the Chicago city limits. She had made him wear the blindfold in the car until they were in Evanston. She didn't want him to know anything more about her secret facility than what he had seen from the cage. He agreed to the blindfold because he had come to accept that cooperating with Olivia was in his best interest. He wasn't sure if he would kill himself when, or if, he was released from the incarceration Olivia had imposed. He had given suicide serious consideration, but he was not fully committed. He would let her try to fix him. She was right about everyone being better off with him in a cage. The world was not safe with him running around when the slightest irritation might set off a cannibalistic rage. He would even make her job easier by being nice to her, to a point. It could only help him in the long run.

Julian gestured with his finger to tell her to turn left onto Sheridan Road. She made the turn and he pointed for her to continue straight. He shifted in his seat to get a better look at the homes of his old neighborhood. As they got closer to his boyhood home Julian saw something he didn't like.

"Shit, that moving truck is parked in the driveway," Julian said referring to an enormous Mayflower truck. "Drive past it and pull over."

As they drove past, they saw a team of movers carrying furniture into the house. A woman who looked like she had just come from the golf course or a photoshoot for Talbots was telling the movers where to put it all. If Julian and Olivia had arrived a few hours earlier they would have found the place empty.

Julian's original plan was to scope it out in the light of the late afternoon and come back when it was dark. After seeing the moving truck and the woman, he immediately started altering his plans.

"You're my wife. Just follow my lead," Julian told Olivia. He got out of the car and waited for Olivia to join him. They walked to the edge of the front yard. The woman saw them standing there and walked over.

"Hi," I'm Ike. This is my wife, Cassandra," Julian said as he gestured to Olivia.

"I'm Rebecca. Do you two live in the neighborhood?" she asked.

"No, but I grew up in this house," Julian said.

"Really?" Rebecca asked.

Julian nodded.

"We live downtown now," Olivia added.

Can we be of any help?" Julian asked.

"That's sweet of you, though it's not necessary. I think they have things under control."

The cordial conversation continued for several minutes. Her husband and their two daughters were staying in New York until school let out. Rebecca said she felt blessed to have found a house in such a lovely neighborhood. When they had chatted long enough for Julian to know Rebecca was a kind and Christian woman, he changed the direction of the conversation.

"I have an odd favor to ask of you, Rebecca," Julian said.

"What's that?"

"It's a little strange, so just bear with me. As I told you, I grew up here. Years ago, when my mother still owned this house, my sister was pushed in front of a train and killed.

"That's awful," Rebecca said.

"It was. I won't go into it, but I will say that I got really depressed. I behaved strangely. I did strange things. I buried a box with some of my sister's things under her favorite tree in the backyard. I never had any intention of reclaiming them until I almost died recently. Now I'm feeling sentimental."

"I can understand that."

"Thank you. So do you mind?"

"Mind what" Rebecca said, not yet fully understanding what Julian was asking.

"Do you mind if we dig a little hole in your back yard? I know you haven't even moved in yet, but it would mean the world to Ike." Olivia said.

"And we'll pay for anything that needs to be replanted or whatever," Julian added.

"Oh, of course you can," Rebecca said as she placed a comforting hand on Julian's shoulder.

Julian took the shiny spade Olivia had bought in the morning out of the trunk. Rebecca led them to the backyard where Julian went straight for the black cherry tree. Most of the backyard was covered by a thick lawn. Under the shade of the black cherry the grass was thin. Julian stood with his back up against the tree and counted off three paces. He planted the spade. After three shovelfuls in the same spot, which made a hole a foot and a half deep, he moved to the right and took three more shovelfuls. Nothing. He looked up and saw Rebecca nervously nibbling her knuckle. He carried on with a third hole, this one to the left. On the second stab he felt resistance against the edge of the blade. He moved six inches to the left and had just put his foot on the blade for another when Rebecca said, "On second thought, I should really wait until my husband gets here."

Julian took his foot off the blade and turned to Rebecca. "What's that?" he said, knowing full well what she had said. He fought hard to control his temper. He took a deep breath and smiled at Rebecca.

"My husband will be here Friday. I think he should have a say in this. Can you wait until then?"

Julian looked at Olivia. Olivia looked at Rebecca, who was flipping her cell phone over in her hand.

"Of course we can," Olivia said as if it were no problem at all. What she was thinking wasn't so cordial.

"Thank you. I'm so sorry."

"Don't worry about it, Rebecca. We'll just swing by sometime next week after you've had a chance to get settled," Olivia said as she gently brushed her hand on Julian's back, hoping it would keep him calm.

Over the years of faking it until she made it, Olivia had become an expert at faking it. It was when she was genuinely trying to be sincere that she struggled. She had no intention of coming back next week.

"Didn't I tell you to follow my lead?" Julian said to Olivia as they got back in the car.

"What was I supposed to do, Ike, tie her up until you found what you were looking for? We're coming back tonight."

That seemed to satisfy Julian, who said, "I'm starving. What about you?"

Julian was unaware Olivia was watching him as he devoured his third pork taco in a little Mexican place in Evanston. She still didn't know how to feel about the man across from her. In addition to the great sex they'd had, she genuinely liked him. She thought, if only for a few seconds, she might be able to love him. She had finally found someone she would consider spending the rest of her life with and he's the guy she locked up in a cage and paid people to kill. Those same people nearly killed his brother. What the fuck was wrong with her?

Julian looked up and saw her staring at him. She flashed him a wistful smile.

"What is it?" he asked.

"Just admiring you. You're quite handsome."

"You're not so bad yourself."

"Thanks," she said. She was almost blushing.

"By the way, Cassandra was my mother's name. It was the first name that popped into my head," Julian said. "I hope you didn't mind."

"Not at all. It's a nice name."

She was about to say she was sorry for dragging him into whatever it was she was doing. She held back. They both had had several margaritas and she had noticed already that her lips, and his, were looser than usual. There was no way he'd be interested in a romantic relationship with her after all the shit she'd put him through. She'd have to settle for keeping him as a science experiment.

Olivia drove down the alley behind the house on Sheridan. The electric Porsche made noise when it accelerated. When it rolled slowly, it rolled in silence. She parked the car close to the six-foot high fence that surrounded Julian's former backyard.

"I'll be right back," Julian said. "Stay in the car."

He took the spade from the trunk and approached the fence. Olivia watched from inside the car as he set the spade on top of the fence and easily hopped over. The house, which was a good 70 feet from the back fence, was completely dark, at least what he could see of it. He hid against the fence and waited to see if the lights would come on. When they hadn't after half a minute, he made his way to the tree.

The moon was a sliver and gave off little light. Julian got on his knees and brushed the ground with his hands to find the holes he had filled in earlier. He sank the spade into the left side of the soft, disturbed earth. He removed more dirt and hit the corner of the hard object he had hit earlier. When he pried at the object, the spade blade scraped against it and made a gritty noise he knew had to have been made by a rock. He stopped and waited briefly for any reaction from someone in the house. There wasn't any. He reached into the hole and pulled out a rock the size and shape of a hefty text book.

He heard thumping against the fence behind him and looked back. Olivia lowered herself from the top and dropped to the ground. Julian rolled his eyes as she approached. He put his finger to his mouth to make sure she didn't try to explain why she had disregarded his order to stay in the car. He would let her do it later. He went back to digging. He knew the box had to be more to the right. The rock took up too much room on the left. After a few more attempts he hit something. He cleared away much of the dirt and got on his knees. With his hands he felt something wrapped in a cloth. He tried to pull it out. A tree root had grown over the top of it, making it difficult to move. He chopped at the root with the spade several times. It was a noisy effort, the spade hitting the root, the root hitting the box.

An upstairs room lit up.

Speed was the new priority. He aggressively dug below the box until he thought there was enough room to wiggle it out from under the root. Just as he was reaching into the hole to give it a try, Rebecca opened the window of the lit room.

"I just wanted to let you know I called the police. They're on their way," Rebecca shouted from upstairs.

Julian frantically wiggled the box back and forth until he finally freed it from its place in the earth. He put it under his arm and ran for the fence with Olivia right behind him. He tossed the box over the fence and it hit the alley on the other side with a loud clank. He jumped to the top of the fence, turned around and offered his hand to Olivia to help her get over. She didn't need any help. She ran at the fence, planted one foot in the middle of a plank and sprung off it. In one graceful move she grabbed the top of the fence and swung her legs over. Julian followed her and scooped up the box from the ground on his way to the car. As Olivia sped up the alley, Julian realized he had forgotten the spade. It didn't matter. Rebecca could use it to fill in the holes.

Olivia looked at the box on Julian's lap. It was slightly larger than a shoebox and it was wrapped up in what now was a muddy, disintegrating tablecloth. She was dying to know what was inside, but she could wait. It contained, after all, the DNA of his dead sister. In what form, she didn't know. As Julian turned the box in his hand to inspect it, it made a muffled rattle, which told her nothing about what was inside.

***

Julian sat in the cage on the thin mat she had given him to use as a bed. He leaned his back against the bars and set the box on his lap. He was wearing the blue silk robe. As soon as they returned from Evanston, she made him change. It was a small thing, but keeping him in the robe gave her an extra level of control.

He slowly peeled the tablecloth off the box, folded it and set in on the floor. He turned the box over and found the small padlock on the front. Olivia, who was 10 feet from Julian, took two steps toward him and stopped. She watched eagerly as he took the lock between his thumb and forefinger and squeezed it quickly two times. The little lock popped open. She took two more steps toward him. He removed the lock from the loop on the box and set it on the folded cloth. Olivia took two more steps. She was now as close to him as she could get without being inside the cage with him. He was too interested in the box to notice her or care.

The first thing he pulled out of the box was a green-haired troll doll in a pink and white tutu. Lara had a collection of troll dolls, each one with different colored hair. Julian had hated the things, particularly the green-haired one Lara had named Lucretia Garfield Hamilton in honor of the real Lucretia Garfield, wife of the 20th President of the United States, James A. Garfield. Lara was a history buff from a young age and had a special fondness for First Ladies. The Dolley Madison troll had pink hair. Mamie Eisenhower had blue.

As Julian examined Lucretia, his smile turned into a little laugh. He set the doll next to the padlock. He pulled out a photograph and stared at it. He put it down next to Lucretia. Olivia could see that it was Lara sitting in the black cherry tree reading a book. He pulled a second photograph from the box. It was a posed shot of the family from when the kids were in their early teens and their father was still alive. They were all in ski gear at the top of Aspen Mountain with the snow-covered Elk Mountains in the distance and the majestic Castle Peak rising above. The last photo was an action shot of Lara waterskiing. It was taken on the lake in Northern Wisconsin where the family had their summer home. Twelve-year-old Lara was stretched out low with one hand on the rope and her hip nearly scraping the water. A wall of spray filled the background. He looked up at Olivia and handed her the waterski photo. Olivia was pleasantly surprised by the gesture.

"Wow! She looks like a pro," Olivia said.

"She fell spectacularly right after that. But yeah, she was really good." He reached out at Olivia and snapped his fingers to let her know he wanted the photo back.

"Thanks for showing me," Olivia said.

"What happened to your hand?" Julian said, referring to an open wound on her palm.

"I cut it climbing over the fence."

"You should get that cleaned up."

"I will," she said, pleased he had shown concern for her.

Next Julian pulled out a chess piece, an equally crude but finished white version of the black queen he had held onto all these years.

"She played chess?" Olivia asked.

"On our 12th birthday my dad gave me a Dremel tool kit that had like 150 pieces. Lara was jealous, so I promised her that I would use it to make her a chess set for Christmas. I got in over my head. I finished six pawns by the next Christmas. Every year I gave her some pieces. I saved the queens for last. She died before I could finish."

"Where are the rest of them?"

"I have the other queen at home, but I don't know where the rest of them are. Maybe my brother knows."

He closed the box. Nothing he had taken out would yield much DNA for Olivia to work with. He stood up, carried the box over to the pass-through in the bars and waited for Olivia to come get it. She gave him a puzzled look.

"You do it," Julian said and pushed the box toward her.

After Olivia took the box, he returned to his spot. He sat on the floor and picked up the troll doll and brushed its hair with two fingers.

Olivia set the box on a work table and opened the lid. The only thing she could see was a white plastic Jewel-Osco grocery bag. Through the semiopaque bag she could see something that looked like a piece of clothing. She took out the bag, untied the loose knot at the top and reached inside. She pulled out the bottom half of a red sweatshirt. She found a few small patches that made it clear to her that it was originally white. She looked at her hands. They were covered with red flecks.

"Is that enough DNA for you?"

Chapter Twenty-one

Aggression Stimulus

Olivia unfolded the piece of sweatshirt, still not certain what it was. When she finally realized the thing was covered in blood, she did her best to conceal her shock. She didn't drop it like a hot rock or react vocally, but it was impossible to hide her horror. She put the sweatshirt in the grocery bag and set the box on the passthrough.

"The train cut her in half."

"I can't imagine anything more awful. I'm so sorry you had to see that."

The 13-year-old memory played in his mind like a film running at triple speed. It was all disorienting jump cuts. Train platform. White sweatshirt. Wriggling nose. Jerome Scarborough. Burn all the liars. Look of terror. Roaring train. Blood, blood and more blood. It was all horrifying. That look of terror in Lara's eyes just before the train hit her haunted him more than anything. His mind went back to it over and over and over again.

"Yeah. Kinda fucked me up," he finally said.

"I'm sure it did. You'd have to be fucked up to keep something like that."

"I stole it."

"Weren't your parents worried?"

"My dad was already dead and my mom was even more fucked up than I was. She didn't even go to the memorial."

Olivia had her own haunting flashback. She saw herself in her bed in Cambridge listening to her mother tell her, in so many words, she was about to slit her wrists.

"I don't want to talk about it anymore. Just go do whatever you have to do with that thing and get it over with."

"Okay," Olivia said as she walked toward her lab space.

"You can cut off a piece if you need to, but I want the rest of it back."

"Of course," Olivia said. Why Julian would want the bloody thing back she wasn't sure.

At her desk in her lab Olivia considered had what had just happened. From the moment he showed her the photograph of Lara waterskiing to the moment he said he didn't want to talk about it anymore, Olivia felt closer to Julian than she had to anyone in a long time. He was concerned about the cut on her hand. He shared intimate details of the worst thing that ever happened to him. No one had done anything like that with her since her mother died.

Olivia took the sweatshirt out of the bag. She took a pair of scissors from a desk drawer and cut out a six inch swatch of sweatshirt. She put the swatch in a ziplock bag. The rest of the blood-stained material went back into the Jewel bag, which she set on her desk. Olivia re-entered the centrifuge room. Julian was sobbing.

"I've been crying for 13 years. You'd think I'd be dried up by now," he said with some difficulty. "I should have left that fucking thing in the ground."

"Julian, this is good. She's reaching out to you," Olivia said. "You saved that scrap of her clothing years ago and now I can use it to help you. And you can use it to heal yourself. It was literally buried. I'm sure you've buried a lot of shit. Not in the ground like the sweatshirt, but you locked it away somewhere. It all needs to come out."

"Maybe," Julian conceded.

Julian knew she was right. Her empathy and counsel was puzzling, though. He didn't know where it came from. He'd come to believe she had no empathy. She was just as surprised as he was. It was hard for him to accept that she could have a genuine interest in helping him. It didn't matter. The woman was still his jailer. He couldn't forget that.

***

The Van de Weghe Foundation's gift had been life and career changing for Lourdes. She could pursue her important work without having to worry about money for years. There was no need to waste time writing grant proposals or taking meetings with the university. The money, however, came with a great deal of pressure. That pressure didn't come from the foundation. The money was an award for her and for her brilliance. She didn't have to spend it on her research. Of course, she never considered putting less than every penny of it into her work. Nor did the pressure come from the university. It wasn't their money. The pressure she felt at work was always self-induced. She put that money to good use right away, which allowed her to hire more help. It also increased her work load. In fact, she had made herself so busy she didn't have time to even think about anything but work. Julian was excluded like everything else that was outside of her professional orbit. She hadn't watched television or read the news for weeks.

While grabbing a quick bite at a campus cafe she eavesdropped on two undergraduate girls in Kappa Alpha Theta sweatshirts. They were already in the middle of the conversation, so she had missed some of the important contextual details. It sounded like they were talking about a horror movie. Two men had been found dead and partially eaten. It wasn't until one of the girls said something about how one of the victims had a trap on his leg and one on his face like he was a tortured bear or tiger that Lourdes thought about Julian.

Lourdes looked up the story on her phone. There had been no developments in the case since it was first reported. The most recent story quoted a police official saying there were no suspects yet. He wanted residents to know that the police did not think they were dealing with someone who was a threat to the greater community. The victims knew each other and were possibly involved in criminal activity. She didn't want to believe Julian had done it, but it sure looked like he did.

She immediately called him. There was no answer. She called him five times over the next hour. He never picked up.

The following morning Vanessa was delightfully surprised when she opened the front door of her house in Lake Forest and saw Lourdes standing on the stoop. She quickly realized Lourdes wouldn't have driven all the way up from the city unannounced for a friendly social call. After exchanging pleasantries Vanessa led Lourdes to the screen porch that looked out to the lake. Simon was in a wheelchair reading Barbara Le Conte's Life in Grayscale.

"Good book?" Lourdes asked after giving Simon a hug.

"It's a great book," Simon replied. "Thanks again for the gift."

It didn't take long for the conversation to turn to Julian and his recent retreat or withdrawal or whatever you would call it. No one wanted to use the word disappearance yet.

"I'd go years without hearing from him when he was in Asia, but we're neighbors now and we have business together. He can't just blow me off," Simon said.

"He started blowing me off before he went to Asia," replied Lourdes, who sat in a soft, overstuffed chair that was in stark contrast to Simon's metal-framed wheelchair.

"Julian told Vanessa the people who tried to kill me were really after after him. You know anything about that?"

"Not much."

"What do you mean not much? Did he say something to you?"

"The only thing he said was some people had tried to kill him in Bangladesh. He was shot twice in the shoulder.

"What?" Simon shouted.

"He thinks they're from Chicago. It's why he came home."

"If the people who tried to kill him are from Chicago, why the hell would he come home?" Simon asked.

"I don't know."

"It doesn't make any sense. Why wouldn't he tell me?" asked Simon.

"I'm sure he didn't tell you because he was trying to protect you."

"Well, he did a pretty shitty job of it." Anger rose in Simon's voice. Lourdes and Vanessa let him be angry. No one spoke for almost half a minute. "I've been calling him for three days. Do you think he's dead?" he finally said. His worry was obvious and genuine.

"No, I don't. I really don't." Lourdes said.

"What makes you so sure?" Simon said.

"I can just feel it. I don't know why." That was a lie. She may not have understood the science of it, though she had witnessed first hand Julian's special abilities that he had somehow acquired from a tiger with a reputation for being immortal. She had good reason to believe he was still alive, but she had promised Julian she wouldn't tell anyone his secret, even after he was dead.

***

"Drink this," Olivia said as she set a shot glass of TB-13 on the cage's passthrough.

Julian got up off the floor and walked to the other side of the cage. He picked up the little glass and looked at it suspiciously. He whirled the glass under his nose and sniffed. He threw his head back in disgust. "No thanks," he told her and set it back on the passthrough.

"In order for this to work, I need some baseline, both physiologically and behaviorally. First, I need to know how your body reacts to this."

"Smells like cat piss. You first."

"I took it every day for weeks."

"Prove it,"

"I can't right now. I stopped taking it so I can run some tests on myself. Stop being such a baby and drink it."

Julian raised the glass and threw it back. His face soured. His body heaved and the vile orange liquid left his stomach and returned to his mouth. He winced as he forced it back down. He shuddered. "Damn that's disgusting."

"Shall we wait to see if it comes back up again?" she asked. He shook is head and spit orange.

"We need to find an aggression stimulus," she said as she pulled a notepad out of her attaché.

"What do you mean?"

"Clearly something set you off before you killed and ate Declan and KP? What made you want to do that?"

"I was hungry," Julian said with a tinge of sarcasm.

"I should rephrase that question." She thought about it a little longer. She kept coming back to her original question so she took a different tack. "Just walk me through what happened. Which one did you eat first. Start with him."

"You really want to know this?" he asked. She nodded that she did. "You're twisted," he told her.

"I'm a scientist. And I'm a little twisted."

"They came for me on the street. I chased KP onto the platform and I freaked out. My anger spiked. I took their car and went to Declan's house because I already knew where he lived."

"You did?" Olivia said with surprise.

"I had done a little research. His house was really the only thing I found."

Olivia exhaled her relief.

"I got there before he did so I looked around. I found the rug and the traps and I went into a rage. It was like I was possessed. I don't really remember much after that. I just did whatever I did without thinking about it, like it was pure instinct to kill and eat him."

"Hmm, interesting," Olivia said as she jotted some notes. "What did he taste like?"

"Shit. Why would you want to know that?"

"Curiosity, that's all."

"Next question."

"Fine. Tell me about KP."

"I don't remember much of anything. I was still going on instinct."

"There weren't many details in the news, but from what I read it sounded like KP got the worst of it. There was a trap on his face. Seems a bit excessive to me. Was there a reason for that?"

"I don't know. That scar-faced motherfucker just gave off the stink of being an asshole. Like I said, I don't remember much. Wait. There was a book. That fucking book." Just talking about it set off something in Julian. He started pacing the cage. The pinpricks were back.

"What book?" she asked.

"It's a journal I found at KP's house. It had photos of people, people he killed, mostly Taliban guys and Iraqis, but there were photos of dead tigers. So many dead tigers. How they were killed. Where they were killed. Dates. Notes."

"Did you see my name?"

"I don't know. I didn't read the thing."

"Think harder. Is my name in there? Or my initials?" She sounded desperate.

"I told you I didn't read the fucking thing!"

Julian's body tightened as anger brewed inside him. He shook out his arms trying to stay loose. "Those tigers, he killed them for you. You paid him to kill those tigers!" Julian raged. He ran at Olivia. She jumped back just as he reached the bars. He grabbed the bars and shook the cage.

"I'm sorry. I promised you it would never happen again. Do you remember when I promised you that?" she asked pleadingly. Despite all the steel between them, her fear was obvious.

Julian didn't answer her. He retreated to the far corner of the cage, which, if not an affirmative answer was at least an acknowledgement of her question.

Olivia knew she needed to look no further to find a test for Julian's aggression. As she made different edits in Julian's genome she guessed she could test the results simply by showing him the book. From what she had seen in the sequencing she had done, she was almost certain his anger and his appetite for human flesh were related, both behaviorally and genomically. A less agitated reaction to the book would mean she was headed in the right direction. Even if it didn't work, she had to find that book. If her name was in it and the police got a hold of it, she was fucked.

Julian sat in his corner with his head between his knees. She didn't want to ask him where the book was. She thought it would be safer if she went alone.

"I'm going out for a bit."

"Leave the lights on, please," Julian said.

"Of course," she said. She reached into her attaché and pulled out a small stack of Playboys. "I found a box of these in my father's room. You can have them." She set them on the bar of the pass through. "For the articles."

***

Olivia and KP's relationship was strictly business. He had never seen her private facility nor had he been to her father's estate in South Barrington. He didn't even know South Barrington was north of Chicago. She, on the other hand, knew where Bridgeview was and she knew his house. She'd even been in it. She had done some snooping into KP not long after he moved to the area. She didn't learn much then and she didn't anticipate learning or finding anything this trip. Still, she had to try.

Olivia pulled in front of KP's house. Yellow police tape blocked the door. She got out of her car and walked across the weedy, overgrown lawn. She didn't care if anyone saw her. She was in her usual professional dress and could easily be mistaken for a detective. She lifted a rock by the door and found the spare she had seen KP hide one of the times she was spying on him. She unlocked the door and waltzed in.

Julian never mentioned what he did with the book. She thought it was unlikely he hid it and she doubted he would have taken it with him.

She assumed it would have been in plain sight for the police to see. The bedpost embedded in the wall suggested Julian had found the book in the same room. She searched the entire house thoroughly, though there wasn't much to search. It didn't look much different than the last time she was there. She didn't find the book. The trip would still be worthwhile if she was able to learn something about the man she had trusted with her dark secrets for more than two years. She didn't find anything like that either. Not finding anything told her he hadn't changed. She knew him to be, if nothing else, a man of his word. She had always trusted him and paid him well to keep his mouth shut. The nothingness of his home reinforced her opinion. If KP did talk, who would he tell anyway? The other three men were dead and KP was such a miserable son of a bitch he never had anyone else to talk to.

Julian was sleeping on the mat in his cage when Olivia returned. The Playboys she had given him were on the bar of the passthrough, though that didn't mean he hadn't looked at them.

She got as close to him as she could and softly called his name. He didn't wake so she called him again. His eyes opened and she saw them search until they found her. "Julian, I need to ask you something."

He closed his eyes, an attempt to ignore her.

"Julian, please, this is important. What did you do with the book?"

He didn't respond.

"Did you leave it at KP's house? Because if you did, the police have it now and that's not good for either of us."

"They don't have it," he said without opening his eyes.

Her body relaxed. She even managed a little smile. "What did you do with it?

He didn't respond.

"I know the book is repulsive, but it's critical for our project."

He opened his eyes and sat up. "Our project?"

"I'm trying to make you better. You know that, don't you?"

"And you can't help if you're in prison."

"That, too."

"It's at a bar," Julian said. "Don't ask me to help you get it. I don't want any part of it."

"At least tell me the name of the place."

"Egan's Four Leaf Tavern."

"I hope you didn't go in for a drink and forget it on a barstool."

"It's on the roof."

Chapter Twenty-two

I Can Always Smell You Coming

After Olivia reminded him that he would rot in the cage if she didn't come back safely from the roof of The Leaf, Julian agreed to provide more information. The book was on the roof near the back of the bar on the parking lot side. He had discovered it sitting on the seat of KP's Buick after he left the bar. He was in such a rage when he left KP's house that he didn't realize he had brought it with him. He threw it on the roof in disgust.

Getting on and off the roof of The Leaf would be harder than putting a few holes in the backyard in Evanston. To dig up Lara's blood-soaked sweatshirt it had made sense to simply walk up to the new owner of the house and ask her if they could make a few holes in her backyard. Even though Rebecca decided she needed her husband's permission and ended up calling the police, it was still the right approach. Julian had lived in that house and his sister had been tragically killed. There was no such connection or sympathy card to play at The Leaf. He described the place as a drab, two-story brick building with a flat roof. The parking lot separated the tavern from a funeral home to the east and a narrow walkway separated it from a podiatrist's office to the west. He told Olivia about the ex-firefighter owner who rarely left his second-story apartment.

When Olivia needed something a man could get for her, a little flirting and vamping got the job done. What she wore and how much of her body she showed off was part of the game. In this situation she couldn't go to work on some maintenance guy who could get her up on the roof. Flashing some skin or flaunting her tits would be pointless. He would want to know what she was looking for. Nor could she ask anyone to get the book for her. It was full of illegal photos of dead combatants and poached tigers, a species even a five-year-old knows is endangered. For this job it didn't matter to her who lived upstairs or who frequented the place. She would do it all from the outside. She did, however, still have to find a way to get up to the roof.

Olivia was too smart to rely solely on Julian's description of the building when there were better resources available. She studied satellite images of the roof on Google. Using Street View she could see all sides of the building, including the one that was just four feet from the office of Dr. Sheldon Gold, the podiatrist. There was a tree in the alley behind the buildings, with a wide gap between the roof and the closest tree branch. If she were desperate enough, a running start might help her clear a jump from the roof to a branch, but she could never make it going the other direction. There was no fire escape or drop-down ladder. Setting up her own ladder was too conspicuous. The exterior walls were relatively smooth and the windows flush. There were almost no features to the building that offered any sort of foot or handholds. Using a body wedge climbing technique in the narrow space between the tavern and Dr. Gold's office was the only real option. She had taken three-months of classes at a climbing gym in the city. She gave them up when she moved into her father's house, but she knew she could do this.

She waited three days so she could go to The Leaf on a Wednesday. An online review said the place was crowded and noisy on Wednesday nights and suggested going somewhere else if you weren't part of the darts league. The crowd and the commotion would provide needed cover and a distraction from what was going on up on the roof. She took three days off from VanPharm and used them to work furiously in her private lab to knock out the offending gene in Julian's genome. Knocking out the gene with CRISPR would be the easy part. Knocking in the stable gene would be the hard part. Knocking in was always harder than knocking out. It didn't matter that she didn't understand how Julian's DNA had mutated by itself. Julian had told her what he knew or could remember about his interactions with Amara. Unfortunately, he didn't know about that one single drop of Amara's blood that fell into his gunshot wound. He couldn't tell her what he didn't know. Even if he could tell her, she probably would have dismissed it. One drop of tiger blood mixed into a gallon and a half of human blood shouldn't make a bit of difference. In Julian's case, it did.

By Wednesday afternoon she was confident that the work she had done showed real promise. Those three days had also given her time for three more doses of TB-13. She was ready and feeling strong. The only detail she overlooked was the weather. The dark clouds that formed in the late afternoon screamed of rain. She couldn't postpone, not if it was going to rain. The book would be ruined.

The noise from inside The Leaf was loud enough for Olivia to hear it as she drove past. She parked one street over and approached from the alley in back. It was after nine and the sun had gone down. The swollen black clouds blocked the light of the moon and stars and gave Olivia the advantage of darkness.

A utility box partially obscured the view of the corridor between The Leaf and Dr. Gold's office from the street, providing Olivia with some cover while she practiced wedging her legs and hands against the walls. She scooted up the wall a few feet and tested the strength of her wedge. She had been taught the technique in the climbing gym, though she was a long way off from mastering it. She got a good start. Her sneakers gripped the wall well, but what impressed her most was her strength. She had never felt stronger. She moved her way up the walls slowly, reminding herself to stay focused and not look down. When she was a few moves from the top she realized the exterior wall of Dr. Gold's office was almost three feet shorter than the wall of The Leaf. She considered two options. The first was to climb onto the roof of Dr. Gold's podiatry clinic and jump across the four-foot gap to the roof of The Leaf. The second option was to make one final power move and launch herself upward, turn her body in the air and grab the ledge of the higher roof with both hands. From there she could pull herself up. She preferred the first option.

When she reached the top of the shorter wall she could see the narrow parapets were more than two feet taller than the deck of the roof. Getting the running start she needed to jump from one roof to the other would require two well-timed jumps, one to reach the narrow parapet, the second going up and across the space between the buildings. Suddenly, the power move was more desirable.

Getting a good grip on the ledge was critical. She had a 30-foot drop onto concrete if she didn't. Maybe it wouldn't be lethal. In her opinion, it would be better if it were. She put herself into a solid wedge and prepared for the move. A raindrop hit her nose. Another landed on the back of her right hand. Still another hit her left hand. If the ledge got wet from the rain, it would be tough to grab. She had to go now. She loaded her leg muscles and sprung upward and made the quarter turn she needed to grab the ledge with both hands. Her left hand easily cleared the ledge and her fingers found solid purchase under the overhang. The fingers on her right hand clung to the ledge by one knuckle. She clawed and scraped at the ledge with her finger tips, eventually finding a secure grip. She pulled her body up and over the ledge. She collapsed on the roof. Lying on her back and staring into the rain she said to herself, "What the fuck were you thinking?" She realized she hadn't been thinking at all. The juice made it so she didn't have to.

She found the book. She didn't open it, preferring to protect it from the strengthening rain. She slid it between the waistband of her jeans and the small of her back. Getting back down would be easier, she thought. She would make the jump from the higher roof to the lower, then go down the way she had come up. As she walked to the ledge she heard voices below. She looked over the edge and saw two young men huddled in the back corner of the corridor. One of them lit a joint and took a big puff. He held the smoke in his lungs for a few seconds, looked to the sky and exhaled. A perfect ring of smoke floated upward, bringing with it the tang of burning cannabis. The smokers tracked the smoke ring's flight, forcing Olivia to pull back to avoid being spotted. The second man took a hit and sent more smoke upward. He passed the joint. A third man appeared, having come into the corridor from the back. The joint was passed to him. The rain came down harder with every passing of the joint, though it didn't seem to bother the smokers. They were more sheltered from the rain than Olivia, who had no cover at all on the roof. She waited 10 minutes before the rain started coming down in sheets and the smokers retreated into The Leaf.

Olivia scoped out the jump to the roof of the podiatry clinic. She took a couple running steps toward the edge and slipped. The downpour had made the roof slick. She fell onto her hip and slid into the raised edge of the roof. She reached down to feel the wall. It was wet and slippery. It didn't matter if the other wall was dry. It would be crazy to use the body wedge technique to descend. She would fall on the first move. If the walls were slippery, the tree branch would be, too. The safest option, at least the one with the least chance for bodily harm or death, was to break into the building via the rooftop door and follow the stairs down to wherever they led her. She didn't know whether the stairs would take her through the second floor apartment or into a more secure stairwell she could use to get to street level. At this point, it didn't matter. It was her only path, unless she wanted to wait out the storm on the roof and climb down when the walls were dry. In that narrow, dark corridor, the walls could stay wet for days.

Olivia grabbed the doorknob and tested it. The knob turned easily and the door opened. As she descended the dark stairwell she used the dim light of her cellphone's lock screen. She could tell she would not end up in the second story apartment, though she passed a door to it. The stairs took her all the way down to the ground floor where there was another door. It didn't face the back alley or the side of the building. It faced inward. She suspected if she opened the door she would be looking into The Leaf. She tested the knob. It, too, turned easily. She cracked the door a couple of inches. It was completely dark, though she could hear the sounds of the tavern. She scanned the room with her cellphone flashlight. It was a supply room full of liquor bottles, cleaning supplies, rolls of paper towels and extra glasses. There was, however, another door on the opposite side, a door that was sure to lead her into the tavern somewhere. After some deliberation she settled on simply opening the door and walking out like she knew exactly where she was going. She cracked the door to get a preliminary view of the tavern.

Gabe was behind the bar reaching for a bottle of tequila when he saw the supply room door open a couple of inches. He had just given a tray full of drinks to Jenny, the cocktail waitress. Alby, the other bartender, was at the far end of the bar. There was no one else in the tavern with the authority to be in the supply closet. He grabbed the baseball bat he kept behind the bar and held it at the ready. He had never needed to brandish it before, but he had no reservations about cracking a skull if he had to. He kept his eye on the door as he crept closer.

Olivia, statuesque and stunning, her wet, white cotton V-neck clinging tightly to her breasts, exited like she owned the place. Gabe dropped his jaw, lowered the bat and watched her walk to the end of the bar, duck under the bar flap and stride out the front door. Gabe simply shrugged and went back to pouring drinks.

As the front door of The Leaf closed behind her, Olivia sprinted through the narrow corridor, into the alley and to her car. When she was a safe distance away from The Leaf, she pulled into the lot of a Walgreen's and parked. She looked at every disgusting photo of men with their heads blown off and tigers that had been snared, shot and clubbed to death. She read every word, examined every pen stroke. Her name wasn't in it, though she saw Julian's name written above an otherwise blank space. She felt great relief not seeing her name. KP was, regrettably, a necessary evil. He had served his purpose. She was glad he was dead, because of what sort of man he was, but mostly because dead men tell no tales. Despite seeing her TB project in such an unflattering light, she didn't consider abandoning it. She had come too far and was too close to another revolutionary scientific breakthrough to give up now. Julian was the only person alive who knew of the crimes and moral compromises she had made in the name of science. She didn't know what she was going to do with him when she was finished nor did she know when that would be.

It was after 11:00 pm when Olivia returned to her private facility. She set KP's death book on her desk. She had left just one light on in the centrifuge room and as a courtesy to Julian and his dilated pupils, she didn't turn on any more before she entered. The light was low, but not so low that she couldn't see that the cage was empty. Julian wasn't sitting in his usual corner, nor was he asleep on his mat. He was gone, vanished into thin air.

"Julian!" she yelled. She got no reply. "Julian!" She yelled again, panic now swelling in her voice.

She dashed into the lab, flipped on all the light switches and ran back into the centrifuge room. Julian was standing in the middle of the cage like a magician who had just pulled off a trick. She gave him a look of relief and anger.

"What the hell, Julian?"

Julian jumped up and grabbed the bars at the top of the cage. He swung his feet and hooked them around the bars as he pulled himself up with his arms. His whole body was flat and pulled tight to the top of the cage. He was barely visible.

"Very clever, Houdini," Olivia said as she walked up to the cage.

Julian let go and dropped to the floor in front of her. She wiped a tear from her cheek and sniffled. He had intentionally tested her and for the first time she had exposed vulnerability. She had a sweet sadness about her when her guard was down. She was beautiful and brilliant, but what a fucked up life she must have had to turn out the way she did. He almost felt sorry for her. Nothing about her was easy. He wanted to understand her better, but whenever she was around him he was too distracted by her pungency. He drew in a deep breath, his exhale as long as his inhale. He always got a rush when he took her in deeply.

"Do you know you have a distinct scent?" he asked.

"I do?"

"Oh, yeah. I can always smell you coming."

"I hope it's a pleasant scent," she said a bit flirtatiously.

"I wouldn't describe it as pleasant or unpleasant. The word I would use is… arousing. I take you in and my insides get tight as a drum. My mind races through all the dirty things I want to do with you. The way you smell makes me feel out of control and feral."

"Is that so?" Olivia asked as she ran her hand across her breasts. She tried to make it look like she was drying her V-neck, which was still wet from the rain.

"And that terrifies me," Julian said. He went to his corner, sat down and hung his head.

Olivia deflated. "I have a lot of work to do," she said. She turned and left, not waiting for any kind of reply from Julian.

***

When Olivia entered the centrifuge room the next morning, Julian jumped to his feet.

"I'm sorry I said that last night. It's not your fault you're beautiful and smell the way you do," Julian said.

"You don't need to apologize. You have a right to be terrified. I've caged you like an animal. And when I see you in there I have to remind myself how much I love science. It's a much better partner. I never have to wonder what it's thinking or if it loves me back." This was all true. What she didn't admit was that she wished it weren't. She wished her relationship with Julian was as satisfying as her relationship with science.

"Did you get the book?" he asked, knowing full well she had.

Olivia nodded. She could see Julian's expression change to dread. She knew he didn't want her to find it. He had hoped some maintenance worker or the old man with emphysema or whatever obstructive pulmonary disease he had would have found and burned it. He worried she would use it as a torture device, that she would employ Ludovico's Technique and force his eyes open to make him stare at dead tigers. He knew she was right about the book being a good test of his progress. He also knew he didn't even have to look at it. Just feeling the book's presence would be enough.

"I need to get some more tissue samples from you," she said.

Julian knew the drill by now. He put his back against the cage and wove his hands through the bars and laced his fingers together behind his head. Olivia cuffed each wrist to a bar with heavy-duty zip ties. She pulled down his pants to expose the firm, muscular flesh below his hip. She disinfected his skin with an alcohol wipe then rubbed in some lidocaine cream to numb the area. She waited a minute and jabbed him with a biopsy punch. She twisted the punch back and forth a few times and pulled out a core sample the size of a pencil eraser. She taped a piece of gauze to the small hole in his skin. She cut the zip ties.

"Thank you for making that easy," Olivia said.

"You're welcome. Now I need something from you."

"I'll have to hear what you want before I can say yes."

"I need you to let my brother know I'm all right," Julian said.

She considered this. "What did you have in mind?"

"I'll write it, You mail it."

"If I approve, of course," Olivia said.

"Of course."

Julian wrote a letter to his brother telling him he was okay. Despite the dearth of details Olivia said he had revealed too much and made him rewrite it several times. The final draft would give Simon no clue of where he was or when he would be back. Julian's forced ambiguity covered him coming back the next day all the way to not at all. He couldn't be specific about anything. Julian asked his brother to relay the message, as meaningless as it was, to Lourdes.

After signing the letter and giving it a final read he thought he had been so vague that his brother may not even believe it was him. For proof of life, he added, "PS. Do you remember Lucretia Garfield Hamilton? Odd question, I know, but the name is stuck in my head."

Olivia objected. Julian explained the cryptic message and she let him leave it in. After all, she had seen the harmless troll named Lucretia. Julian addressed the envelope to the Water Tower address. He didn't remember the address in Lake Forest. He was sure Simon would get the letter in at least a couple of days. Olivia went out and put it in the mailbox. When she returned she looked somber.

"What's that look," Julian asked.

"We have work to do."

"The book," Julian said reluctantly.

"It's the only way."

"Fine. Let's just get it over with."

Olivia went into the lab and returned with KP's death book. She flipped a few of the book's pages and marked with her thumb the one she thought was the least offensive.

"Ready?" she asked. Julian nodded.

Olivia approached the cage and showed him a photo of an Amur tiger lying dead on a blanket of snow and ringed by a forest of Siberian birch. There was no blood, no trap. The enormous cat could have been mistaken for being asleep if the photo had appeared in a book in which death wasn't the sole context. Julian's heart rate sped up. He felt hundreds of invisible spiders scurrying up his arms and legs.

Olivia flipped the book to a photo of a Bengal tiger lying in an awkward and lifeless position in a soup of gray mud. A cable snare on its leg had become tangled and knotted during the tiger's struggle to free itself before it was beaten to death with a wooden club. The club lay on the ground beside the tiger. Julian only glanced at the photo before he started pacing.

"Okay, that's enough."

"You're still exhibiting control. I need to know if this book can make you lose that control completely." She flashed another photo. A tiger's belly was split open.

"Fuck that. Give me that fucking book!" Julian yelled. He thrust his arm between the bars and tried to grab the book out of Olivia's hand. She pulled it away quickly and Julian missed, but he snagged the cuff of her jacket. The book fell to the floor. He tightened his grip on the cuff and pulled on the jacket so hard that Olivia was jerked off her feet and into the bars of the cage. Julian didn't let go.

"Give me the book," Julian said.

"No," she insisted.

Julian yanked on the jacket sleeve. Olivia's face smashed against the bars.

"Give me the fucking book!"

"I couldn't even if I wanted to," she said. The book was still on the floor and out of her reach. The pain in her arm was becoming unbearable. If he kept pulling on her jacket the way he was, she was sure her arm would snap. "Let go of me. You're going to break my arm."

"Swear to me you'll give me the book if I let go."

"You know I won't do that," she said.

He pulled her sleeve to his face. He opened his mouth and bared his teeth. Her hand was so close he could taste her. A stream of saliva drooled out of his mouth and into her palm. She quickly squeezed her fingers together to make her hand more slender and yanked hard. The back of her hand brushed his slobbering tongue before it disappeared into the sleeve. Her arm was free. Its sudden release sent her falling to the floor and made Julian stumble backward with her jacket still in his hand.

Olivia grabbed the book and without looking back at Julian ran into her lab. She locked the door behind her and killed every light, leaving Julian in a room so dark even with his enhanced night vision he couldn't tell if his eyes were open or closed.

Having so little control over his anger upset him. She had intentionally provoked him. She knew what she was getting into. She knew the risks. As much as he tried he just could not figure out what made her tick. She could be sweet and evil in the same breath. Most of the times he looked at her she was drop-dead gorgeous from head to toe. When she did something heinous, like show him photos of dead tigers, it didn't matter how beautiful she was. He couldn't see it. Every bit of her was as ugly as that troll doll. Even when she was ugly, her scent was irresistible. It was maddening. What he did understand was he still needed her. He hated needing her. If she really was as brilliant as she claimed he would play her game for a while longer. If she wasn't, he'd end up killing her. He was sure of that. He didn't have much hope of controlling himself if she didn't help him. He would probably eat her, too. He wondered where he would start if he did? All of her looked so delicious. Her breasts? Her hips? Her legs? Definitely. He would start with her legs.

Chapter Twenty-three

The Fix

Olivia's scent woke Julian. Next to him was the bloody sweatshirt. Olivia had put it back in the plastic grocery bag and pushed it through the bars. He could tell she had been there only a minute before. The scent was still strong.

Olivia entered the room wearing a lab coat and pushing a cart with five of the two-liter vials. Julian watched as she went to each of the five points of the centrifuge and loaded the vials into the compartments. She picked up a pair of ear protectors and put them on. She took a second pair and put them on the pass-through of the cage.

"Put these on," she said flatly. He didn't move. "Suit yourself," she said and walked to the centrifuge control console, flipped on the power switch, turned the key and pushed the green button. The alarm sounded three times and the centrifuge started to spin. As it spun faster and faster, the whir grew louder and louder. It was like standing next to a jet engine. Julian put on the ear protectors. Olivia sat in her swivel chair and watched, only once looking back at him. He was as entranced as she usually was.

"Mesmerizing," Julian said as the centrifuge finally came to rest. "I don't remember thinking about anything."

"It used to have the same effect on me. Now there's one thought that always—." She cut herself off abruptly. She hoped he hadn't heard her. He didn't appear to be listening.

"Go on," he said after several seconds of silence.

"Never mind. It's not really appropriate."

"Now you have to tell me."

"I think about what would happen if I threw myself at it." She didn't elaborate, fearing it would hit him a little too close to home. He was already upset about the way she provoked him with the book.

"And?" he asked.

She studied him to gauge his comfort level. She proceeded cautiously. "Would it throw me and turn me into a goopy stain on the wall or would it hold on to me until my brains exploded?"

"My money's on the goopy stain," Julian replied, apparently not bothered by the prospect.

"That would certainly be the kinder death. But as a scientist I'm more curious about how long it would take until my brains came out my ears," Olivia mused.

"That's fucked up." Julian said.

"Yeah, it is."

Olivia went to the nearest centrifuge compartment and took out the large vial. Like before, 90 percent was cloudy gray. The remaining 10 percent, however, was not bright orange. It was bright green and resembled Chartreuse. Olivia smiled, pleased with the result. She turned her back to Julian, snuck a whiff and retched. She collected the rest of the vials and carefully poured off the green liquid into five smaller vials for each of the larger vials, for a total of 25 small vials, just as she had done with the TB-13. She tightened the caps on 24 and put them on the table next to the centrifuge's control console. She set the 25th on the passthrough.

"Bottoms up," she said.

Julian shuddered and put his hand up in protest. "Pass," he said.

"This is different stuff. Honestly, I don't know how it tastes."

"You first. You created it. You deserve the first taste."

"It's not for me. This is specifically formulated for you and only you. It's a booster for the injections I'm going to give you."

Julian took the small vial. The pungent green liquid assaulted his senses from a full arm's length away.

"If all goes as planned you'll be out of that cage in three days. But you have to drink that stuff in order for the injections to work that quickly."

He drank. The taste and stench was far worse than the orange stuff. For a half minute he valiantly fought the urge to throw up. He gave up the fight when his stomach cramped. He heaved luminescent green froth.

"Congratulations on the world's most expensive vomit." She placed another vial on the passthrough. "Let's try that again."

"No more, please."

"Wash it down with some of this." She put a bottle of ginger ale next to the vial.

The ginger ale did the trick. Olivia pushed the cart to her lab and returned a few minutes later with a mop and a bucket on wheels, which she left in front of the cage. She pulled a microinjection syringe out of the pocket of her lab coat.

"Assume the position," she said.

He put his back against the cage and wove his hands between the bars. He was accustomed to the routine and Olivia's trust in him had reached a point where she no longer needed the zip tie handcuffs. She pulled down his pants a few inches and jabbed him in the butt with the needle. She pushed the plunger.

"Injections and the juice. Twice a day for three days," Olivia said.

"I have to drink that shit six times?"

"If it works. More if it doesn't." She looked down at the pile of bright green vomitus. "As pretty as that is, you better mop it up before it dries. I'll see you later. I have family business to attend to."

By noon he could feel the effects of the shot and juice. The sensation was subtle. He didn't notice any particular changes. It was more like having a really good day.

In the evening, after the second round of the treatment had time to work its way into his system, she tested him with the book. While he was still agitated, his reaction was considerably subdued compared to the first time. With each subsequent injection he made more progress without losing any of his physical abilities. He could still jump high and easily crank out 50 pull-ups from the bars at the top of the cage. Most of the effects happened in his mind. He had more focus than he could ever remember having. Most importantly, he felt hopeful.

***

Simon's doctors marveled at his speedy recovery as much as they had at his survival. He felt so good he drove his 1960 Maserati down Sheridan Road all the way to the city just to pick up his mail. It was the first time he had driven it, or any car, since he was shot. Feeling the wind in his hair as he drove through some of Chicagoland's most beautiful neighborhoods took his mind off the unknown fate of his brother, whom he hadn't heard from in a couple of weeks. It was a welcome change to be able to think more pleasant thoughts, like reassessing his future. He thought about cashing in all his chips and finding a new path. He mused about taking up painting or opening a gallery. He didn't know what he would do with the rest of his life. He did know what he didn't want to do with it. There would be no more cooping himself up in an office in the sky at a job that didn't even allow him time for lunch. He thought about keeping the house in Lake Forest. If he retired from his finance career there would be no more commuting hassles. Life in the burbs could be enjoyable under those circumstances. To say he saw getting shot was a blessing would be an exaggeration, but he was certainly focused on the positives.

Simon parked the Maserati in the building's garage, collected his mail and took it upstairs to his apartment. He set the mail on his living room table and spent a few minutes staring into the Rothko. He made a call to the director of the Smart and told her he wanted to return it early. It belonged in the Smart. He didn't tell the director he was ashamed of throwing his money around just so he could have a $75 million painting as a sort of emotional support animal, which was how he felt. He did tell her that all the money he had given the museum as part of the deal was theirs to keep and there was more on the way.

Simon had looked at every piece of mail before his brother's letter fell out of a flower bulb catalog that wasn't even addressed to him. He recognized the loopy handwriting immediately. The thought of opening it made him nervous. The postmark was Chicago and it had been sent just three days earlier. Considering how long it had been since Simon had last heard from his brother, he expected any letter from him to be postmarked Kathmandu or Kolkata.

The vagueness of Julian's letter was puzzling. It wasn't a suicide note and it offered little help in understanding what Julian was involved in. Simon did remember Lucretia Garfield Hamilton. He had despised the little green troll as much as Julian had, even more. That part of the letter was as puzzling as the rest of it.

Simon exited the elevator in the lobby and went outside to see who was on duty. Eugene, the longtime day doorman, was sweeping the sidewalk when Simon asked him if he had seen his brother.

"Not in quite some time," Eugene said. "Come to think of it, I hardly ever see him."

"He's a bit of a night owl." And a pain in the ass, Simon told himself.

"That would explain it," Eugene said.

All the way back up to Lake Forest the letter was on his mind. When he got home he called Lourdes to pass on Julian's message and to get her take on it.

Simon asked her if she knew anything she hadn't told him yet. She was conflicted. There was so much about Julian she hadn't told Simon. There were some things she had vowed not to tell anyone. However, the part about Julian telling her to stay away from him because he was dangerous was different. She had never vowed to keep that a secret. Simon was, after all, Julian's brother. He had a right to know at least some of what was going on.

"He told me to not call him anymore and to stay away from him. He thinks he's dangerous."

"You mean like he's a danger to himself?" Simon asked.

"I don't know. Maybe. Did you go in his apartment?"

"No. He never gave me a key. I should have had someone let me in. I'm gonna call the police to do a welfare check."

Lourdes did not want the police involved. "Could you arrange for me to get in?" she asked.

***

Eugene turned the lock and pushed open the door to Julian's apartment. He gestured for Lourdes to enter.

"I have to go back down," Eugene said. "Please lock up when you leave."

She nervously stepped inside and wandered from room to room. There was no change or addition to the apartment made by its new owner that made it look or feel any different from when it was owned by a middle-aged widow. He had bought some new clothes and that was about it. Aside from a dead body, she didn't know what she was looking for. It felt to her like she was in a hotel room. She found the black queen on the table in the living room. She picked up the chess piece to examine it more closely. She knew the whole story behind the handmade pieces. She felt a tug of sadness. She wrote a quick note on the back of receipt she had in her pocket. She put the note on the table and the queen on top of the note. Unwittingly, she set the queen facing the opposite direction of how she found her.

Julian had been through some radical changes in his life recently. He would never be the same man she fell in love with when they were really just kids. There were remnants of the old Julian she still loved. As a whole man, she didn't know if she could love him they way she had. They never had the chance to grow and change together. Until recently she had been willing to take the time to find out what a life with Julian would be like, even with the potentially dangerous changes he had gone through. Now, she wasn't so sure. What kind of relationship could she have with someone who kills and eats his victims?

Johnny had just come on duty when Lourdes returned to the lobby. They had only met once, but Johnny immediately knew who she was.

"Is Mr. Hamilton home?" Johnny asked excitedly.

"No, he's not," Lourdes said.

"Oh, man," Johnny said, clearly disheartened by the news.

"When was the last time you saw him?" she asked.

"Seems like a couple of weeks."

"Was he coming or going?

"Going out. We chatted for a bit like we always do and then he left footin' it with some woman he ran into in front of the hotel."

"Did you get a good look at her?"

"I got a real good look at her, but only from the back and from a distance. Still caught myself peepin."

"Peepin?"

"Long legs. Short skirt. Nomsayin?"

"I think I do," she said. She handed her business card to Johnny. "If you see him, please call me."

"I will. And please do the same for me."

***

Julian grew impatient as he sat in his cage waiting for Olivia to come in and give him his final injection. He hadn't seen her since the morning. She told him she needed to go to her office downtown. He didn't know if she actually went. He was pretty sure she was in the next room. For the first time he thought he could smell Olivia through the insulated walls. He had never been able to figure out why her scent was stronger some days more than others. She knew even less about her scent than he did. She had reduced her dosage of TB-13 to once a week because she had started to feel like a junkie. She was well aware of the dangers of the stuff. She had seen firsthand what too much of it could do to someone. It had led to her father's ignoble death. Still, she couldn't give it up completely. It made her feel too good to quit. Further scientific study of Julian would help her understand how much she, or anyone else, could handle.

Julian was correct. He had smelled her. She had taken a dose just after she gave him his morning injection. Olivia was in her lab, though she wasn't working. She was stewing over a text she had received from Lourdes. The text read, "Hi, Liv. Worried about Julian. I heard you might have seen him some days ago." Who could have seen her with Julian. What did Lourdes know about the two of them? Had Julian told her they slept together? Did she know or witness anything herself?

Olivia doubted it. Still, she couldn't be sure. Friend or no friend, if Lourdes got in the way she was willing to do whatever needed to be done. For now, the safest thing to do was not reply to the text, to pretend she never saw it.

Olivia entered the centrifuge room carrying a syringe in her right hand and a vial in her left. She stuck Julian in the ass and pushed the plunger. She gave him the vial and he forced down the putrid green liquid. He chased it with ginger ale.

"Let's get this over with," Julian said. "Show me the book."

"It doesn't work that fast. We should wait," Olivia said.

"I don't need to wait. I'm already fixed. I can feel it."

"And how does it feel?"

"It feels fantastic. I don't know what you did, but you're a fucking genius."

Olivia was flattered, which was strange because she never really cared what other people thought. It felt different coming from Julian. She knew she was a genius. An IQ test told her that when she was 13. Still, it was nice to hear Julian say it. She, too, already knew he was fixed. She had observed the successful edits in his DNA. What she had done was revolutionary stuff. Anyone would admit that. The downside was her work was ethically dubious. She couldn't brag about her brilliance or her accomplishments. The scientific community would roast her for it. Her success created other complications. She was now the largest shareholder of VanPharm. News of her misdeeds could tank the company. Selling her interest would put her in a financial position to continue her work on her own terms indefinitely.

Olivia rarely did anything just to be recognized. She didn't cure her father of arthritis and impotence to help him. She did it to prove to herself that she could. Her overheated desire to prove herself to no one but herself almost always blew up some other part of her life, usually a relationship with a lover or potential friend. She had worked on cooling that desire. She had little success. She eventually gave up trying to control the collateral damage. Her latest quest had gotten four people killed. A few years ago that might have bothered her. At this point in her life she was too committed to her work and too far gone to care.

Olivia pulled out the death book and turned it to the image of KP standing over the dead tiger. Julian looked at it blankly. He didn't feel that inner switch being flipped like the other times he looked at the book. There were no pinpricks. He didn't feel the urge to sink his teeth into human flesh.

"Satisfied?" he asked her.

She showed him another photo. Nothing. She showed him his name written in the blank space. He had no aggressive or violent reaction to anything in the book. She walked closer to the cage. She set the book on the passthrough.

"Pick it up," she told him.

He picked up the book.

"Look at the photos."

He calmly leafed through the book page by page. Dead tigers would always make him furious, but he was able to control that fury. It didn't control him. He still thought about killing every motherfucker who had ever killed a tiger, but he had no desire to eat them. Telling Olivia that wouldn't help his cause. He set the book on the passthrough.

"Are you going to let me out now?" he asked her.

"Are you going to hurt me?"

"I promise on my sister's grave I will not hurt you," Julian said.

"I'll get the key," she said.

She turned her back and took a step toward the door to the lab. She heard him inhale deeply and loudly through his nose. She stopped and faced him. He pulled at the sash of his robe. The robe fell open.

"Hurry up and get that fucking key," he told her.

She displayed no urgency as she walked to the lab door, the death book in her hand. She entered the lab. She reappeared and walked back at the same teasingly slow gait. A key on a string dangled from her little finger. Julian, his robe hanging open, watched her approach. She stopped in front of the cage door. She put the key between her teeth and started to undress unhurriedly, carefully setting each item of clothing in a tidy pile on the floor. Julian shook the bars of the cage as she undressed. She unlocked the door and left the key in the lock. She opened the door and slinked over to Julian at the center of the cage. He set his finger on her chin, ran it down her neck, between her breasts and all the way down. She reached for him. He gently blocked her. He was in charge.

"On your back," Julian said.

She complied.

"Eyes closed. Legs open."

Obedience.

Julian kneeled at her feet and put his hands on her knees. "I want to know if you taste as good as you smell," he said.

"You're not going to eat me, are you?" she asked playfully, though there was a hint of nervousness.

"Only in a manner of speaking. Where should I start?" he asked as he moved his hands up the inside of her thighs.

"That's a good place," she said when he got to the top.

He inhaled her earthy musk. It was still pungent and enticing, its effects still visceral. He could, however, resist it. He was in control now. He liked the feeling.

"Keep those eyes closed," he said as he slowly removed his hands from her body. "I'm going to take off the robe."

"They're closed," she assured him.

"Good girl."

A second later she heard the door of the cage slam shut. She looked up and saw Julian turn the key and remove it from the lock. He was on the other side, the box with Lara's things in his hand.

"What are you doing?"

"What does it look like?"

"You lured me in here just so you could trap me?"

"You did it to me."

"You bastard."

"I promised I wouldn't hurt you. How else was I supposed to get you in there? I doubt asking you to trade places would have worked." He tossed the pile of her clothes into the cage. "Get dressed."

Olivia grabbed her shirt and put it on.

"Where are my clothes and the rest of my things?" he asked.

"In my desk. Now let me out."

"I'll only let you out if you promise to leave me alone."

"This wasn't the arrangement. You said you'd help me."

"I've helped you enough. And I mean it when I say don't ever come looking for me. If you do, I'll break my promise not to hurt you."

"Fine, I won't ever come looking for you." Olivia appeared strong. On the inside she was deeply wounded.

"Good," he said.

"But you'll come looking for me."

"Don't flatter yourself."

"You still need me."

"What do you mean?" Julian asked. Anger simmered inside him.

"The injections were a saline solution. The real fix is in the juice. You need to keep taking it every three days or you'll go back to what you were a week ago, a man-eating killer. A violent cannibal."

"You're lying."

"A few minutes ago you said I was a fucking genius. Do you really think I wouldn't keep an insurance policy?"

Julian's heart dropped into his gut. The bitched fucked him over. She had him by the balls and he knew it.

"How many vials are left?" Julian demanded.

"Eighteen. That's two months at most."

The tiny smidgeon of hope he had seconds ago blew up. He was no better off now than when she had him locked in the cage. He walked to the control console of the centrifuge. He flipped on the power switch.

"What are you doing?" she asked.

He turned the key.

"Julian, don't mess with that," she asserted.

"Just push the green button, right?"

"Please don't." She tried a more pleading tone.

"You know, I've been thinking about what you said about this thing. I mean about whether you'd make a goopy stain on the wall or if you'd spin until your brains came out your ears. I wonder what would happen if we did it together, at the same time. Maybe one of us would hit the wall and the other would spin to death. Kind of romantic when you think about it."

"Julian, don't do this."

"Whatever I do is on you. If it weren't for you I wouldn't have killed or eaten anyone. I'd be back in Bangladesh without a trouble in the world."

"Only because you're a coward and you ran away from all your troubles here." Olivia immediately regretted this personal attack, but she wouldn't apologize. Julian looked directly into her eyes as he pushed the green button. The alarm sounded three times and the centrifuge started to spin.

"Turn it off. It's not balanced to run with the compartments empty. It'll crash." Olivia yelled.

Julian ignored her. The centrifuge gained speed. As it did, it got louder and louder. Julian took the ear protectors and put them on his head. She yelled over and over to turn it off, knowing full well that even with his enhanced hearing he would never hear her.

The light on the control console lit up, indicating the centrifuge had reached full speed. Julian walked to the cage. He stuck the key in the lock and opened the door. Olivia retreated. Julian walked in, grabbed her. She punched. She kicked. She flailed. He was too powerful. He squeezed her arms and legs tightly as he carried her out of the cage and within a foot of the furiously spinning centrifuge.

"Julian, no! Don't do it! Put me down!" she screamed as she wriggled in a futile attempt to escape his grasp.

He stared at the centrifuge blankly, coldly.

Her forceful commands, useless and inaudible, turned to sobbing appeals. "Please, Julian. Put me down." Tears streamed down her face as she cried and begged for her life. He could neither hear them nor see them. He was entranced by the centrifuge.

There was a loud clunk and the centrifuge listed. It wobbled and rattled. With every revolution it was closer to breaking off its anchors. Julian stared at it calmly, but Olivia squirmed frantically.

He looked at her for what he was sure would be the last time. In her eyes was the same look of absolute terror he had seen in his twin sister's eyes the instant before she was hit by the train. That look hit him like a baseball bat to his head. He dropped to his knees, releasing Olivia from his grasp. She fell to the floor. She lunged at the control console and punched the kill switch. An alarm sounded and the centrifuge began to slow and level off. Olivia collapsed on the floor.

"Where are the rest of the vials?" he asked when the room was quiet again.

She didn't answer.

"Where are the vials?" he said with threatening force.

"In my desk with the rest of your things."

Julian walked toward the door without saying another word.

Olivia cried out, " Julian, don't leave me. Please. I love you." She lay on the floor in a pathetic, sobbing heap.

Chapter Twenty-four

Another Slap In The Face

Julian searched Olivia's desk drawers and found his clothes, wallet and 18 vials of the chartreuse juice. His phone was not there. He didn't remember if he even had it the night he ran into Olivia on the street. Atop the desk was the death book. He put it in the box with Lara's things. He got dressed and walked out the door with the box under his arm.

The first thing Julian saw was a cracked, weedy parking lot. The building was an old warehouse, just a windowless concrete rectangle on a small side street that could not have been less impressive. The only clue he had as to where he stood was his internal compass tuned to the lake. He always knew where it was. He walked east until he found a sign for Superior Street. He guessed that no matter how far west he was, if he walked north one block he would hit Chicago Avenue, where he could get a bus that would eventually drop him off a block from his apartment building. He didn't want to go home. He had other plans. After a few more blocks he saw a sign for Cicero Avenue. That gave him a better idea how far west he was. He headed south on Cicero Avenue. Ten minutes later he was standing under the Green Line tracks.

He stood at the bottom of the stairs to the platform and looked up. He put his hands in his pockets and pulled out the vials. He counted them and did the math in his head. Olivia was right. One vial every three days would last him barely two months. And then what? Back to killing and cannibalism? He put the vials back in his pocket. He climbed the first flight of stairs to the platform and stopped. He drew in a deep breath and continued. He pulled the Venta card he had bought but never used out of his wallet and passed it over the card scanner to pay his fare. He walked onto the center platform that ran between the east and westbound tracks. He looked west to check for an eastbound train. There was no train in sight. Standing near him was a girl around 16 or 17 years old playing with her phone. Julian approached cautiously.

"I'll give you $20 for one quick call with your phone," Julian said.

The girl looked at him like he was some kind of pervert and turned away. Julian took out a twenty and held it out for the girl.

"I know it sounds creepy, but I need to make an important call and I can't find my phone. I won't leave this spot. I promise."

The girl was still unsure. Julian peeled off four more twenties. "Make it $100. Here, you can count it first."

The girl slowly reached out for the money. She counted the bills. She opened the phone app and handed him the phone.

"Thank you." He dialed the number and waited for an answer.

"Simon, it's me."

"Oh my god. You're okay," Simon said on the other end.

"Yeah, I'm okay. Did you get my letter?"

"Yeah, I got it. Where the hell have you been? Wait a minute. Who's number is this?" Simon asked.

"What's your name?" Julian asked the girl.

"Uh, Tiffany," the girl said tentatively.

"I borrowed it from a nice girl named Tiffany. I'm sorry that I haven't been in touch. I hope you weren't, I mean I'm sure you were worried."

"Damn right I was. I thought you were dead."

"I've been going through some really weird shit lately. You wouldn't believe it if I told you. But that's all over now."

Julian again looked down the eastbound tracks. A train was noticeable in the distance.

"I wanted to tell you that I'm..." Julian paused to catch his breath. The train drew closer. "I wanted to tell you that I'm about to do something really difficult and I needed to hear your voice."

"Dude, this is really weird. You're scaring me," Simon said.

"Nothing to be scared of. I gotta go. I love you."

"I love you, too." Simon said, a little confused but sincere. "Don't hang up."

Julian ended the call and handed the phone back to the girl. "Thanks, Tiffany. And you should never have your phone out on the platform. You're just inviting trouble."

"Okay. Thanks, I guess," Tiffany said, also a little confused.

Julian walked out to the blue rubber safety strip and waited nervously. When the Green Line train was close enough to make the platform rumble, Julian inched his toes all the way to the edge of the blue strip. His eyes were closed, but he could hear and feel it getting closer. It was just a few yards away.

His heart raced. His breathing was forced. He opened his eyes, flinching slightly as he saw the train almost upon him. After the first car roared past, he relaxed and watched the rest of the cars rumble in. They were so close they blew back his hair. When the train came to a stop, he was standing in front of the door of the sixth and final car. A man carrying a lunch box stepped out and nodded hello as Julian cautiously boarded and found a seat. He bounced his knees nervously. The train pulled out of the station. He hugged the box with Lara's things.

Julian rode the Green Line to Adams and Wabash, reminding himself to breathe all the way. He hesitated at the threshold. He dabbed his foot on the platform as if he were checking the firmness of a frozen pond. He stepped onto the platform. He felt great relief as he put one foot in front of the other toward the stairs. By the time he reached the street he looked like any other straphanger on his way home from work. The mundanity thrilled him. He felt like a kid who had just learned to ride a bike. He looked to the sky and blew a kiss to Lara. As he walked north across the river on the Du Sable Bridge he took a good, long look down the Mag Mile. The sun had been down for nearly an hour and Michigan Avenue was glowing. When he got to his building Johnny was standing at the door.

"Mr. Hamilton, where you been? I thought something awful happened to you."

"Nope. Been gone for a little bit, but feelin' better than ever."

"I'm glad because there's some bad people out there. Nomsayin?"

"So you keep telling me."

Johnny led Julian into the lobby and called the elevator for him.

"I got a little sumpin sumpin from Tomasina," Johnny said. "Thank you."

"Who's your favorite tenant now?"

"I can't believe you even need to ask."

"And you're my favorite doorman."

"I know." Johnny said with a big grin. "I'm everybody's favorite."

The elevator doors opened. Julian said goodnight and stepped inside. He pushed the button for his floor and the doors started to close. An arm reached through the narrowing gap and forced the doors open. Howard Erlacher stepped into the elevator.

"Howdy neighbor," Howard said cheerfully.

"Howdy to you," replied Julian as he hit the 37th floor button for Howard.

"How's your brother doing?" Howard asked.

"He's doing well. I just talked to him a little while ago."

Julian and Howard chatted politely as far as the 37th floor. As he stepped out of the elevator, Howard asked Julian to give Simon his regards.

"I'll do that, Howard."

Inside his apartment Julian found his cell phone charging on the kitchen counter, right next to the business card Sarah Redstone had given him. He set the metal box on the counter, removed the white queen and took it into the living room. The unfinished black queen sat on an end table. Beneath her was Lourdes's note. "Couldn't stay away. Hope you're safe. Lou," was all it said. He smiled.

Julian set the two queens on the table so they looked out at the night sky and the Chicago skyline reflecting off the lake that looks like an ocean.

Julian walked back to the kitchen and poured a glass of bourbon. He picked up his phone and Sarah Redstone's business card. He tapped in her number as he walked to the couch. He suddenly realized he was nervous and he didn't know why. He'd never made a call like this before. It went straight to voicemail. The first couple of seconds after the beep was just a throat clearing sound Julian made while he thought about what he was going to say.

"Hi, Sarah. It's Julian Hamilton. I, uh, rode a Green Line train today. Uh, no need to call me back, unless you want to. Oh, by the way, I loved the story you wrote. It helped me get on that train. I should have told you that earlier. Sorry. So, okay. Bye."

He took a long sip of bourbon and relished the burn in his throat. He closed his eyes and drifted off. Half an hour later a knock on the door woke him. He went to the door after a second knock. Through the peephole he saw Lourdes. He opened the door. They stood at the threshold and looked at each other in silence for a long moment. He couldn't read her stony expression. He had no idea what she was thinking. She raised her hand quickly and slapped him hard across the face.

She turned around and walked to the elevator. She pushed the button and the doors opened immediately. He wanted to go after her, but didn't. He could see tears in her eyes as the doors closed on her.

In his kitchen Julian leafed through the death book. After seeing the entry with his name on it he shut the book. He took a large metal pot out of a cabinet and turned on the gas burner of the stove. He put the death book to the flame, set it in the pot and watched it burn. He enjoyed the control he felt and was able to exercise. He still thought about killing every motherfucker who had ever killed a tiger, but he didn't know what to do about Olivia. He needed her and he hated that. She had gotten lucky. If it weren't for that look in her eyes, she'd be a goopy stain on the wall. So would he.

Ross J. Burns is a former middle school teacher, real estate broker, special effects producer and compost salesman. His writing has appeared in print, online and on radio and television. He has lived up and down the West Coast from Seattle to Lima, Peru, and points in between. He currently lives in the Sangre de Cristo Mountains near Taos, New Mexico.

Made in the USA
Middletown, DE
16 January 2022

58755095R00187